FIRE

the

BLADE

by *Drayton Mayrant*

PEOPLES BOOK CLUB

CHICAGO

Dedicated to
the best Bible student I have ever known...
my father, S. Lewis Simons

THE only authentic history of the wife of Pontius Pilate is written in thirty-eight words in the nineteenth verse of the twenty-seventh chapter of the Gospel of Saint Matthew. Although I have used in this story numerous legends, I have tried all through it to picture a woman revealed to us in that brief but urgent message by which she tried to save Our Lord from crucifixion.

DRAYTON MAYRANT

*"First the blade, then the ear, after that
the full corn in the ear."*

ST. MARK 4, 28

PART ONE
The Island

1

AROUND the island lay a sea of periwinkle blue. It changed from misty turquoise, when it stretched silk-smooth in the dawn, to sapphire at noonday below the shelves of stone. It darkened with dusk to purple; and off toward the mainland the child Procla could watch the sparks that were the fishermen's torches.

Her life had always been pent by the enforced self-sufficiency of the isle. Unlike her mother she had no ties with any other place. It had never occurred to her to wish to leave Pandataria. She was the child of winds and waves and that bit of dark volcanic rock that an emperor whom she never saw had chosen for her mother's prison.

Her mother was not unkind when she remembered her or had leisure. Unless Julia was overwearied from pleasures of the night before, Procla was taken by old Bruna every day to Julia's apartment. There she was petted by mother and grandmother and given gifts of sweetmeats or painted dolls which had been brought from foreign lands by the legionaries.

For Julia, daughter of the Emperor Augustus, lacked nothing, although she was supposed to be banished and disgraced. When first transported to the volcanic isle she had suffered the privations her father intended. But that punishment had not endured. Her old associates had found her out. Now her lovers brought her not only all delicacies of food and wine but gifts of jewels, money and clothes. Officers crossed in small boats from their encampments ashore. Idle patricians sailed directly in private galleys from Ostia. It had become the fashion both to cheer and

3

to share the outlawry of the granddaughter of Julius Caesar's sister.

As long as her babyhood lasted Procla looked forward to those daily visits to her mother. She realized no lack in Julia's languid interest, which soon died and resulted in a petulant dismissal. She was flattered by her grandmother's embraces and intimate questions. She was too young to discern underneath Scribonia's words a desire to rip apart and destroy all happy things. She took it for granted that those two, regal-looking and indolent and always self-important, were busied with affairs so great that they could spare her only this short time.

When dismissed by the wave of a jeweled hand, she made the small obeisance that Scribonia had taught her and that always brought applause. Then she turned slowly and carefully in her full, trailing robes and preceded Bruna out of the apartment.

Once in that hall which the exiled princess had had built in nostalgic imitation of a Roman house, Procla picked up her skirts and ran to her own apartment, calling to the old woman to come and change them for simpler garments.

In the little knee-length toga which was childhood's everyday dress, she could wade in the slow salt tides and climb the rocks that shelved from the beach. She could lie flat upon them and watch for small boats with ocher sails or for great war galleys passing.

When the tide was low and there were no waves, she could even see the shark that cruised back and forth off the south cliffs of the island. That was where the slave Ennius threw all the waste from the kitchen, and the dead birds and animals after the sacrifices. She lay on her stomach on the rock that overhung a small beach below, and watched for the dark triangular fin that cut the sea like a lateen sail. Sometimes she stood up and threw a stone as far out as she could. Then the monster would wheel at right angles from its course and dart inshore toward the splash. Fascinated she would watch the wake of its rushing body, and see it slow and circle in its hunt for expected food. Sometimes in hunting it rolled clear of the surface, and she made out the long pale belly and crescentic gash of its mouth. When she first saw that she screamed aloud and turned to escape—and found Psiloriti's arms around her.

Although he scolded, her tutor held her close. "I have told you not to come alone to the south cliffs. They shelve outward, and if you fell you would fall in deep water."

"If I fell," she implored, "would the shark really eat me?"

He felt her shivering, but he knew that he had to warn her. Her nature was too fearless and alien to danger. He understood her better than did mother or grandmother or the hag of a nurse called Bruna.

"It would tear you to pieces and devour you, as the small carnivorous fish in the pond devour a mouse thrown to them. Its teeth are knives"—he caught her hand and spread out the slender fingers—"longer than the longest of your fingers, Procla."

She shuddered again, then reached out and put the slim hand in his. Her education had already begun under Psiloriti. He told her that this Mediterranean Sea was the center of the world and the oldest of all known waters. He told her that there were a thousand islands in it and that most of them clung to its northern or European shore. He was Greek and had no interest in or knowledge of Africa. He had been captured as a child about as old as she was now, when the Romans conquered his island home of Crete. For years he had been a political slave, but time had made him a freedman. Time also had made it too late for him to return to the Isles of Greece. Those whom he loved and those whom he knew would long have been gone from his birthplace.

Since he had no love for Rome and he longed for the

sea and solitude, he had been willing to come with Julia into banishment. But wherever he went beauty remained his creed, and he longed to instil it in this little girl who had no other teacher. He made learning such a joy that she begged for it and loved him best of all those in her small world. Throughout the daylight hours she followed him foot to foot along paths bordered by almond, peach, apple, quince, and other flora native to the soil or planted by the exiles. She tried to follow him when he rose from old age's sleep in the daybreak and went out where low mist trailed pale scarves over the crags. But old Bruna always caught her and put her back to bed.

"Not until the sun is up, you wicked child," she scolded. "There is poison in these miasmas that rise from the marsh and the sea. Lie there until I bring your fruit and bread and warm milk and sweet wine."

"Bruna, I saw the shark yesterday. He was swimming out by the south cliffs."

Bruna stopped short and began to mutter an incantation. Then she picked up the thin-stemmed gold pitcher. of wine and turned toward the altar which she had placed in a corner of the child's bedroom. Procla sat up on her couch to watch.

The little image which was the Lar looked back with a sexless blankness. She had always wondered whether it was a boy or a girl. Its hair was a halo of badly molded plaster and its legs thick and stumpy below the full, short toga. Its left hand extended a miniature cup and its right held a drinking horn high.

Bruna approached it, muttered more words, and poured a few drops of wine in its cup.

She turned on Procla. "I've told you not to speak of death before sunrise. It is well for you that I am here to propitiate the household god."

"How can it help me?" asked Procla. "It is made of plaster, and besides its legs are too fat to move."

Bruna at once darted upon her and shook her. "Now I shall have to give it a dove as well as the wine!"

The small white face looked up at her from thick, tangled hair on the cushion. The gray eyes reminded her of her one look at Augustus, and the red mouth was reminiscent of one of Julia's rages.

"If ever again you give it one of my pet pigeons, I'll break it to pieces and I'll kill you too!"

Bruna knew when to conciliate. She was sly as well as cruel.

"It is because I love you that I warn you about the shark. Signs have foretold—and Ennius will bear me witness in this—that death will come to this island and the course of your life will be changed because of some man-eating fish."

Procla thought about that while she enjoyed her breakfast. She glanced several times at the Lar, and was sure that she caught it once grinning at her. Bruna's augury had impressed her enough to keep her from making faces at it, as she often did. So she held her peace, and as soon as permitted she ran through the door to hunt for Psiloriti.

Between the low pillars of the façade she stopped and looked around her. No one was in sight. She could hear the surf; and closer at hand she heard a sound not unlike it. It was the soft, rhythmic roaring of imprisoned doves and pigeons. She thought of the Lar and laughed aloud as she visioned it tortured by hunger.

Nobody saw her as she stole around the big house. She opened the doors of both the large dove cage and of the smaller one where her pigeons were kept. Then she crawled inside and shooed the last bird to freedom.

She watched them circling overhead like a sudden gust of snowflakes, until the servants rushed screaming from the back of the house. Then she turned, still laughing, and ran like a little goat off toward the high meadow where she knew she would find Psiloriti.

2

AS Procla climbed the ascending path she drew nearer to the sea. At the crest of the cliff she could see it foaming and tearing below. This was the western and least protected side of the island. She had never seen the shark here. Ennius said that sharks feared rough water and that was why he fed it in a more sheltered place. But she knew that the south cliff was nearer to the kitchen and it was easier for him to carry the offal there.

She was now beginning to meet the goats: nannies and half-grown kids. Bruna had told her never to pass a goat without touching its horns for luck, so she slowed up and turned aside toward a young grazing billy. But he reared to meet her, pawing the air with his small, black, cloven hooves, and thrusting his short horns belligerently.

Procla took refuge behind the mother goat, and caressed her long, limp ears while she went on nibbling grass.

With its back to a rock in the high meadow was the little hut of the herdsman. It was built of rough small logs with goatskins stretched tentlike over them. Clods of earth mounded around its base kept it snug from the east wind. More than once she had seen from afar a figure disappearing into it, but she had not yet met the goatherd face to face.

Psiloriti filled her thoughts, and she went on in search of him. As usual he sat on a stone, gazing east into the distance. She poured out an excited account of the hostile billy goat.

But he only smiled and said that goats were for meat

8

and for milk, not for luck. "He was only mischievous, Procla. Do not let him make you afraid." He paused and scanned her eager face for signs of fear. He was proud of her courage. "Had you picked up a stick and gone forward instead of running away, he would have turned tail and fled from you. Remember that; because it applies to people as well as to goats."

He sighed, recalling that last scene in Rome. For the Emperor Augustus had chosen not to hide his shame but to publish it. Trumpets in the Forum and the shout of *Proclamete!* Tramp of the Praetorian Guards as they went from house to house arresting noblemen of the city. *Proclamete!* Let it be proclaimed that these men were doomed to execution or exile and that the Emperor's daughter was banished and publicly shamed!

She—Julia—had no shame. But she was angry at being deprived of sybaritic banquets in palaces of friends; of mad chariot races through the streets of Rome, when the drunken young patricians driving not only lashed with their whips at pedestrians but tried to run them down; of nightly excursions into unsavory byways, after which the Emperor's bodyguard had more than once picked up at dawn the Emperor's daughter and her companions sprawled in disarray and asleep in the Forum. . . .

Of all that this child knew nothing, and she loved Pandataria. She had been born into its small world, more lovely because of its smallness. For that reason she could hold it more closely against her heart. When not with Psiloriti she made herself happy with solitary games in the shade of oaks that leaned on the landward slope to the meadow. She loved to escape from Bruna and hide in that evergreen coolness while the nurse yelled and scolded and Psiloriti laughed. It was while hiding in these trees at high noon of a summer day that she unexpectedly came on the herdboy Yod.

She almost stepped on him as she ran into the grove. In

fact she saw him just in time to jump over him instead. He was stretched out on his back with his hands beneath his head, and he sat up and looked at her out of big, bright black eyes.

"Daughter of Emperors," he said, "I am small enough already. That is why they called me *Yod*, for the littlest letter in my alphabet."

She knew that superstition too. It was one of the oldest in the world and was not confined to any one land.

"Lie back," she said, "that I may step across you from the opposite side. It may be that will undo the evil I have done and let you grow to a man's size."

He had laughed and thrown himself back, his dark curls clustered around his face. As she stepped carefully over him she saw he was not much taller than herself, although stockily built and strongly muscled. She spread her skirts around her as she sat on an oak root.

"Who are you, Yod?"

"I am keeper of the goats," he said, still lying at ease in the green shade. "I come here to rest when the sun is hot. If you tell that I shall be beaten."

"I will not tell," she promised him. She had twice seen slaves beaten. "I like you because you are small like me, while all the others are grown up. Are you one of my lady mother's slaves? How old are you?"

"I am fifteen," he said ruefully, "although but the size of a ten-year-old. I am a slave." For a second she saw a red spark in his dark eyes, then he moved his shoulders in a gesture that might have been a shrug. "But you would neither understand nor care about the wherefore of that."

She gazed at him, puzzled. To her a slave was a slave: a servant destined to serve and to foresee a mistress's wants. He pushed himself to a sitting position with his arms braced stiffly behind him on the ground, and he looked back at her as proudly as a young lion.

"There are slaves in your household whose birth is as

noble as your own. The steward of your villa is an Ethiopian prince."

She knew the steward, proud and tall and ebony-black, with his hair dressed high. Only infrequently did she see the girl who was his wife. She saw them walking when work was done through the garden by the fishpond that was ringed with wild hyacinths and marigolds. They walked each with an arm laced around the other, and the slim young woman leaned on him as if she needed support. But he walked as straight as the spear that he always carried in the hand that did not clasp his wife's waist.

However it was of Yod that she wished to know. He was nearer her own age than anyone else on the island.

"Why have I not seen you before? I go to the goat meadow often."

"You have not seen me because I did not choose you should see me."

She remembered the goatskin hut and the figure that disappeared within. "That was unkind of you, and discourteous. I am lonely."

"Unkind?" he said. "Discourteous?" and he seemed to spit the words. "What has a Roman princess to do with a slave from Palestine?"

"There are political slaves," she said, "who rank almost as high as hostages. What is your status? Will time not bring you your freedom?"

But Yod refused to speak either of his own past or the past of the Ethiopians. He told her instead the names of the goats and what they liked to eat, and he sang for her the sad little wailing songs that he sang to quiet them while he was milking.

"I live apart in the hut," he said disdainfully, "and I kill and cook my own meat."

"Why do you not eat with the others what the cooks prepare?" she demanded.

"It would be against the law of my religion," he said.

"Which of the gods has decreed that? Which one presides over your house? The gods of the Julio-Claudian line are Mars and Venus."

"War and love," he sneered. "It is an appropriate choice."

She challenged him then, for she understood the tone. "Is your god more powerful than mine? Over what things does he hold sway? Is he the god of wisdom or harvest or rivers or sea?"

He frowned and spoke as if to himself. "My God is the god of all."

That puzzled her. "Tell me his name? I know all the Roman gods, and Psiloriti has taught me the gods of Greece."

He rose to his feet with a bound like a goat. "I see the kids straying too near the cliff edge and I hear the wind rising. One was blown over seven days past, and the kites found it before I did."

"Oh," she cried, sad for the baby goat, "could you not save it?"

"It fell on a jagged ledge of stone, and I had no way to reach it. It probably died at once and felt no pain."

He was going, and she cried after him: "Will you come again to this grove? I like to talk with you."

He waved a hand. "I will come again—if you tell no one but the Greek scholar."

She watched him wistfully as he went, then turned back to the villa. When she and Psiloriti walked out again she told him of her new friend.

"He said I must tell nobody but you. If my grandmother Scribonia and Bruna know, they will say unkind things of him, as they do of everyone else."

He smiled reassuringly at her. "The boy from Judea is a good boy, and you have done no harm. I will keep your secret, little one."

"Why have I never seen him before? Why did he always go in his hut when you and I went to the high meadow?"

He could not explain to her a Jew's hatred of Romans, or the bitterness and stubborn racial pride. He said: "It is time now to return. The wind from east is blowing and twilight will soon fall."

She forgot Yod and asked him: "Psiloriti, why is it that the wind from east blows with a sound like thunder?"

"It is because it blows from east," he said. His face looked strange to her. "Across the sea and across the years and across Italy, it brings to my ears from the caves of Crete the bellowing of Minoan bulls."

3

THE wind from east still blew across the Adriatic Sea, across Italy's spinal column of the Apennines, across the bay and across the small island beyond it. Myrtle and cypress and pine, which rooted in fertile fissures, bowed their feathery boughs before it. Winter was coming, and the fruit of the ilex grew gold and red. The goats still played in the pasture, but they were now housed at night. In the garden the flowers died, and the slaves replaced them with evergreen. But the bright fish in the fishpond felt no change in their spectral world. They rose to the mirrorlike surface whenever they heard voices, and they darted and snapped and tore at quarters of goat flesh thrown to them. They were cannibal fish, and they often fought fights to the death among themselves. Julia and her guests enjoyed tantalizing and watching them. Sometimes she gave orders that they should not be fed for days. At the end of that time the smaller ones would have disappeared, and the larger would have grown heavy and bloated. Procla used to look down through still, stained water and pale green reeds and see them waiting motionless, with fierce eyes and pulsing fins.

It was at this time that she first found out what Lalibela did. The Ethiopian princess was the seamstress for the household. Her slim, dark fingers made magic of the lengths of silk and cloth of gold which were brought as gifts to her mistress. She seldom spoke, but when she did her voice was soft and kind. And always as she moved her wrists the heavy bracelets of beaten silver clashed and jingled with strange, barbaric music. Bruna said that she was no good for harder work than sewing because she had a sickness which made her cough blood from her chest.

When the wind blew too cold for the child to go out of doors, she would climb to Lalibela's room in an upper wing of the villa. It was hung with lion and leopard skins, and they carpeted the rough stone floor; for the sick woman suffered intensely from the climate. She sat close to a small metal box that stood on short legs on the floor and that her husband took care to keep filled with charcoal. She would shiver uneasily although all openings were sealed tightly, and the air would be heavy with perfumes that were strange to Procla.

She loved Lalibela for her gentleness and courtesy. Nobody else was as kind to her. Bruna always scolded; Julia was short of temper; Scribonia was sharp of tongue. But the dark girl in the upper room smiled swiftly and spoke slowly.

"Lalibela," the child would say, "I had a strange dream last night. I saw things I had not seen before. Do you believe in dreams?"

"The Lord has appeared to kings and to men in dream," said Lalibela. "But one must be careful of such things. They verge on abomination."

Procla did not know what abomination was. She said: "I feel as if in my dreams I go farther than my eyes can see, and I hear things I would not hear if I were awake."

Lalibela thought it best to change the subject. She was homesick, and she was a born storyteller. While she was talking her listener saw ancient Cush. She saw the great men's strongholds built on peaks. She saw the warriors with shields of rhinoceros hide, crossing rivers in boats made of papyrus and lashed together with vines.

"How I would like to go in a boat! Did you go in those boats, Lalibela?"

The dusky noblewoman shook her head. She was too modest to explain that her rank kept her in strict bounds.

"Only men go in the boats," she said. "They have strength to drive them with poles. But village women go each day to the nearest spring for water. They dare not go far because of the mountain leopards. Sometimes they are charged by rhinoceroses. Our men go forth to hunt these strange beasts with horned noses, in order to make from their thick skins shields which will blunt any weapons."

"I would like to hunt them," said Procla, whose disposition was without fear and whose age was that at which a child wishes to do everything.

Lalibela smiled and shook her head as she smoothed cloth stiff with gold.

"You would be there a great lady, as you are in your own country. You would sit beneath an awning made of the skins of bright sunbirds. Servants would bring you raw meat and fruit and cakes made of flour ground between two stones. They would fan you all through the heat of the day, and if the dust devils blew or the hailstones began to crash down, they would bear you on their shoulders to your father's house."

Procla thought about that. She knew that she lived in her mother's house, but a father's house sounded more safe and important.

"Where is my father?" she asked. "And where is his house?"

Telke came in as she spoke, bringing live charcoal for the brasier. He heard and he knew that they were on dangerous ground. Behind Procla's back he signaled his wife to be silent.

"Your father is the great general Tiberius. He has palaces in Rome and villas on the island of Rhodes."

As he spoke he fingered the little gold cross he wore around his neck. Unlike Psiloriti, he had not come willingly to this penal island with the pale-faced, evil Julia. Perhaps the holy merit in the talisman would offset the wickedness of which he lived in dread.

The child saw it. "You have a cross like Lalibela's, Telke. Is it an amulet? Why do you wear it?"

There seemed to him no harm in telling the tale. Like his wife he pitied and liked the lonely child.

He rose from his knees by the brasier and folded his wide scarf around him. "There was a queen of my country whose right foot was deformed."

"How sad," cried Procla, "for a queen! Could she wear a sandal upon it?"

"That I do not know. But this queen, whose name was Makeda, heard rumor of a great ruler in a city called Jerus Alem. This ruler was called Solomon and was king as well as doctor. So Queen Makeda set out from Cush with caravans of rare spices and priceless wood and jewels and gold to visit Solomon."

"Did the great doctor cure her foot?"

"I think that Solomon healed her ills. She stayed a long time in his country and was so impressed by his customs that she left her son Menelik to be reared and trained in his temple. This son was afterward a king of my country."

"Then he came back from Jerus Alem? He did not stay with the ruler?"

"When he had grown to manhood he returned to his home and his people. He brought back gifts more price-less even than those his mother had taken. For he brought the Ark of the Covenant and the Ten Laws of Moses."

"Was Moses a senator? Are his laws the laws of the Roman Code?"

"No; they are very different from the laws by which you live. They were given him on a mountaintop by God."

"By which god?" asked Procla, daughter of the Caesars.

"By the God of the wise King Solomon, who is also the God of my land. I think that Bruna awaits you down in the hall, small princess."

But as she turned, she saw that Lalibela's hands were clasped together and that her lips moved in a faint but solemn whisper. *"I am the Lord thy God,"* were the words she heard.

"Is the Lord thy God then Jupiter of the Romans, or Zeus of the Greeks?" she demanded. "Will you not tell me his name and the names of his companion gods?"

"There are no others," Lalibela said. "It is forbidden us to bow down to other gods or to images."

"I find that strange," said Procla thoughtfully. "For I do not see how he can preside over all things at once. When Mars takes the field with the Legions, Ceres must stay at home to give us fuller harvest. Truly I pity your God that he has no others to help him."

"The first of all His laws," said Lalibela in her soft voice, "is *'Thou shalt have no other gods before me.'*"

Procla was puzzled. She looked at Telke. "But—"

He stopped her there with a gentle push.

"Go now," he said, "little princess. As I came through the hall I heard Bruna calling you. It is better for you and for us that you leave us and go to her."

4

AMONG Julia's associates at this time were the tribune Andrus Draco and the patrician Lexus Paulus. The latter was old and was steeped in all the evil of his time. The former was young and handsome and quick to learn and rise. The military tribunes were considered apprentices for either the Senate or the Equestrian Order.

Procla was growing up, tall and lithe with bright chestnut hair. Old Bruna dressed it with a thick fall of bangs in front and an unbraided pigtail tied in the back. That fashion had passed in Rome, but she was not aware of it. She tried with fumbling fingers to make her charge attractive by arts in the elegance of a bygone day. This was not hard to do, for the child was lovely. She had no prettiness in the way of curly locks or dimples. Her mouth was the Julio-Claudian mouth: full and strong and sulky. But where her mother was heavily built, she was slender and pliant. Instead of round dark eyes under lids like hoods, she had long eyes, gray to blackness, underneath dark, level brows.

Julia's lovers admired Procla. She was now twelve years old, and Roman girls were given in marriage when little older than that. They made much of her when she was brought to banquets. They discussed omens which might bear upon her return to Rome; for Julia believed implicitly in omens.

Procla liked the excitement of arriving guests and banquets. She liked the blazing lamps and the golden dishes, the heavy armlets and signet rings on arms and hands of the officers, the atmosphere of laughter and ease. Most of all she loved the gifts that these men brought when they came. Last and loveliest, to her, of gifts was a piece of diaphanous muslin that Draco had bought from a legionary returned from the East. It was delicate as veiling and shimmered with rainbow threads. It changed its color with changing light and was stiff with embroidery of small pearls. Fortunately there was not enough for Julia's ample figure; so it had been turned over to Lalibela to be made into a tunic of occasion for Procla.

The occasion on which she first wore it was at the opening feast of that year's Saturnalia on the island. The villa was crowded with guests; for both labor and military movement came to a stop for dedication of the winter sowing. Procla, in wild excitement, ran from place to place, exchanging the *Io Saturnalia* of greeting and accepting tokens of figurines made of clay and of small wax candles. She carried them up to the goat meadow to show to Yod.

"Come to the villa and play with me! I'll show you the lion made of mosaic at the door. Draco told me a general of the Legion brought it back from Judea."

"He probably did. Your soldiers bring back all things which are not fastened down."

"At this time you may come with me, Yod. Psiloriti told me that for these days all slaves are free. It is their opportunity to say whatever they please and to insist upon any wrongs being righted. He says that in some houses they recline at table and eat with their masters attending upon them."

"But not in the Villa Julia," said Yod.

"There will be a great feast tonight. I wish you to see me in my new dress."

"If I am to see you in your new dress you will have to come to me."

He seated himself on the grass and leaned his back

against a rock. "Not even to see your new dress, will I risk a flogging."

"Nobody is flogged during the Saturnalia," she said. "That would be wrong and would offend the harvest gods. Even the worst criminals are not then put to death."

He jeered at her. "How kind of the gods! I see you are well learned in laws of the idolators."

The word gave her no offense, but teasing angered her. "You are ill-mannered," she told him, and she stamped her leather sandal.

"The manners of my people are not the manners of yours. We do not make a religious festival of overeating and of drunkenness."

She thought that over, for she had a mind of her own. She had always been accustomed to seeing her mother's friends in various stages of intoxication. Lexus Paulus, bald-headed and bulbous-nosed, had once seized her with his fat hands and put his wet lips against her neck. She had twisted away from him, tearing his toga and tripping him up. The others had shrieked with laughter as he sprawled on the floor, revealing the strips of woolen cloth which old people wrapped around their legs for warmth and which were considered a sign of infirmity.

She thought drunken people rather ridiculous, but no one had ever told her that drunkenness was wrong.

"If you like you may choose one of my dolls of clay and keep it, Yod."

"No," he said. "They are images."

He was always independent. Although she was a princess and he admired her, he was stubborn and aggressive about his own opinions. He had no longer any fear of her telling what he said. By this time he knew her well enough to realize that although she would quarrel with him she would protect him from others.

"Give me one of the candles," he said. "I have no light in my hut."

She divided them with him.

"I must go now and let Bruna dress me. The tables are laid in the garden since the weather is still warm, and my couch is next to Draco's. Will you not come, only as far as the fishpond? From there you could see me."

He turned his face away and spat.

"I will stay with my goats. I will not go one step toward that place of abomination."

She walked back slowly and sadly; for he was her only playmate and she had wished him to see her in the glittering muslin. She kept thinking about it while Bruna arranged her hair for the first time in a knot on the back of her neck, and secured it with golden pins like tiny daggers. Then the old woman lifted the iridescent folds of the full tunic and slipped it over her head. While she was fastening it with a broad golden girdle, Procla was holding at arm's length her metal toilet mirror and trying to see every inch of her new dignity.

She sighed with satisfaction. "Lalibela is clever."

Bruna was jealous. She scolded. "I have told your mother that you spend too much time in the quarters of that heathen. She comes from the uttermost end of the world, and she will teach you things as black as herself."

Procla's temper flared. "Keep your advice to yourself unless I ask for it! You are as brown as Yod's ram goat and just as ugly. As for Lalibela," she said—and did not know she was quoting—"Lalibela is black but beautiful."

As she went out the door she saw that the hanging lamps and the torches on their tall standards were being lighted. It was one of Julia's grievances, and she said they lived like barbarians, because the villa had only one small dining room. It could not accommodate the diners at a party of this size.

She walked slowly through the garden, holding her long skirts high above slippers which were only soles of matting laced with ribbons. Trellises wreathed with vine leaves had been erected to hide the musicians. Vines were garlanded around the stone edge of the fishpond. As she leaned across the screen of evergreen to look, she put out a hand to steady herself. But she reached too high and instead of encountering solid rock it pushed through leaves and plunged her arm into water. There was at once a rush and a swirl, and she felt a pain like the stab of a knife. She threw herself back on her knees and looked at her dripping arm. A small piece of flesh had been torn out just below the elbow and blood was running down across her wrist and palm.

Draco picked her up. She was sobbing with terror.

"The—nasty fish—they bit me! They tried to eat me." Her voice broke with horror at the thought. "Draco, command that they be destroyed! Have boiling oil poured into the pond!"

He lifted her over to his couch which was next to hers, and he sat by her and comforted her. He called a slave for linen and oil, and he cleansed the wound and bandaged it.

"I am treating you like a soldier of the Legion, Procla. The legionary's cure for every ill is oil and wine. Nay! Do not cry out at the sting of it. Remember that you are a Roman."

He soothed and fascinated her, with his gay voice and his strong, sure hands. He was very gentle and yet quite stern with her.

"No Roman girl should shed a tear because of a little blood and pain—least of all the most beautiful Roman girl that I ever saw."

He finished the bandaging swiftly, and she winced but did not cry out as he tied it tightly in an effort to check the bleeding.

"Now you must act as if nothing had happened," he told her. "You must laugh and eat and drink and let nobody know."

She was shaking all over, and she felt her sleeve folds cold and wet and slimy. But he again lifted her, this time across to her own couch, and he gave her no sympathy.

"I shall be ashamed of you if you whimper like a whipped slave. Laugh, Procla, and forget the fish. Or while you laugh be thinking of some way in which to give them torture even worse than boiling oil. So you must be, I tell you, if you are a Roman."

She managed to laugh all during the feast. The men paid her compliments, and Draco plied her with wine. He did it in kindness, for he knew that she still suffered. His bands were so tight that they kept the blood from flowing and her hand and arm lost all sense of feeling. Her head felt strange too; but he held his golden cup to her lips. He was handsome, and she was too young to see her mother's angry glances and the guests' malicious smiles.

When the last courses had been served and basins and napkins had been brought for them to wash their hands, Julia looked down the table. "I will have Catus the younger and Andrus Draco upon either side of me," she decreed.

He left Procla without a look. Already he swayed upon his feet. He went to the coarsely handsome woman in the purple tunic and put his arms around her and dropped his face in her hair.

The others amused themselves likewise. Procla sat alone and erect on her couch, a little giddy from the red wine, with her arm and shoulder throbbing faintly.

The swinging lamps flared in the sea wind and the musicians played louder. There seemed to her to be an offensive blare of sound and light. The soiled cloth and uncovered dishes on the table offended her.

It was then she thought of the goat meadow and the path along the low cliffs. It would be quiet there. Instead of the smoky torches would be only the full moon as it rose across Italy.

She reached down for her sandals which had been removed by a slave before the banquet began.

None of them even saw her go. They were by this time overcome by wine and occupied with love-making.

She ran by the fishpond and up the short slope to the rocks that bordered the ocean. She knew that this was the shortest way from the garden to the pasture. In daylight she liked the shade of the oaks and the descent through the ravine; but at night and alone she was afraid of the shadows. She wished to show Yod her party dress and tell him about her accident. And although she did not realize what the longing was, she longed for the clean-cut sturdiness of the Jewish boy, for the gay friendliness of the little goats, and the salt wind on the high meadow.

Through her thin shoe soles she felt the jagged, uneven stone of the path. But she knew that the cliffs were not very high and that the way was not very long.

The moon was rising as she ran around the peak at its highest point. Forty feet below her the waves crashed in and broke. She had made the turn and started down when something reared up before her. Its Pan-like head had a beard and two horns and it stood on two feet and was six feet tall.

Yod, lying outside his hut, heard her scream as she stopped short. Then the brown ram goat which she had startled from sleep lowered his head and charged her.

5

YOD, running at full speed up the small peak from the other side, saw the ram standing stiff-legged and staring down at the water. He knew at once what had happened, and he struck it with his staff.

"Beast of sin," he screamed at it, "you have done an evil thing!"

He dropped the club and began to descend the slippery, volcanic shelves. The waves lashed up to meet him and tried to tear him from his precarious hold. All below him they foamed and boiled and sucked at the pitted stone. Whatever they had in their grasp they were dashing against the side of the crag. He knew that the girl might be there, hidden from his sight in their turmoil; but he knew that if she was she could not still be alive.

Perhaps . . . with ropes and nets and the help of other men. . . .

He bounded in on the revelers like a shaggy faun from the night.

"The child," he shouted—"the Roman child has fallen from the cliff into the sea!"

Those who could still sit up did so. A few were able to spring to their feet. He stood in their midst, stocky and short, with his wet black curls half hiding his face. His short, coarse kilt dripped water and clung to his heaving body. Beneath it his knees and his hairy legs were lacerated and running blood.

"If you are men and not unclean swine, follow me back," he shouted.

The shock brought Draco's wits back to him. He called

to the slaves to bring torches, and he wheeled to follow the boy. Julia clutched him, shrieking, and he pushed her roughly away. He tried to concentrate his mind and to make his limbs co-ordinate. But he could not overtake the boy, although he was running with longer steps and with the sea roaring louder at each step against his ears.

As they reached the peak, both he and the boy saw that the island was now alarmed. Lights were floating like fire-flies in the darkness below them, and torches gathered and converged as they moved toward the place. They heard shouts and saw dark silhouettes against the sky and along the path.

"I will go down," said Draco. "Bring me a rope, shep-herd!"

There was one at the hut that he had woven of goat's hair in lonely hours. He ran for it. As he disappeared Draco looked over the cliff. He was not a physical coward, and he had great strength and was a trained swimmer. But he did not know the terrain and was too dulled by drink to see the scanty footholds which had taken Yod halfway down. In the moonlight it looked smooth and sheer and almost overhanging, and forty feet down the tide roared in against it. He felt quite sure that the girl was dead. A wave of sickness swept over him.

Just as Yod came back with the rope Catus and several slaves arrived. Draco was ungirdling and dropping his outer tunic. They fastened the rope around him just below his arms. His head was swimming horribly as he went over the edge, with Yod and Catus gripping the long brown line and playing it out by inches.

He could get no purchase of hand or foot upon that slimy wall. He swung free of it helplessly, and then was dragged back against it. It ripped his close-fitting inner tunic and tore deep gashes in the flesh beneath it. When he tried to fend himself off he broke his fingernails to the quick. He was a stoic about pain, but he was suffering mentally. For befuddled as he was, it came to him in flashes that if he had been sober he could have done more than this.

The waves leapt up to meet him. They had taken Procla and had tried for Yod and failed, and they hungered for a new victim. The salt burned cuts and skinned places like fire, but he did not even notice the pain. He was trying desperately to make brain think and body act.

Now he felt loose rock and pebbles under his bare feet. He stumbled and clutched for support, went under and came up again. The tide stood well above his waist and every wave broke over his head. But he breathed between their onslaughts and their cold wash cleared his thoughts. He untied the rope and left it hanging and began to make his way along the base of the cliff.

"Procla," he shouted. *"Procla!"*

And the sea shouted back at him.

He felt with his feet under water, for he knew that a small body might be floating submerged, sucked back and dashed up again. More than once he clutched madly at rafts of soiled foam that had taken iridescent hues from the moonlight. But they were even more fragile and diaphanous than the little rainbow dress he had bought from the legionary.

He could now hardly stand against the backwash of the turning tide, and his brain was reeling with confusion and self-reproach. He saw her sitting, grave and pale in the palely shimmering muslin. She had looked like a nymph of moonlight then, and now she was drowned in a moon-lit sea. Why had he not been more tender with her when he bound her arm in the garden? He had left her to go to Julia who was no more than a courtesan.

But he had been aware of the girl beside him all during the banquet. He had been angry when he saw young Catus' eyes upon her. Now she was drowned, and that slim body beneath the bright veiling was being battered and bruised by waves against saw-toothed rocks. If only he were himself—were not swayed by this shuddering nausea—he might yet be able to find a way to save her.

"*Procla!*" he cried. "*Little Procla!*"

And he could have sworn that he heard faintly from the depths of the solid rock a childish voice implore him in answer: "*Draco. . . .*"

He beat upon the cliff face with his fists, and he fell again and again. He finally managed to find the rope, and he was half mad when they drew him up. Julia had come, upheld by two slaves. Her gilded chaplet was over one ear and she whimpered and wailed. She threw herself upon him, but he shook her off.

"Do not touch me, wanton! Your child is in Pluto's caverns. I tell you I heard her voice crying—" his own voice rose—"from the caves of the dead!"

A tall figure all in white stepped between him and Julia. It was the steward, and he dared to seize the Roman's arm.

"Do you know what you are saying, or are you too drunk to know?"

Draco was drunk, but he drew himself up in pride and anger. He tried to break the man's grip, but the muscular fingers tightened.

"Tell me, as you value the life of the little Princess Procla! Did you hear her voice while you were in the sea at the foot of the cliff?"

Draco forgot his pride in his grief. He dropped his face in his hands.

"I heard her calling, I tell you! I heard her faintly but plainly—and I did nothing for her!"

Sickness again surged over him and his knees buckled beneath him. But as he fell he saw the Ethiopian cast his scarf aside. With a leap like that of his own mountain antelope, he reached the verge and poised himself, supple and dark in his white loincloth. Then he sprang upward and dived far out to avoid the fanged rocks at the cliff base.

6

PROCLA told Lalibela all about it. Although strong, she had caught cold, and fever kept her indoors for days. She did not yet suspect the reason, but she already felt that this room where the dark girl sat with the little cross around her neck was a refuge from trouble in that unquiet house.

"When the goat butted me off the cliff a big wave caught me and rolled me. It rolled me through an arch in the rock and up a slant of stone."

Lalibela inclined her head. "My husband knew there were caves."

"I was terribly frightened. It was dark, with a sound of thunder; and I had to crawl higher and higher as the water rose around me. Besides, I didn't know what the thing on the cliff had been, and I feared it might pursue me."

Lalibela looked up at her in surprise. "You thought that the ram might leap from the cliff and pursue you through the water?"

"It stood upon two cloven feet, and I feared that it might be Pan. He can easily change his shape, you know, to a man-goat or to a goat-man."

Lalibela shook her head. "No other gods before me."

"Why do you always say that?" Procla demanded. "It may be that Pan himself struck me from the cliff. Yod laughed at me when I told him so; but he cannot be sure, for he did not see it happen."

"Yod knows too that there is but one true God. The Ten Laws were brought from his land to mine. How can you exalt and worship a monster, half animal, who would take pleasure in throwing a young girl into the ocean?"

"Would your God never do so—not even if he were angry?"

"Never," said the African girl; and her soft voice was certain. "He exacts justice and must have an eye for an eye and a tooth for a tooth; but He does not go in obscene shapes doing evil things to His people."

But there was another facet of the matter in which Procla took an even deeper interest. She spoke shyly. "Psiloriti said that Draco went down the cliff on a rope and tried to find me before Telke got there."

Lalibela recognized the reluctance of that tone. Always before it had been a child's voice, eager and unabashed with any inquiry. She herself had not gone out to the cliff that night. When the news reached them and Telke rushed away, she had stood and watched from an upper window, then dropped on her knees to pray for him and for the child. When he came back he had told her all, fairly and impersonally. The young Roman had risked his life unhesitatingly, but had been too maudlin to accomplish what he tried. Telke had concluded generously that there must be some good in the man since, overwhelmed by shame and horror at his failure, he had left the island next day without even seeing Julia. In consequence Julia had been for days in a black fury.

Procla had reason to know that. She had been ordered from the room when she went to her mother the morning after the near tragedy. Julia had ordered her out of her sight, screaming after her that she was willful and had not only spoiled the banquet but probably provoked the gods by disturbing their festival. Procla had no suspicion that jealousy of Draco's dawning interest in her was behind that anger and unkindness. She had asked Psiloriti what to do to propitiate Saturn. His calm, untroubled philosophy had poured oil on troubled waters and steadied her small, storm-tossed bark in a sea of crosscurrents. She had questioned him bashfully about Draco too. The young patrician was known by all to be on the rise in Rome. To the old Greek's sharp and worldly eyes, he seemed Procla's best chance of escape from Julia and Pandataria. In all the world Psiloriti cared only for beauty and for this child. He felt that she would be fortunate if Andrus Draco took her for wife and shared with her wealth and glory, no matter how he attained them.

So Psiloriti had made much of what Draco had done, and had made no mention of any defection in Draco. She recalled that he had spoken out in praise of Draco's courage. But she saw that Lalibela was hesitating now. She looked at the older girl with big eyes which were almost black from anxiety.

"I had crawled as high as I could in the cave. I thought I was going to be drowned. I tried not to cry, because Draco had said a Roman girl must not shed a tear. But I was so frightened, Lalibela!

"After a long, long time I thought I heard Draco's voice. So I slid down off the rock and tried to get to the cave door. But a big wave came driving in and knocked me down and rolled me around and strangled me. I finally managed to get above the water again. And then, suddenly, I heard Draco shout 'Procla!'"

As near as that, Lalibela thought, and too stupefied to find her.

"He was shouting 'Procla! Little Procla!' He must have been close to the mouth of the cave, for I heard him clearly. I was afraid to get down again, but I cried back to him. Then I listened . . . and waited. . . .

"But he must not have heard me. I had given up all hope and I was crying and sobbing when I saw Telke before me and he picked me up in his arms. At first I hoped —I mean I thought—that he was Draco come back for me."

Bruna had interrupted them there, scolding and calling

for Procla. She had been indignant; for in the villa only she cared at all for its mistress. She had served Julia from Julia's babyhood; and all of the woman's wickedness had failed to kill the old nurse's love for that baby. She slapped Procla, which was a mistake. It aroused characteristics inherited directly from her beloved mistress.

"You she-goat! You ugly old devil! I'll have you thrown to the fishes. Draco told me to find them a death even worse than boiling oil. If they eat your unclean body they will be poisoned and die."

It happened in the hall. The household slaves, in delight, gathered to watch from entrances or from behind statuary. They all hated Bruna, and she knew it. She heard their laughter, and it enraged her more.

"I shall see that you are forbidden to go again to the Ethiopians' room."

She paused to search her mean little mind for other punishment.

"Your lady mother has every right to be angry with you and beat you. Your behavior with her friend the Lord Andrus Draco was unseemly, and you ruined her banquet."

Procla drew herself up. Telke, who had heard the noise and was watching in apprehension, thought that she looked a princess as she faced the old panderer.

"Not you and not my mother, and not anyone else in the world, dare lay a hand upon me. If anyone does I shall go straight to my grandfather the Emperor Augustus in Rome."

Then she spun on her heel and sped from the reception hall, out into the garden and on toward the high meadow.

Bruna turned slowly and, although the watchers were hidden, cast a glare of malignance around the huge hall. Then she went across to Julia's apartment to report the matter to her in detail.

As Telke climbed the stairs he could see through the

pillared façade a slim figure running up the low hill by the oak trees. His wife rose to meet him as he closed the door behind him, and she saw that his face was grave.

She did not question. She went to him and put her arms around him. He held her close, as if he feared she would be taken from him.

"My own flower of gold, for the first time I regret that I offered myself as a hostage."

She lifted her face and looked him proudly in the eyes.

"What else could a prince have done when the Roman cohorts prowled like lions?"

"You were gay and free as a sunbird there. If harm should come to you . . ."

"*He* is our refuge," she said clearly; and she released herself and went to get the scrolls of holy writing.

She put them in his hands and drew him down on the wooden settee with its thin cushion of straw, and she sat beside him with her head against his heart.

And he unrolled the papyrus and began to read aloud: "'Make haste, O God, to deliver me; make haste to help me, O Lord.'"

7

BACK in Julia's apartment Bruna spat poison like a viper.

"They conspire against you, my lady—all of this house except me."

"Why not you too?" inquired Julia. She spoke between her teeth, and she was no longer handsome as she lay fat and flushed with her face deep-lined by temper.

"Because I love you, my lady," the old servant entreated. She preferred lying to speaking truth, but it was truth she spoke now.

Julia roused from her misery of jealous brooding.

"Bring me clean linen and dress me! I will lie here no longer. Where is the violet toga that I wore on the last night I dined?"

"I gave it at once to the black woman to mend. She should by now have done the task. But instead she spends her time on her knees making heathen incantations. She works her spells on your daughter to steal her affection from you."

"You lie," said Julia. "My daughter never loved me. She is even at her age a slut, and she is working her own spells to steal from me the one man I love."

She fell back on her couch and wept tears of rage and self-pity. She was growing old, and what looks she had were raddled with debauchery. Men who had loved her despised her now. They came less frequently. It was she who had to invite and plead. Only the old servant cared and tried to comfort her. Bruna sat now beside her and smoothed the matted hair, discolored from years of dyeing.

"Your daughter would love you were she not under Africa's enchantment. She is still so young."

She realized that was dangerous. She knew that Julia wished no contrast with Procla's youth. So she hastened to continue: "Procla is a scrawny child. I mean that she is unripe in both body and mind. There is no man who would look at her twice while he had you to look at. Also she is wild and untrained."

That was another mistake. Julia sat up and flung her violently aside.

"If she is wild and untrained it is your fault, you old cow!"

"It is not my fault. I cannot break witches' spells. I tell you the steward's wife teaches her things unfit for a Roman lady."

"A Roman lady?" raged Julia. "My father made me an exile. I am denied the splendor in which he lives and rules. It is *his* fault if his granddaughter grows up a barbarian."

"Sooner or later," Bruna crooned, "your father will take you back. Did you not tell me that the great lord Lexus Paulus was using all his influence for you?"

"He swore that he would," wept Julia. "But he lies. He is an old goat. Oh, Bruna, what can I do? Must I spend my life on this island? I had hoped—I had hoped that Draco would take me away!"

"And so he will," crooned Bruna. "He loves you. He will come back."

"Bruna, do you think he will? What can I do to draw him back?"

That was the question Bruna wanted. She had to turn her face to smile. She knew that in order to get back the young tribune, Julia would sacrifice anyone else on the island.

"Calm yourself, my lady. Do not spoil your beauty by fretting. Then do these two things: first loose your child from the barbarians and put her back under my authority; and, secondly—"

She paused, and her mistress looked eagerly at her.

"Secondly, send the Greek Psiloriti to Rome. Instruct him both to intercede with Augustus and to interview the Lord Andrus Draco. If the Emperor refuses to allow you to return, have Psiloriti tell your lover to come for you in his private galley and take you with him to Athens or Alexandria."

It was so exactly what Julia wished that she could persuade herself Draco might wish it too.

"Dress me at once," she cried, "and then summon Psiloriti. Where is my daughter? Nay; she can wait. Hers is the less important affair."

Psiloriti came and heard her incoherent instructions. His expression did not change. Except for one fear that worried him, he was glad to go to Rome. He knew that the Emperor did not want his daughter back, and he knew that Draco did not want her at all. But he saw danger for the child in the situation. He knew that Bruna was venomous and he dreaded leaving Procla with the two unscrupulous and jealous women.

"I will do your errand, noble Julia." He was flattering her deliberately for his own ends. "You have made a wise decision. I can think of only one thing else which might further your case in Rome."

"What is that thing?" asked Julia. She had recovered herself and was again vital and bright-eyed with hope.

"Let me take with me to Rome this granddaughter of Augustus. Surely the sight of her will soften his heart toward you."

"Take her!" cried Julia—then stopped short, recalling that Draco was in Rome.

"Take her," said Bruna viciously, "and my lady's case is lost. The Emperor will keep Procla in Rome and leave her mother in exile."

He knew then that he would not be allowed to take the girl with him. All he could do was to warn them that they should be made to account for her.

"I shall do as you bid me. In so doing, I shall tell Augustus that I left the youngest member of his family well and alive and beautiful on Pandataria."

They looked back at him, for they knew he was driving a bargain. He smiled.

"She is both beautiful and intelligent. I feel sure that your father will be more inclined to receive you if he knows you will bring her with you just as I describe her."

He saw the hate in Julia's eyes as she stared back at him. But he knew that throw of the dice was his, and he continued to smile. "May I go?"

"Yes—but send me Procula. What mischief is she now doing?"

"She defied me in the hall," said Bruna. "Against my orders she ran out to the goat meadow. She thinks that I do not know, but she visits the Jewish herdboy."

Psiloriti went for her and found her on the cliff with Yod. She had been making Yod repeat the story of Draco's exploit. She leaned and looked down. Although not as heavy as on that night, the surf at the cliff base was always rough on account of the rock formation.

"It is steep and dangerous, Yod. Only a brave man would have dared. And suppose the shark had come?"

"The shark stays in calm water," Yod told her scornfully. "Besides, the Roman was tied with a rope and too drunk to know his danger."

Psiloriti lingered with them and told them about his forthcoming journey to Rome.

"I wish that my mother had consented to let me go with you," she said wistfully. "You have taught me about Rome and its Seven Hills."

Until now the island had fulfilled her heart's desire. But now she looked north across that periwinkle sea. . . .

"I would like to see my grandfather—and the officers of his legions."

Her voice dropped to a caress. Draco was one of them. Psiloriti read her thought as if she had spoken it aloud.

"If I see the tribune Draco, what word shall I give him?"

"Tell him," she cried—

Her face blazed into radiance, and the young Jew and the old Greek were amazed by its beauty. She looked from one to the other, and her color died to paleness.

"No," she said softly and fearfully. "I have nothing to say to him."

But Psiloriti had to warn her before he left, and it was hard to do without telling her what her mother was.

Yod understood. "It is better, I think, that she stop coming here."

Psiloriti nodded; but Procla's eyes filled and she cried: "Oh, Yod, I shall want to come oftener while he is away!"

"Yod is right," said the old man. "It will only make trouble for you."

"What trouble?" she asked him angrily; and she rose and drew herself up. "Am I not Augustus' granddaughter? What have I to fear?"

He took delight in her newfound imperiousness.

"True," he chuckled, "my princess. But you had better recall that your grandfather did not hesitate to banish his own daughter to this island. That daughter inherits his temper—as you yourself seem to do."

Then his face sobered and his voice grew grave.

"Little one, I implore you to walk carefully during the days that I am not with you. Do not provoke your mother or Bruna by spending time either with Yod or with Lalibela."

"They are my friends," she said. "Shall I let fear of punishment make me desert friends who have been kind to me?"

"Assuredly you should. All sensible people do so. The gods are themselves frail and appreciate human frailty. Always think first of yourself and secondly of friends."

"I will not do so! There is a God greater than all the gods of the Greeks and the Romans."

He turned a horrified face to Yod. "Did you teach her this?"

"By the prophets, no! Do you think I wish to be strangled or crucified?"

"Lalibela told me. I choose Him for my God!"

Psiloriti had seldom known fear, but he was frightened then.

"Do not even speak such words aloud!"

"I shall do so. For I now believe there are no other gods before Him. He is just and severe, but He teaches justice to others. His religion bids you think of others before you think of yourself."

Psiloriti rose and shrugged. He looked old and tired.

"It sounds like a most inconvenient religion," he said. "Why should you choose it in preference to gods who are like mortals, and who can be bribed or flattered into allowing mortals to do as they choose?"

His eyes searched her young face but found it set and strained. He spoke slowly. "If you are really thinking of your friends before yourself, I warn you to tell Julia nothing about all this."

He left next day in a fishing boat. But before he went he had another brief exchange of words with Julia.

"Tell my father the Emperor," she commanded, "that I named this daughter Procula in memory of his old friend Proculeius, who captured the witch Cleopatra. I wish her called that, you understand. Forget this childish 'Procla.'"

"I shall do even better than that, Lady Julia," he replied. "I shall name her to Augustus as 'Claudia Procula.' Surely you have not forgotten—and it will remind him— that she comes of the imperial Julio-Claudian line."

8

DURING Psiloriti's absence the slow months dragged, unbroken by either trouble or joy.

Procla, forbidden to go to her playfellow Yod and discouraged by him when she tried to do so, spent even more time with Lalibela. Lalibela knew by heart lovely singing psalms. The daughter of pagans listened, her big gray eyes intent.

One day Lalibela opened a little box of spikenard wood and lifted from its fragrance two massive golden armlets. They were thickly engraved with symbols: the lion, the star, the dove, the rose of Sharon, the sacred scrolls and the cross. She balanced them in her thin hands.

"They are now too heavy for me to wear. It is the custom of my land for two sisters who love each other dearly each to carry one. Since I left my land, you are the only one I have learned to love. Will you wear this, Procla, while I keep the other in memory of our affection?"

Procla seized it with delight, and then embraced Lalibela so hard that she lifted her from her feet. She turned the heavy ornament on her slim, strong young arm.

"It is beautiful, and its workmanship is different from ours. Yet, Lalibela, although your religion is different you have told me yourself that your God is a God of wrath." Her voice was wistful. "I have sometimes wondered whether there was any God who loved us enough to forgive us, without bribes and sacrifices."

"The Hebrew prophets have foretold that God would one day send a Messiah to save us all."

Procla was thinking about this so deeply that as she

41

went out on the terrace she came upon the sacrifice of doves that she hated and always avoided. The birds she had allowed to escape had long since been replaced. A white wing fluttered weakly as old Bruna crouched over it and examined the hot entrails.

"You nasty old woman! I hate you and Ennius for killing that dove!"

"Ah," breathed Bruna, "the omens show that a messenger of some kind is near."

She wiped her bloody fingers on her already dirty clothing, and turned to carry that report to her mistress.

And just then a shadow fell on the small stone altar.

Procla and Bruna and Ennius started back in horror. Nothing more inauspicious could occur than the fall of a shadow upon a sacrifice. As they looked up they saw a dark streak and heard a whistling sound. A small hawk which had seen from above the bloody feast on the marble dropped like a plummet upon it, dug in his claws and rose. For a second Procla saw him: beautiful, wild and hungry, with wings upraised to a sharp point above his lean, taut body. Then their downbeat lifted him. He was gone with the mangled dove, and Bruna and Ennius were screaming and running into the villa with their skirts thrown across their eyes to hide the unlucky sight.

Procla looked up until the hawk had disappeared. She hoped that this portent of ill had nothing to do with the safe return of Psiloriti.

Julia, upon hearing the news, had seized and shaken Bruna violently.

"Why did you or Ennius not strike down the hawk? Its sacrifice might have helped to counteract the evil it did."

"The trouble was done once it had cast its shadow on the altar. The taking away of the dead dove cannot affect the omen."

Julia bit her lips and began to pace her room. For weeks and months she had kept to it, alternating between hope and hopelessness and seeing no one except Bruna. Bruna acted like a drug and translated her by flattery to a false world where a young soldier loved her. Bruna raised brown claws of hands and cried out admiration.

"Never before have I seen hair so thick and lustrous as yours! How well its red-gold becomes you!"

Its red-gold did not become her. Her complexion was a natural olive and was sallowed by years of dissipation. But Roman women of fashion dyed their hair that shade regardless of the color of eyes or skin.

Now she stopped to stare at herself in the round shield that hung for mirror on her wall. She saw a woman of medium height, compactly and strongly built. Her limbs were well proportioned and rounded and her throat and bosom still fine. But it was getting difficult to make her tunics hang flat across her stomach.

"If I ordered Lalibela to make my tunics striped from neck to hem, it would make me look taller and more slender."

"But my lady, that is the mark of senators and knights."

"I did not mean to use purple, you old fool! I could have mine striped with gold or crimson."

"Indeed you could, my lady. It is a clever idea. Besides, it would give the African more honest work to do and leave her less time to make magic to steal your child away."

Mention of Procla brought back the double terror: fear of any comparison with youth and doubt of Draco's intentions. Julia snatched a metal hand mirror and revolved before the shield. She saw herself as broad of beam as one of the squat freight galleys that plied its trade between Ostia and Rome.

"My tunic falls too full," she raged. "Take it to Lalibela. Tell her she shall be punished if she is too clumsy to make it fit me across the back!"

Bruna returned with Procla. "I told her you wished to

see her. The woman will do more careful work if she is left alone."

"You did well," said Julia.

She eyed with no affection the slim figure already as tall as herself.

"I do not interfere with Lalibela's sewing," said Procla indignantly. "She knows her prayers and her laws by heart, and we only talk while she sews."

"And learn all manner of evil from the talking," said Bruna. "You refuse to obey me, and she encourages you."

"You lie," said Procla. "She teaches me only good. I told you just now that I would not come with you. But Lalibela bade me remember the Fifth Law."

"What witchcraft is this?" asked Julia.

She had no respect for Lalibela's laws or for any other laws. But she saw that Procla was lovely and that her chestnut hair had glints brighter than any dye could give.

"What spell is it," she repeated, "that can make you obey at mention of some heathen law, when otherwise you defy me? Tell me at once what is this Fifth Law?"

"Honor thy father and thy mother," Procla told her.

It diverted her spite to Bruna. As the girl went she turned on the woman.

"The Ethiopian teaches her what you failed to teach her. How dare you so misrepresent things? For the first time in her life she has been taught to honor me."

Bruna saw that her malice had come back like a crooked stick thrown. But long years of scheming had taught her means of recovery. She wagged her head wisely.

"So it sounded, my lady. But have you not always heard that Africans are devious? Do you not see that by such speech the witch can fool you and make you believe she is your friend, and at the same time implant in your child's mind the idea that *you do not honor your father?*"

Being self-centered, Julia always saw what she wished

to see. She dashed the small mirror across the room in a rage.

"Order the woman brought here at once! I will have her whipped. She shall be flogged until she confesses what evil spirits she invokes against me through my daughter." Bruna turned, laughing silently as a dog, toward the door.

But Procla was bursting through it. "Psiloriti is coming," she cried. "We saw the boat from the cliff—Yod and Telke and I!"

Julia's heart stood still and all laws were forgotten. She was thirsty for news from Rome after the long, arid years of exile. But the news she craved was not of her father's welfare, or of her older children. She was mad to hear of Draco, and she screamed at Procla: "Are you sure it is Psiloriti? If you disappoint me . . ."

"The boat is close to the south beach where the water is calm and it can land. Already the sailors are furling their sail, and Psiloriti waved at me."

"I am dressed to receive him," cried Julia. "Bring him! Why do you delay?"

But as Procla came back with the Greek, Julia turned on her and Bruna. "Leave us! This matter is between the Emperor and his daughter."

So they waited outside: Bruna anxious as to the effect of the messages on Julia, Procla anxious only to see her old friend again. He kept his voice too low to be overheard, but more than once they heard Julia's rise in anger.

"How can he be so cruel as to refuse me? Did you tell him my time was spent in mourning because of his treatment?"

"I told the Emperor what you told me to tell him."

"You must have in some way displeased him, and so injured my cause."

"I did not displease him. He has made me a Roman citizen and appointed me magistrate of this island."

He wanted her to know it at once, to forestall threats of punishment. Even the Emperor's daughter could not lay a finger upon a Roman citizen. Augustus had been generous and wise in his laws concerning the freedmen. He had opened to them various minor offices. It had occurred to him that this Greek, who had both learning and humanity, could better protect himself and keep Julia in bounds if invested with a magistracy.

She paced the room. "Oh, Juno, hear! He has denied his daughter's request and given power to one who was both alien and slave."

She stopped as she passed him, as if to strike him, then paused.

"Tell me every word that my father uttered! Magistrate or not, do not leave out one, I command you."

He smiled in his beard as he told her.

"From the first I saw that it was hopeless. He told me that not even if the goddess of wisdom advised it would he permit you to return to Rome. He is angry too with your daughter Julia and your youngest son Agrippa. He has banished the former to an Adriatic island. Seeing that those two had inflamed him more against you, I told him of his youngest grandchild. I told him she was growing up—beautiful, regal, intelligent—and suggested it might be well to have both her and her mother in Rome. I told him that men were already attracted by her."

"I care not for Procula," Julia screamed. "What did he say of me?"

Psiloriti was silent, but she urged him: "Tell me!"

"He spoke ugly words and cruel words. I ask you to excuse me."

"I will not excuse you. I order you to repeat them!"

Psiloriti's face was grave, for he hated all things ugly.

"Augustus told me, in a public hearing, that he looked upon you and the younger Julia and Agrippa Posthumus as his 'three cancers.'"

She clenched her hands and looked back at him with a hatred meant for her father. She did not care how he looked upon her; but his latest insult told her she would never get to Rome. And she was determined to get to Rome—to get to Andrus Draco. She had put off her question about him only because she feared to hear its answer. In spite of Bruna's flattery and her own determination to have her way, fear was closing in on her heart like a vise. But even if he would not come, she might win him back if she got to Rome—if she were re-established there as the Emperor's daughter. . . .

"Am I dismissed?" Psiloriti asked her.

He need no longer have asked. For a Roman magistrate, however small his domain, was a person of importance and entitled to respect. But the philosophy that was his religion had taught him that courtesy has more in common with beauty than has discourtesy.

She wheeled on him and unclenched her hands and struck them together. "No," she screamed, "not until you have told of your other errand."

"I could not do that errand," he told her gently; for he was beginning to pity her now.

Her whisper was harsh with anxiety. "Did you not go, as I bade you, to Andrus Draco?"

"I went to his house and asked for him, but he was not there."

Her face was contorted with rage and grief. "Where is he? Could you not get word to him?"

"No; for I could not follow him, and this is a private matter. Twelve years of exile have made us lose track of Rome and her affairs. But there has been trouble in the East, and the legate Varus has had to turn from Syria to wage war in Palestine."

"What has it to do with Draco and me? Tell me what has transpired?"

"Herod is dead and the Jews have sent an embassy to

Rome asking for a protectorate. There have been out-
breaks."

"What do I care for their turbulent tribes? Tell me of
Andrus Draco!"

"Their turbulence concerns him, noble Julia, for he is
in Judea. As soon as he returned to Rome from Pandataria he requested foreign duty. I was told that he is stationed at Caesarea in command of an armored column of
mounted men."

9

SO he had chosen to go to some savage province, instead of returning to take her away and establish her as his mistress. She had not waited to send that message by the Greek. She had suggested it to him in a dozen different ways. She could not fool herself that he imagined her unwilling. But he preferred his career as a Roman soldier. He preferred campaigning in eastern deserts and leading his heavy cavalry into battle against the bowmen of the tetrarchs. He preferred risking loss of his life to living it with her.

Fear and hope and doubt and distress crystallized into cold fury. Bruna, entering the room, looked at her and dared not speak. With her face flushed purple and her eyes glittering she paced the bed chamber, stepping like a tigress in spite of her weight. The only way she could rid herself of this venom of hatred would be to punish someone . . . to see someone suffer. . . .

Procla, waiting outside the door for Psiloriti, slid her hand into his and pulled him away.

"I have been so lonely without you. I could not go to Yod. I tried to do as you told me to, but the time was long."

He looked down at her, thinking of Julia's face contorted with passion and longing for revenge. At whatever cost to others he was determined to use his new power to further Procla's interests. All his pagan philosophy—beautiful, shallow, easy—centered on her youth and beauty. It was as if he, like a sculptor, had fashioned her by his teaching and care. She had nothing in common with Julia

49

who had given her birth. He would take care of her, he vowed, whatever befell.

They walked the path by the almond trees and he told her about Rome. "I saw and spoke with your grandfather Augustus."

"Although he is my grandfather he cares nothing for me."

He knew that she had no reason to love parents or grandparents, but never before had he heard her speak of their neglect. She is growing into a woman, he thought. I must keep her away from Julia. Julia will never brook a daughter who draws men's eyes from her. Julia will thwart and suppress her—perhaps do worse to her.

"Always in Rome," he said, "I wished that you were with me. I have been thinking of ways and making plans and trying to arrange for you to go there."

She shook her head. "My grandfather does not want me, and I will not go unwanted. I would rather stay on the island with you and Lalibela and Yod."

He stopped and took her by both hands and looked down into her eyes. "You cannot stay here, Procla. I fear for your safety."

She looked steadily back at him. "I am not afraid."

"But I tell you that I am and that I intend to get you away. If once the Emperor sees you, he will accept you."

"He will never see me. Had he wished to see or accept me, he would have told you and you would already have told me."

He reflected that she could think straight and speak directly. He knew that he need not be afraid to speak as plainly to her.

"Before I left Rome I sent the Lord Draco a message by a friend of Tiberius who was going as far as Crete."

Her eyes widened, then wavered. "Is Draco in Crete?"

"No, he is in Judea. But this man Pilate seems to have influence in high places. He promised to see that my letter was relayed on to Draco. I took care to let him know that for its delivery both Andrus Draco and the Emperor Augustus would be beholden to him."

"What message did you send?"

"I sent him word that you were in danger and that if he cared for you, he should come at once or send someone else to take you to your grandfather."

She flushed crimson. "He does not care. It is no affair of his. You have done wrong. Besides, even if willing, what can he do for me?"

"He has more power in Rome and more influence with Augustus than any other of your mother's friends. He is the only son of a powerful and important house. Too, he has in his own right prestige as a soldier. He distinguished himself with the legion sent to Varus' help on the Rhine."

She listened wide-eyed, and he added tenderly: "Did you not know that, little Procla?"

"I know naught of him save that he is one of my mother's friends. I will not even speak of him. Let us go on to Yod's pasture. Surely I may go there if you are with me."

But Psiloriti had delayed in his apartment, and before they reached the meadow Yod had news from Ennius. "Why did you bring her here?" he asked the Greek. "There is trouble at the villa, and I would not be involved."

"Has anything happened since my arrival?"

"Telke has been sent away in the sailing boat in which you came. Ennius says he is going on a long journey, but Julia gave him hardly time to say good-by to his wife. I wish I'd been sent in his stead! I would never return."

All three of them knew that the Ethiopian prince would not only scorn to break his parole as hostage, but would never leave his wife. They knew also that this was Julia's reason for choosing him. Psiloriti guessed the errand to be an appeal to Draco. But he could do nothing about it.

So he told the young Jew what news he had heard of his country through political gossip in Rome.

"Herod is dead; but before he died he butchered Alexander, Aristobulus and Antipater. A story in Rome runs that Augustus told the ambassadors from Judea he would rather be Herod's pig than Herod's son."

Yod's face was bitter. "Nightly I wail for my turbulent and tormented land. Yet—" and he turned his dark eyes east—"I would go back to it if I could."

Psiloriti went on, and his voice was thoughtful.

"Rome's gossip says that strange things are taking place in it. They tell of a child that was born in a cattle shed in a small village. This child was poor and of plebeian family; yet kings and scholars from far places arrived upon that very night and said that his birth had been forecast and hailed him as a Messiah."

"Oh," cried Procla, "perhaps he is the one of whom Lalibela spoke! She said that her prophets had foretold that a Messiah would come."

Yod shook his head. "There have been impostors before. They have been beheaded and stoned and strangled."

"So have I heard. I am telling you the latest gossip from Judea. It must now be close to fourteen years since this child was born, yet men still speak with awe of the strange events attending his birth. I had it from reliable sources that a star never seen before rose and stood over this birthplace. Princes from Greece and Egypt and India and other lands set out by the guidance of this star and met at Bethlehem."

"It was my village," Yod said. "Jehovah grant that I see it again!"

Procla, enthralled by the story, found her voice and gasped: "I must go at once and tell Lalibela!"

They watched her running like a deer, with her white skirts flowing backward. She flew through the entrance-court and hall and up the stairs. The house was strangely deserted; for the steward was away and Bruna had urged Julia to walk in the dusk in the garden. There under the quince trees she followed after the heavy, middle-aged woman, uttering scorpion compliments that carried stings in their tails.

"You move like a nymph, my lady. Only as compared with a child could anyone fail to associate you with youth."

Julia just then spied Procla running like the young Diana.

"It does me small good to have a wild and uncouth daughter. It may be that her unseemly behavior toward the Lord Draco is keeping him away."

Bruna nodded wisely. "It is like she offended him with barbarous ideas that she gets from the Africans. Hold still, my lady, and let me look. . . . Ah yes, I am now sure of it. It is only the clumsy folds of that tunic below your girdle that give you the appearance of stoutness. Were it cut properly you would look ten years younger."

"Go," said Julia between her teeth, "and bring me Lalibela!"

10

LALIBELA'S busy hands lay still as she listened. Her great eyes, exotically tilted in her small triangular face, were blazing with an unearthly light.

"It is the Word of the prophets made flesh! Oh, to see Him before I die!"

"Perhaps you will see Him," said Procla. "Do you think He is really a god?"

"I think so, and I pray so: God made man, come to earth to save us."

Procla was puzzled. "But how can one be sure? Yod says that other men have pretended to be saviors. They were killed, and their teachings were trampled and forgotten."

Lalibela shook her head. Her great black eyes were still burning.

"If He is the true Messiah—and something tells me He is—neither His own people the Jews nor the great Roman Empire will be able to trample Him into oblivion. Some blade of His teaching will take root, like a shoot of green in stony ground. It will take root in the hearts of men and someday come to fruition."

Her face saddened. "I think it is He; but I know that I shall not see Him."

"You and Telke are hostages, not slaves. When your land is at peace, you will be free to go as you choose. Perhaps you will then go to Judea."

The dark girl was seized with coughing. She could only shake her head. Just then Bruna came through the door.

She was panting but triumphant, for she had found a scapegoat.

"The noble Lady Julia commands the sewing woman to come at once to her in the garden."

Lalibela rose and laid aside her work. Procla looked from one to the other.

"I will go with you and you can lean on my arm, Lalibela." She turned on Bruna. "It is too far for her to walk alone."

"She will walk alone nevertheless," said Bruna with satisfaction.

"She will not, you nasty she-goat!"

She picked up the heavy cloak and laid it around the fragile shoulders and drew its warm hood over Lalibela's head.

"It is near the twilight and getting cold. Where in the garden is Julia?"

"By the fishpond," said Bruna. "Once again I warn you that you will only anger her by going along with us."

Procla delayed only long enough to stick out her tongue. Then, with a strong young arm around the too-slim waist, she started walking slowly with her friend.

They met no one. For the servants, knowing the steward absent, were either resting or visiting together, and Psiloriti and Yod were still talking in the meadow. As they passed under the quince trees dusk shut in upon them and Procla felt Lalibela shudder.

"Are you cold, or weary? Shall we stop to rest?"

Bruna, walking behind them, said: "My lady does not wait patiently."

Procla began: "Hold your tongue, you—"

But Lalibela checked her. "I wish to go on to the lady of the villa and have this matter concluded, whatever it is."

Julia's figure loomed ominous and thickset in the pale

light that filtered through the trees by the fishpond. She said sharply: "I sent only for Lalibela."

"So I told them, my lady. So I told them both. But your daughter is not herself. She is influenced by magic."

"Go," said Julia to Procla. "Get out of my sight! After all the harm you have done me, do you presume to come whenever I call a slave to account?"

"Lalibela is not a slave. Bruna makes this trouble. It is said in the Ninth Law 'Thou shalt not bear false witness. . . .'"

"So you defy me with words taught you by this black heathen? I order you to go at once! Am I not your mother?"

Lalibela said softly: "Go. And remember always that thou shalt honor thy mother."

Procla turned then and walked slowly away.

Behind her, Julia wheeled on the slim black girl. "Accursed witch! By what magic do you make my child obey, when she defies me to my face?"

"There is no magic, Lady Julia, in the Ten Commandments given Moses."

"There is evil magic, you sorceress! You control her, and neither her nurse nor I can do it. You sit in your quarters, weaving your spells like a spider."

"Aye," said Bruna, wagging her head, "she not only weaves her spells but she teaches their incantations to your child. You heard her quoting one of them just now. No matter what orders I give her, she tells me 'Thou shalt not do this or that.'"

Lalibela was silent. She was exhausted and trying not to cough. She swayed with fatigue, like a dried flower stem in the folds of her cloak.

"I have always done as I chose," Julia raged at her. "I am daughter of the Emperor Augustus. I am above law. Why should I not take from life anything that I want and put to death anyone who tries to prevent me?"

"Because," said Lalibela—and she spoke faintly but clearly—"the Eighth Law of Moses says that thou shalt not kill and the Sixth Law that thou shalt not steal."

"How dare you dispute me and quote your barbarous laws to me? I tell you I am a Roman and an emperor's daughter. How dare you corrupt my child? What other dark things have you taught her?"

She was advancing, and Lalibela backed away in terror. She backed into the tall marigolds that grew around the fishpond, and their rank, weedy fragrance came up in a wave to her nostrils.

"Sixth Law," Julia jeered. "Sixth spell of witchcraft!"

"It is so," urged Bruna. "Even now your child wears upon her wrist an African armlet engraved with strange figures and incantations."

Lalibela gathered her failing strength for one last attempt to justify herself.

"I do not deal in spells. I only try to keep my laws. I just now told you the Sixth and Eighth in answer to your question."

"You shall then tell me the others. I will hear all of them and get to the bottom of this mischief." Julia had worked herself up to madness and her hands were clenched into fists and her mouth twisted away from her strong teeth. "You have told me your Sixth and your Eighth Law. What is then your Seventh?"

Lalibela whispered: *"Thou shalt not commit adultery."*

Augustus had not whispered it. He had roared forth *"Proclamete!"* All the bitterness of those years of banishment seethed in his daughter. She lashed out like a wounded panther at the fragile woman before her. With her two clenched fists and with all her strength she struck her full in the chest.

Lalibela went over backward, without a cry.

And as she touched the water it boiled with the rush of the cannibal fish.

11

O F all the household Procla was the only one who did not know. She was still too young and too clean, and Julia was her mother. None of them dared, or even wished, to tell her the truth. She lay on her narrow couch, weeping all night long. She had listened to Bruna's story, then ordered her away.

"It was the woman's own fault. She went too near the fishpond. I had warned her to keep away, but she became dizzy and fell."

"It is your fault, because you made her go out in the garden. I knew she was weak and dizzy, and I wished to stay with her."

"You could not have helped her. She might even have pulled you in with her as she fell."

"She couldn't. She was no taller than you and thin as a stem of marigold. More than once I have lifted her, as I lift a doll. You caused it, and I hate you! Go away! Never come near me!"

The servants, as they passed her door, heard that spasmodic sobbing. Each one in turn paused as he heard, then shivered and hurried on his way, thinking of the absent Telke and wondering. . . .

Horror and fear and suspicion and hatred hung like a miasma over the island. Julia kept to her room, while her jackal Bruna prowled. But the others avoided her and turned aside as she approached. Not even fear of Julia could make them endure her. They knew that Lalibela's blood was on her head as well as on Julia's. Psiloriti knew

58

it too but knew that he had no proof. Incoherently Procla
had sobbed out the story.

"When I left them I ran on to the cliff. Oh, Psiloriti, if
only I had stayed! If I had stayed with her and kept my
arm around her. . . ."

He saw that she could tell nothing and he knew she had
loved Lalibela. So he tried to divert her thoughts to other
subjects. "Why did you go to the cliff? You may meet that
wicked ram again."

"Yod keeps him down in the pasture. I was looking for
a ship."

Since she had been so small that he helped her toddle
along the path, she had liked to look for any ship passing
the island. But he wondered now if she was looking for
any ship or had in her mind the galley of Andrus Draco.
He hoped so; for he knew now that he must get her away.
He was sure of two things: that Julia had done murder
and that she could not be punished by the law. He had
questioned her in his official capacity. Cold, contained
and callous, she had answered his every question. Yes; she
had summoned the woman. It was her right to call to
account any servant on the place. It was neither her fault
nor Bruna's if the woman fainted and fell in the pond.
Why make such a fuss about an Ethiopian girl who would
in any event soon have died from a flux of the lungs? No;
she would not have the fish destroyed, no matter how the
servants felt. They probably pretended horror because
they were too lazy to clean the basin and supply fresh
water. The fish amused her, and the slaves would be
whipped if they complained.

Bruna nodded agreement, and supported her story
word for word. Only the two of them had been witnesses.

A few weeks later Ennius brought a message to Procla.
Yod asked her to meet him in the grove where they had
first met.

She knew it must be important, because he discouraged

her visits. She was glad to go, to have something besides the horror to claim her thoughts. As he saw her coming he thought that she had aged years in those weeks. She was now a head taller than he, and she was thin and pale. He remembered how lightly she used to run. Now she walked slowly toward the ravine.

"Why did you send for me? But whatever it is, Yod, I am glad to see you again."

"I sent for you," he said bluntly, "only because I could not leave without telling you good-by."

She drew a quick breath. "Are you being sent away?"

"I am running away. One of your slaves is escaping."

Tears filled her eyes. "Did you ask me to come only in order to be unkind?"

He was ashamed. It was his pride and his hatred of Rome that had spoken. But he had always been blunt of speech.

"Does not my telling you of my plan speak more plainly than my stubborn tongue? Not only am I trusting you with my secret, I am asking you to help me."

Her face lit. "I will help you. What can I do? When and how are you going?"

"I have been trying for months to buy my passage to Sicily. This morning a sailor brought me word that a smuggler bound for that island would send a small boat in for me before midnight."

"Yod! Yod, I shall miss you! But I am glad you are leaving. Since—since Lalibela's death—I hate this island. I too would leave it if I could. I will do all I can to help you."

"Will you then hold two-thirds of the price that I am paying these bandits? I am not such a fool as to pay them all. If they once got it they would throw me overboard as soon as they got underway. I have told them I would pay them a third of all that I have, and leave the rest with someone here to be paid when, on their next voyage, they stop at Pandataria with the message I will send to you."

"It sounds like a game," she cried in delight. "That message will be a secret?"

He nodded grimly. "It will be a secret. Only you and I shall know the words. And you may be sure—" his face grew more grim—"that if they try to force it from me on the way, I will give them the wrong words before they kill me."

For the first time since Lalibela's death Procla was taking interest in something. In her room later she gathered together what coins she had, and then slipped from her wrist the massive gold bracelet that had been Lalibela's gift. Lalibela would wish her to use it to help Yod to freedom. She had gone early to her room and closed its door and extinguished the lamp. But she had not removed her dark blue tunic; and time after time she slipped silently through the hall to look at the water clock in the entrance-court. Yod had told her that he would meet her in the oak grove three hours before midnight. She was proud and happy that he had trusted her and appealed to her.

He stepped free of the shadows as she came toward the place. "I know that the darkness frightens you; but we cannot go along the cliff for fear we may be seen in silhouette from the villa."

"I do not think that anything could frighten me tonight," she said. "Yod, am I really the only one? Do none of the others know?"

"None of the others know," he said somberly. "That is well, both on my account and on theirs. The least word or look could betray me to the vulture eyes of Bruna. On the other hand, when my escape is discovered their innocence will be sincere. If necessary you can uphold it. Psiloriti will protect you from abuse. But a magistrate cannot prevent an owner flogging or branding a slave."

"I will bear witness that they did not know. He can then forbid punishment. But Yod, you said you were using all your savings."

"I am using them in a good cause."

He stopped by an ilex tree whose unripe berries shone with faint opalescence in the dimness, and he handed her a small bag made of goatskin.

"There is the two-thirds payment for you to keep and deliver only when they bring you back the secret words from me."

She took it. "What are the words, Yod?"

He said slowly: *"The brown ram has broken his fence and runs free."*

She repeated the words twice. "They could never guess that."

"Never—until I tell it. Also it is a safe message to be sent to you." She saw him smile. "You have always liked my goats and, to your own grief, have met the brown ram face to face."

"I shall say it over three times a day and never forget a word of it. But Yod, you will have no money when you get to Sicily."

He shrugged. "That cannot be helped. I am strong and I will find work. The agreement with the Sicilians was that I should give them all I had saved, and I do not lie to any man."

"You promised them only what you had up to the time you bargained with them. I ask you to take this."

She caught his hand and thrust the coins into it, then held out to him the golden armlet.

"I will take the money," he said gruffly; "but I cannot take your ornament. I would be accused of stealing. Besides, I know that you love it."

"I love it. That is why I am giving it to you. Do you not see that if you take it and sell it you will be letting both Lalibela and me help you get back to your land?"

He took it then. "I thank you—and her. But I think I hear oars."

Two men stood on the beach below the overhanging

shelf of rock. Yod whistled softly, and the men looked up.
In the starlight she saw them plainly: a fisherman who
was evidently acting as guide, and a dark, knife-faced
fellow with a head kerchief and with huge hoops of brass
hanging from his ears.

"I am coming," Yod told them.

Then he turned and whispered: "May the God of Abra-
ham and of Isaac and of Jacob watch between you and me
until we meet again!"

He was gone, bounding like one of his goats from ledge
to ledge of the cliff until he dropped on the beach.

Standing above she watched him pour his coins into the
outstretched hands of the Sicilian. Then he looked up at
her, knowing that she could not be reached from that
place below.

"The Princess Procla," he said, "holds the rest of the
money. She will pay it to you when you return to this
island and give her the secret message which means that
I am safe."

The smuggler slapped his hands on his hips and burst
into laughter. He raised his narrow face and she could
see its every feature. "More like she is your doxy and she
will keep it," he said.

Procla stood there like a figurehead, with a cold rage
freezing her. Her dark garments blew back with the wind
and her face was chiseled marble.

"Foul beast," she said, "you are speaking of your Emperor's granddaughter."

The Sicilian laughed again; but the fisherman grasped
his arm.

"She is Augustus' granddaughter. Of that there is no
question. Whether or not Tiberius will acknowledge her
as daughter . . . but the Emperor is her grandfather."

"I am the Emperor's granddaughter," said Procla. "Hold
your unclean tongue while you hear my command! You
are to take this herdsman, who was a slave in my house,

to Sicily and set him on his way to Judea. When you have done so he will give you the secret message. When you bring that message to me, I will give you what he has promised. But harken to me, outlaw! If you play us false, I will hunt you down in every port between Rome and Lilybaeum. You will have no chance of escape, for I have seen you and know you. And when you are caught you will be nailed on a cross head down on the Appian Way. I am a Julio-Claudian. In my house we keep our word."

If Yod did not believe in idols, the smuggler believed in nothing. But the fisherman from the Campania thought of the young Diana. He cast one more look up where she stood: slender and sculptured by the wind, angry and inaccessible. Then he followed the other two into his rowing boat.

And Procla stood on the shelf of rock in the starlight and watched them go.

12

WHEN she told Psiloriti that story next day he saw that she was no longer a child but a woman. Lalibela's death and Yod's escape had changed her. He saw that she feared neither the responsibility for what she had done nor the wrath which might be consequent upon it.

But when Julia was informed she was surprisingly careless.

"Have we not enough slaves to furnish another goatherd? Must I be annoyed with such matters?"

"I have already sent Ennius to care for the flock," Psiloriti told her. "Everything has been arranged. But it is your right to know."

"Bruna has often told me that the Jewish lad was a surly fellow and that he presumed in talking with Procula. He is no loss; but I hope he drowns in his attempt at escape."

He saw that her mind was on other things and that it had not occurred to her that Yod was obliged to have someone's help in order to leave the island. He was glad of that. For although he could and would have stood between Procla and harm, he preferred always the smoother way. As he turned to go he found out what was occupying Julia's mind.

"Stay!" she called. "I wish you to send a watchman to the island's highest peak. I wish to be notified as soon as a galley is sighted. If the man on watch should fall asleep or delay, he will be sorry."

So she is mad enough, he thought, to believe that Draco is coming for her. She has evidently been counting the days since she dispatched Telke and reckons that a ship should by now be arriving.

For weeks and for months that watch was kept. Infrequently galleys were sighted. But always they passed under oar or sail on the sea lanes leading north and south. For days after each disappointment Julia would weep or rage, and would order cruel punishment for the slightest offense. Tension was mounting all through the household. Psiloriti could feel it, as taut as a drawn bowstring. Procla was moody, and her eyes were made huge by violet shadows. She used to climb the cliff path and sit half the day with the slave on watch.

At last came the day when a galley was sighted and reported and continued to head in toward the south beach.

Message after message came: *"It is some officer's galley. It has turned directly in and is rowing toward the anchorage. The figurehead can now be seen, and it is the Young Diana."*

Procla, who had watched on the cliff, had gone to her room as if afraid to face what the outcome might be. Psiloriti followed her and spoke to her through the drawn curtains.

"The Young Diana," he told her, "is Draco's figurehead."

But she would not even answer, so he went on down to the beach.

There was movement and bustle. A seaman had rowed in and said that the officer in command of the galley was not himself coming ashore but sending his message by the Ethiopian prince Telke Yezaker, who was aboard.

So, thought Psiloriti, both messages have converged and Andrus Draco is sending his answer by Telke. The tribune thinks enough of Procla to dispatch his own galley in response to my call. Surely Telke will bring word that the girl is to be taken to Rome into the keeping of her grandfather the Emperor.

The very announcement that Telke was aboard made
him sure of this. For in his letter to Draco carried by the
man named Pilate, he had warned Draco not to trust his
reply to anyone on the island except Telke or himself,
Psiloriti.

So wrapped was he in concern for Procla that, until he
saw the tall figure step from the rowing boat, and Ennius
and Laros scurry forward to meet him, he forgot the awful news with which the slaves would greet the steward.
Willing to leave those tragic tidings to them, he turned
back to the house and reached it before Telke did.

He found it still hushed and expectant. The servants
whispered in corners, and Bruna flitted like a bat. The
curtains of Julia's and Procla's rooms remained drawn.
Misgivings descended upon him like moths out of the
dusk, and their wings of uncertainty seemed to flutter
against his brain. Why was Andrus Draco not himself
coming ashore? Was he craven enough to fear facing
Julia? How would Prince Telke react to the death of his
princess?

He was not even sure of Procla's feelings. He could not
know she was watching from her dark little room with her
pulses throbbing so fast that her slim body felt shaken. It
was this strange and never-before-experienced excitement that had frightened her into retreat. Did Draco
really care enough to come and take her away? If so he
must be tender and kind, as well as strong and brave.

Through the past months she had subconsciously fought
against her dawning love for him. She was so young and
there had been so little between them. Only a young officer helping her when she was hurt and risking his life to
seek her when others thought her drowned. Memory of
his friendship for Julia was easily brushed aside. She had
been brought up to think such friendships and such revels
were customary for all Roman matrons. But young as she
was, Procla was already the kind of woman whose pride

forbids her to own even to herself that she loves a man until she is sure that he loves her.

Now she could be sure. Now she realized that she had cared from the moment when he lifted her in his arms and bound her wounds and spoke sternly to her. She had held him ever since in her heart but had not dared to own it. She could own it now and need not be ashamed, because he had come for her. He would take her and her friend Psiloriti away from this horrible place, and from its unnamable suspicion and terror. Life would be clean and beautiful, as it had been in her childhood. Her grandfather would acknowledge her and she would live in the Eternal City which was Draco's home. All this happiness would be intensified because Draco would have brought it to her. He must care, since he had come. She was now of age to be married. Perhaps . . .

She stopped there, not daring to let herself even think any further.

But she was so wrapped in her dream that when she heard steps in the hall she flung the curtains of her room aside and stepped out to meet Telke. He was coming in with Psiloriti, and Psiloriti was questioning him. He walked as straight as a spear and his face was an ebony mask. Both it and his voice were expressionless as he spoke.

"The message," he said, "is for the Lady Julia."

Her heart stood still. And then she thought, he would notify my mother, of course. He is a Roman officer, and he knows law and courtesy.

She knew that her mother would oppose it, would argue and rage and forbid. But she knew that argument and rage could not stay the Emperor's order. Julia had never given her cause for love or obedience, and she had now no reason for regret or self-reproach. This interview, she told herself, was an unpleasant interlude necessary as a threshold to freedom.

She was so sure that Telke's message was about her that she followed him to the door of Julia's room. As he went through its curtains she stopped, but she could hear his voice plainly.

"The tribune Andrus Draco," he said, "sends by me to the Lady Julia assurances of his undying respect and of his renewed affection."

Julia's voice sharpened with triumph. "Yes! Yes? Has he come ashore?"

"He has not come ashore because he awaits you on his ship. So eager is he to take you away that he dares risk no interference."

"I will go with him," cried Julia. "Bruna, you witch, make me ready!"

In her anguish Procla did not notice that the rich, soft voice of the steward was harsh and monotonous. It sounded as if he tore each word from an agonized and constricted throat, but had to fulfill a mission from some power stronger than he.

"I am to tell you that Bruna cannot go with you. The Lord Draco engages to serve you in every way."

"What do I want with the old hag? Tell him I will come alone."

"Do so—unless you wish to be stopped by the magistrate. Bide your time, and slip away from the house and come to the south cliff. The galley is waiting off that beach, and the Lord Draco will meet you. He will meet you at the height of the cliff and make your descent swift and sure."

13

PSILORITI'S ears were less keen than Procla's and he did not hear the words. But he was watching her face, and it told him disaster had struck her. He went forward and stretched an arm toward her protectively, but she backed away from him and covered her face with her hands. Before he could reach her she wheeled and ran for the nearest exit.

She ran as a wounded animal runs for the shelter of loneliness. All she sought was escape from human beings. It was they who had given the wound: a mother and a supposed lover. It was worse than if her world had collapsed in Jovian thunder, or in Vulcan's fires spouting from his forges underground. In that would have been dignity and a chance for memory. In this was only corruption and the stink of age-old evil. The man whom she had exalted with her first love had passed her by and returned to a sordid affair with an older woman—and that woman was her own mother.

She ran for the cliff by the goat meadow. It had always been her refuge. At its foot she tripped and fell in deep grass and tangled vines. She did not even try to rise. She lay with her hot face against cool earth and leaves wet with the salt spray. . . .

After a while she sat up. Off in the east a silver fan of light was slowly unfolding. Far out across Italy a full moon was rising, as large and as bright as a legionary's shield.

She put her hands across her eyes. Legionaries . . . and Draco. . . . She wished to weep, but could not. She must go back to the villa and force herself to behave as if nothing had happened. Tomorrow the household would know, and she must be prepared. She must by then have a mask to hold between their eyes and her heartbreak.

But when she rose, her feet carried her up the rocky ascent instead. There was a place she recalled, halfway on that climb, from which she could see the south cliff. She would force herself to look at Draco's galley—perhaps make herself watch its departure. That would prove to her wild heart that neither he nor Julia could beat her to earth.

The great rock jutted seaward, and she was surprised to find how close in the moonlight lay the scene at the south beach. The galley was anchored between it and the place where she stood. It lay low and black as a long shark, with its riding lights flickering yellow. Beyond and close inside on the smooth flood of that sheltered cove, she caught a glimpse of a gliding triangular fin.

But her eyes were now caught by a lantern down in the garden. It moved so slowly and jerkily that she knew it was carried by Laros. He was crippled and timid, and Julia would have chosen him to light her through the shadows. He would never dare to tell until quite sure she was far away.

At the foot of the south cliff the lantern stopped— waited for a few moments—and then began to jerk its way back into the alley of quince trees. Procla lost it there. The moon was rising higher, but it did not yet show the landward path by which Julia must be ascending.

Very suddenly she emerged in silhouette on the crest of the cliff. She was wrapped in a long cloak and her head was hooded. But she stood in conspicuous relief, for the cliff overhung the sea. Procla recognized each familiar movement: the eager and yet imperious gesture with which she turned. . . .

For a man had come up the other side of the cliff, on

the path that wound down to the landing beach. He stood for just a second, as clearly outlined as Julia: tall and straight, with his officer's cloak blowing back from his shoulders and the moonlight flashing like jewels on the high coxcomb of his Roman helmet.

Then he moved forward as swiftly as the woman was moving to meet him.

Procla saw his arms go out—saw him clasp her and in spite of her weight swing her up and high above his head.

Procla's eyes followed—although her stunned mind could not—the violent outthrust of those arms with their burden, and the tangle of garments hurtling through mid-air and down toward the sea. She could hear no sound, but she saw the full tide divide and splash high where the body struck.

And before she turned and ran shrieking toward the villa, she had seen a long pale wake outlined by phosphorescence where the great shark was rushing toward its feeding place. . . .

PART TWO
Rome

1

THE Emperor's galley held close to the shore as it
moved north to Ostia. Although a royal yacht, it was
small and inconvenient, and its commanding officer felt
safer in sight of land. From its deck where she stood
Procla could see the uneven, indented coastline, with its
dark thatch of forest and with the hills beyond. Day after
day she gazed, trying to realize that Pandataria and childhood were left behind. She was remembering how she
had hoped that Augustus would send for her to come to
Rome. Her eyes darkened as she recalled that her reason
for the hope had been the expectation that she would see
Draco. Now she could only hope never to see him again,
and to forget that she had ever seen him. To accuse him
of murder would have been useless. Telling the sordid
story would not bring Julia back. If Draco denied it, she
had no other witnesses.

Procla had told herself that over and over again. She
was of course fighting, although she would not admit it,
the impulse to shield the man who had murdered her
mother. It was a thought too dreadful to be admitted to
light. It had caused her to live for months in a twilight of
horror. Although she had not loved Julia, she pitied her
deeply and tried now to think of excuses for her faults and
her unkind deeds. Her death had been dreadful enough
to mitigate any sin. The recollection of it filled Julia's
daughter with sincere grief and with hot rage.

Psiloriti, knowing only half of what had transpired, had
watched over her and tried to help her. He was thankful
when the Emperor's galley finally came for them; but she

had shown no pleasure at the prospect. She had gone aboard pale and listless, but with her head held high.

He wondered now as they wore slowly through that periwinkle sea how much she knew of the matter and whether she knew more than he did.

Bruna, crazy with grief, insisted that the Lord Draco loved her mistress and had come to take her away. She screamed that Julia's death had been foul play and had been accomplished by a member of the household. "None of you loved her," she concluded truthfully.

Psiloriti knew that, and he was besides quite sure that Andrus Draco had not loved her. It was his opinion that at the rendezvous the tribune had informed her that he was done with her, and that she had then thrown herself into the sea. He knew how she had longed to escape from Pandataria, and he knew the violence of her nature. Loss of that last chance, in addition to loss of Draco's love, might have caused her to destroy herself.

That checked with Procla's incoherent story. Procla, running like a wild thing and almost out of her head with grief, had reached the villa crying for help to rescue Julia from the shark.

They had run to the beach and launched a boat but had found no sign. The galley was already moving out with the first ebb; but Procla had kept them searching until the tide was at its lowest and the moon stood directly overhead. At daybreak the next high water had brought in a long, dark cloak.

Ennius, who was truthful but dull-witted, gave Psiloriti the most information. He had not seen Julia fall into the sea, but he had heard the commotion and arrived on the spot shortly afterward. He and Procla were able to bear witness for crippled Laros. In fact Laros and his lantern still wobbled through the garden when Psiloriti and Procla rushed out of the villa. The other servants followed them back through the garden to the cliff. Telke, leaping downstairs from his lonely upper room, had overtaken them and taken command. Time after time he had swum out from beach or boat, recklessly disregarding all warnings about the shark.

In that stark dawn when the cloak was washed in, he had come through the surf with his face a gray mask. His lips moved stiffly as he spoke to Psiloriti. "There is no use to search longer. Let us give our help to the girl. In my own grief and shock last afternoon I failed to tell you that the Lord Draco had promised to prevail on the Emperor to send at once for you and the Princess Procla."

However, two things still troubled Psiloriti. First, Draco had sent a message to Julia before he sent the one about Procla. Next, why had Draco himself not come ashore as the galley arrived, and faced Julia and told her that he did not love her and that he intended to have Procla taken from her and carried to Rome? His only excuse for not doing so might be that he feared Julia would then take out her spite on the girl before he could get her away. That line of argument discounted Bruna's story, but Bruna was known to be a liar. Psiloriti thought it probable that no matter what message Telke had brought from Draco, Julia had rushed out to try to persuade him to take her.

So Psiloriti held formal magistrate's court the next morning and examined everyone on the island. Laros, the only suspect, was cleared by Procla, who stated she had seen him turn back from the cliff's foot before she saw Julia come up on its height.

"Was anyone with her?" questioned Psiloriti.

"I told you Laros had turned back. She—she came up on the cliff alone." At that point the girl broke into convulsive weeping. "To my knowledge and upon my oath, I saw no one of these people. Why do you question us? I cannot stand any more!"

So Psiloriti had let her go and had talked with Telke. The steward admitted that Bruna was right inasmuch as the message he brought from Draco had told Julia to meet him on the cliff. But he shook his head at the idea that Draco loved Julia.

"Then," said Psiloriti, "two explanations remain. The tribune is a hard man. He may have been determined to tell Julia in his own merciless way that he was weary of her. If that be the case, the violence of her nature could well have caused her to throw herself into the sea."

Telke's lips did not move. He bowed his head.

"Or," continued the magistrate, "the tribune could be her murderer."

Telke shook his head. "The tribune had no reason. Women like Julia are always their own destroyers."

That was behind them, thanks to the gods; and the long-suffering magistrate was thankful for every puff of wind and every stroke of oar that carried them nearer Rome's seaport. He looked at Procla, standing like a statue at the prow, and wondered how she now felt toward the young patrician. He had not missed that qualification "I saw no one of *these people*." He reflected that she might have seen Draco stand by while Julia committed suicide. He reminded himself that Draco had no reason to kill Julia. Telke had been right in defending him. And he reminded himself even more emphatically that a Roman tribune was far above the reach of his magistracy.

He reviewed the evidence: Telke brief but precise; Procla in an almost-unaccountable passion of grief; Ennius vague and stupid; the others ignorant. When he had said farewell to Ennius, he had left the old slave sitting on a stone, playing his reed pipe out of tune and wearing a rusty helmet low down upon his head. He had found it, Ennius said, in the surf, and thought it lost from the Roman ship. Psiloriti saw that it had belonged to a man with a much larger head; only Ennius' long, sharp nose and the plaintive pipe stuck out of it.

The galley was now approaching Ostia, and they sighted

first the fort commanding the river mouth. Psiloriti seized
the chance to go and stand beside the girl and in his role
of tutor tell her about the great port of Rome. "Here," he
said, "Vulcan was enshrined above all other deities. It is
because of the lava rock from extinct volcanoes. They bear
witness that the Lame Smith had his forges here."

But he saw that Procla was not even listening. She was
gazing without expression toward the ships lying at anchor. There were freighters and merchantmen from Alexandria, Puteoli, Aquileia; from Joppa and Ascalon and
almost every other seaport of the known world.

The galley which carried them threaded its way across
that busy roadstead and worked slowly upstream as it met
the Tiber's amber flood. Sails fell slack. The oarsmen were
straining on their benches. Procla was looking down at
the long sweeps. Like the legs of a huge spider, they lifted
and fell—and gripped the soiled tide—and pushed forward
the galley's body.

Against that foaming current their progress was slow.
The lights of Rome glowed out of the night ahead. Procla
still stood on the forward deck, motionless and silent.

As soon as they dropped anchor a messenger came
aboard. He was an officer of the Praetorian Guard, and he
told Psiloriti that two litters were waiting. The Emperor
wished him and Procla at the palace without delay.

Although silent, Procla gazed from side to side as the
slaves carried her through the streets of Rome. The lamp-
lit windows on the hills seemed to climb up to infinity.
Their pale light showed her marble façades and columns
that soared into darkness. When the bearers halted, Psiloriti helped her out of the litter and led her like a child
up steps between bronze lamps whose light fell on eagles
and fasces. They were conducted into an imposing hall
where marble statues stood around a central fountain.
There they waited. . . .

There was no sound in the hall except the splash of

water. Procla looked at the intricate mosaic floor at her feet, then up to the skylight of the dome through which she could see the stars. That surprised her. She had never seen or heard of glass. Only the Emperor could afford its ultramodern luxury. She thought she was looking through an opening in the roof. Rain will come in, she told herself, and spoil the wall paintings and gilding.

And then the Emperor entered from the court.

She was surprised, for *Augustus* presupposed majesty. This was a gaunt, gray-eyed, grim-mouthed man. He looked more like a fanatical priest who had once stopped on the island than like a ruler or soldier.

Psiloriti had seen him before, but it was not his place to speak.

Instead he watched Procla, and saw her head go high on her slim throat. She looked into those cold gray eyes with pride and dignity, and with no sign of fear.

"I am Procla, daughter of Julia," she said. "Are you my grandfather, the Emperor Augustus?"

He stopped and looked her up and down. He said: "You are Claudia Procula of the Julio-Claudian house. The Emperor Augustus is dead. I am Tiberius, Emperor of the Romans—" he hesitated there, then added—"and your father."

2

PSILORITI had not known that Augustus was dead; but he had become apprehensive the moment Tiberius appeared. This dour and unhappy man was unpredictable. Upon his recent visit to the Eternal City the Greek philosopher had heard gossip of his strange behavior. Rome and her rewards had been unable to tempt him. He had dared the wrath of his father-in-law Augustus by retiring to Rhodes and losing himself in the occult study of stars. While Rome held mastery of the world he longed for knowledge of other worlds. He who had been a soldier had turned astrologer and lived a life of dream instead of action. Some said he was heartbroken at being made to set aside the wife he loved and forced to marry Julia, who was his stepsister although not related by blood. Some said he was trying to efface himself to make way for the Emperor's own grandsons. Some said that his ambitious mother Livia had thrust him into a role for which he was not fitted, and that he was by nature scholar and anchorite. Whether any of this was true or whether nature had cursed him, he had now returned to Rome and regained imperial favor and succeeded Augustus as Emperor.

But foremost in Psiloriti's mind loomed the fact that Tiberius had acknowledged Procla as his daughter.

He had acknowledged her, and had established her near him in a small but lovely house. It was north of the Palatium and overlooked the Forum. It was built of soft yellow-gray stone, and was set in a garden of cypress and ilex. West were the ancient fortifications of the city, and

the four-hundred-year-old town wall built of the same
neutral-colored stone.

When Procla and Psiloriti were carried home that night
from the Emperor's palace they found all in readiness,
from the bronze lamps burning at the door to the cushions
on the settees. That human dynamo Livia had herself
staffed it with a modest but adequate corps of slaves, and
moved into it one of her own elderly relatives to act as
duenna.

It was a far cry from Pandataria: from the high meadow
where the little goats played, and the loneliness of volcanic shelves, and the ebb and flow of tides.

But Pandataria had already done its work. It had
shaped this girl as surely as its waves shaped lava rock.
Its insular loneliness had taught her to stand alone. Its
spaces of periwinkle sea had given her perspective. Its
winds had swept her heart and mind clean of the clutter-
ing little things that crowd the brain in cities, as refuse
crowds their gutters. She had already a better education
than was given in the unsystematic Roman schools. Psiloriti had taught her first the customary reading and writing and arithmetic. He had grounded her as thoroughly
in the Greek literature then fashionable as in her own
Roman writers. But he had been to her companion as well
as teacher. In their long hours together he had, by dis-
cussing these subjects, made her completely at home with
them. When talk turned to poetry or philosophy of either
tongue, she could take her part and hold her own.

Julia's only gift to her daughter's development had been
a negative one: the destruction of a belief. Before her
mother's death Procla had accepted certain excesses as
customary in Roman society. Now, although she could
not but see that they were still customary, she knew them
for what they were and was armored against them.

This was the young Claudia Procula whom a Greek
philosopher brought from exile into Rome.

But even he, had he not known, could never have guessed that she was not accustomed to Rome and its life. She had needed some outlet for the intense vitality that she had expended in her wild, free childhood, and which in girlhood had focused upon a premature and tragic love. She had enough strength and intelligence to transmute it now into the channels along which her life as a woman must run. She could accept new friends and new ways, yet remain in her heart aloof and mistress of herself.

She was a woman now, and she had servants and a home to rule. Between the ilex she had crossed her own threshold into a square entrance hall with a little fountain playing. Back of this and on a slightly lower level was the enclosed court, surrounded by bedrooms, dining rooms, kitchen and small library. She had no dog; but upon her door was painted a ferocious one, with the warning *Cave canem* inscribed beneath it.

While not as large as the island house, this house was far more convenient. All the rooms had pierced shutters which could be drawn or left open. For breakfast there was one dining room with windows to catch the morning sun. Slaves brought the dinner meal to another with western exposure. The little library had books and papyrus scrolls. She and Psiloriti read aloud to each other as they sat on the hard, backless chairs which were covered with cloth of bright colors.

From the very first Claudia Procula had been intrigued by the city. She had her own litter and bearers and could go as she pleased, provided she was accompanied by either Psiloriti or the widow Catella. On these outings she soon learned the Clivus Victoriae, where every house was a palace inhabited by, or haunted by the ghost of, some great man of Rome. She saw the palace of her grandfather Augustus, next to which Tiberius had established himself. As she gazed upon it she wondered how different her life might have been had the grand old soldier of whom she had dreamed in exile lived to welcome and advise her. Although she had never seen him, she felt between him and herself a bond which was totally lacking between her and the man who claimed her as daughter.

Augustus' widow Livia summoned her at once. As she dressed for the interview her duenna sat by, eating almonds and urging her between mouthfuls to make her best appearance and to try to please the Empress. In trepidation Procla arrived at her grandmother's house. She found a small woman of commanding presence in a house whose wall paintings were notable even in Rome. Although in complete discord with her imperial son, the Emperor's mother was still a ruler in Rome. It was she who decided where her granddaughter went, and whom she met of the many who were eager to know her.

But that night as the girl lay in her room that opened into the court, she dreamed of Draco.

Although she had never seen him so, she saw him in battle dress and mounted as an officer of Roman cavalry. She saw the charge sweep forward, the horses rearing and plunging and the standards of the signifers dipping and rising again. Draco was riding at their head, superb in his fighting harness. She saw his coin-cut features beneath his helmet's crest. His equestrian cloak blew backward as he leaned with his horse while he rode.

She woke in the dawn. Helmet and cloak . . . and moonlight as clear and as cruel as steel to light the scene on the cliff. . . .

She did not weep. Tears never came with ease to Claudia Procula. She clenched cold hands and stared dry-eyed at the pale daybreak in the courtyard.

Then she put Draco from her thoughts as she put the garment she wore at night from her body. She arose and dressed herself for day and went to walk under the cypress trees which threw long shadows to west in her garden. The rising sun made a silhouette of the old gray wall she

loved. She stood—a slender figure in white—gazing northwest at it and thinking of men who had builded it and
defended the city behind it. She filled her mind with old
tales of the past and left no corner open for a young soldier riding with the Legion in Judea.

3

O F Livia's many callers the most frequent and devoted
was a man in early middle age whose name was
Pontius Pilate.

He was one of the first Romans whom Procla met at the
Dowager Empress' house, and she saw that he was one
of her grandmother's favorites. His manner was dignified
and his bearing assured. He was strongly built, with a big
head and a curved, fleshy nose. His cleft chin was prominent; but the small mouth between those two good features was contradictorily weak.

Procla found him polite and pleasant, but he made little
impression on her. He was nearer Tiberius' age than her
own, although no one would have guessed it. He looked a
man in his early prime, with vigor and confidence. Where
Rome's Emperor was ravaged by the doubts that beset the
sensitive, this man appeared sure of his own ability. It was
that quality which made him congenial to Livia. She had
in turn ruled two husbands, two sons, and numerous
grandchildren. Had Augustus and Tiberius not been the
men they were, she would have attempted to rule the
Roman Empire.

Even in friendships and in social affairs she tried to
form the opinions of others. She watched her granddaughter's reaction to every new acquaintance, and she
found it unsatisfactory in regard to Pontius Pilate.

One day as he left them after one of her small and intimate breakfasts, she turned and looked intently at the
girl.

"That young man is of equestrian rank. Your father Tiberius approves him, as I do."

Procla looked back at her with eyes wide between dark wings of brows.

"I find him courteous, and his stories of Gaul and Iberia interest me. Yet—" she frowned as she paused to find words to express her thought—"he is different from other men whom I have met at your house."

"You have sharp eyes," said Livia, half in reproof and half in honest admiration. "He is the son of Tyrus, prince of one of the Rhenish tribes."

"A barbarian?" asked Procla.

"Curb your tongue! It is sharp as your eyes. His people became Romanized long years before his birth. He has held office in the auxilia and served honorably in those lands of which he has told you tales. It is not to his discredit if he is different from certain young Romans I know."

"If he is a prince's son," asked Augustus' granddaughter, "why does he not hold a prince's rank in Rome?"

"Because his mother was not Tyrus' queen. She was the daughter of a German miller named Pila. Various stories have been circulated about him. He has made himself a person of importance and is accepted by the nobility of Rome."

"But he bears only his mother's name," said Procla.

Livia's eyes narrowed. She could have replied to that. But she had agreed with Tiberius that he should acknowledge this girl whom Augustus had sent for before his death. It was she who had urged her son to announce at once that her name was *Claudia* Procula. That was by far the best way to silence wagging tongues. Neither she nor Tiberius had Augustus' soldierly bluntness and his habit of driving straight to a point regardless of criticism. It had always seemed to her foolish to publish a scandal when it might be concealed, or even used to advantage. Now,

since she had seen and appraised Octavian's granddaughter, she was doubly glad of the decision. The girl
walked like Diana, and there were many men who enjoyed pursuing Diana more than being beckoned by
Venus. With her youth and her look of race she could be
used in a marriage needed to draw some man of power
closer or bind securely one whose allegiance wavered.

She was hoping now that the tall, slim girl had nothing
of Julia in her. She had witnessed pitched battles between
her stepdaughter and Augustus. She—Livia—preferred diplomacy to violence and knew how to conceal an iron
hand in a velvet glove.

"So you do not like my friend Pontius Pilate?" she asked.

"I do not dislike him; but I do not like his mouth."

"What is your objection to his mouth?"

"It does not suit the rest of his face, which is strong and
heavy."

Livia smiled. "I agree with you. But your own mouth,
my child, is completely at variance with your other features."

Procla looked back at her in surprise. She explained.
"You are built slim and straight as a nymph. Your brows
are delicately drawn and your eyes change gray to black.
Your hair is as fine as gossamer and the color of dying
leaves. Your brow and chin and cheekbones are chiseled
cleanly and coldly."

She paused in amusement as she saw the flush that was
creeping up from pale throat to color those cheekbones.
This young goddess, she told herself, is only a girl. I can
lead her.

"I am no sibyl," she continued, "but I have listened to
almost every kind of fortuneteller. Between you and me,
I believe in none of them except the ones who judge by
your bones and the shape of your head. For we are obliged
to answer the urges that quicken our blood, to shape in
our lives the fate shaped in our bodies. If strong enough

we can influence others, and so carry destiny beyond ourselves. That is all there is to it. Sacrifices are nonsense.
How can an animal's insides affect the Roman Empire?"

She was taking Procla's breath away; for Procla had not
yet discovered the skepticism that was prevalent in Rome.

"I hate the sacrifices. But what of auguries such as the
darkening of stars or the flooding of waters. And—" she
spoke very slowly—"do you not believe in dreams?"

Livia frowned. "If there are gods, they may speak to us
in dreams. But clouds hide the stars, and rain causes flood.
Your destiny is within you. What you will do in time to
come is because of what you are. Whatever Pontius Pilate
is to accomplish for good or evil is written now in his
beaked nose and aggressive chin and weak mouth."

Seeing that Procla showed no interest in her favorite,
she added tartly: "Above all, do not forget that he is a
member of the family Pontii. Adoption in Rome is just as
strong a tie as birth."

But Procla still said nothing, and she was anxious to win
the girl.

"Your own destiny, my dear, is in your loveliness. No
more occult reason causes young Lepidus to haunt my
house and just now to appear in my garden. I could have
foretold his coming in the leaf-brown hue of your hair."

"But," said Livia's granddaughter, "but—"

"But except for Andrus Draco, who is in the East with
his Legion, Lepidus is considered foremost sportsman of
Rome. His chariot and horses win almost every race."

"But," pleaded Procla, "before he comes, tell me why
you said my mouth was different from my other features?"

"It is the Julio-Claudian mouth," said the widow of
Augustus. "It belongs to Venus, who is one of your deities.
My husband, who was your grandfather, had strength
enough to keep the balance between her and his other
patron Mars. We have yet to see what you will do about
it, Claudia."

4

BUT Procla, taking part in the gay but lazy life of
Rome, was surprised to find that young Lepidus did
not drive his own chariot. He rented a chariot, charioteer
and a trio of gorgeous horses imported from Spain. His
charioteer was Diocles, one of the greatest drivers in
Rome's history of racing. Since the patrician could afford
to buy these famous services and then sit in the circus and
bet heavily upon them, he was hailed as a sportsman and
a charioteer of note.

He brought his team to the yellow house in the cypress
garden, to show to the girl who until she reached Rome
had seen no larger quadruped than a goat.

She had no fear of the restless, dancing, fiery stallions.
She stroked their white coats and stiffly roached silver
manes and fed them sweetmeats from the basket that
stout Lucia Catella always had at hand. True to her trust,
Lucia had followed her charge out of the house. But her
only interest in the affair was that her nectared nuts and
fruit were disappearing rapidly between the horses' strong
back teeth.

"I shall have none left," she protested, "and the animals
will bite you."

Procla hardly heard. She had stepped into the low chariot, and as the team felt the touch of weight they reared
together and pawed the air. Diocles tightened his hold on
them. Lucia Catella shrieked—and choked on a mouthful
of almonds.

Procla was leaning against the curved guard which

closed the light body in front. Her eyes blazed, and the sun blazed on her dark red hair.

"Oh, Lepidus, bid your charioteer drive me through Rome and out to the Campus Martius!"

But both Psiloriti and Lucia Catella forbade it. She jumped lightly down and ran to Diocles.

"Why do you wear this heavy belt wrapped from beneath your arms to your hips?"

"To brace my body against the pull of the running stallions, lady. My driving reins are attached to that belt. My hands are for whip and for guidance."

"But," she cried, "were you overturned or thrown out, you would be dragged."

Quick as a flash he had the short knife out of his belt and in his hand. His teeth gleamed in his dark face. The short blue toga stopped just above his knees. Below, his thighs were laced for support with strips of leather. Upon his shoulders were stout pads; his legs were armored in leather; his feet were incased in sandals soft and flexible enough to grip and balance and give stance as he swayed to the chariot's pace. His head was protected by a padded and helmetlike cap, which was decorated upon one side with a blue cockade.

"We learn to draw quickly, lady. Few understand as you do. To see a charioteer dragged and killed but adds to their excitement. In case of a spill, my only chance for life is to slash the reins as I fall."

Lepidus was looking bored.

"What matter unpleasant details? Diocles has won more than a thousand races. His prize money amounts to at least thirty-five million sesterces. Do I not deserve credit for having the acumen to choose a charioteer capable of such attainments?"

"Perhaps," said Procla. "But I should not care for or count the money. Had I such horses I would stand in my chariot and drive them."

The widow Catella screamed again—and louder this time, since no sweetmeats filled her mouth. Lepidus was amused in spite of his boredom. But Diocles flashed her a look of fellowship.

"My lady, chariot drivers are not merely taught, they are born. We see that every day in the circus where new ones are trained. Veterans are sent around the track beside them, to guide them at first and then to foul them, so that they may beware of such tricks at the games. Nine out of ten, after having a wheel taken off or a horse thrown, get up in such a state of fear that they are at once dismissed."

But although not allowed to ride in the chariot, Procla's time was filled with other amusements. She attended the theater, and she was guest at all the great houses of Rome. Among those who gave banquets in her honor were Lepidus, Pontius Pilate, and old Lexus Paulus. The last was now senile and was always accompanied by two painted Egyptian slave boys. Lexus Paulus, as well as the younger men, entertained so magnificently that the feasts in Julia's garden paled by comparison. But always, at Julia's daughter's side and next to Julia's daughter's couch, reclined one soldier guest whom the others did not see. So real was he to her that more than once she lifted and looked at a slim white arm which had worn his bandages. Then she shook her head with its hair dressed in scallops like autumn leaves, and turned to drink from the proffered cups of both Lepidus and Pilate.

Pilate had the latest news from the East. He helped himself largely to peacock tongues and then leaned nearer to her.

"Changes are taking place in Judea. The Jews have always been a turbulent race. It is my opinion that they need a firmer hand than that of their present procurator."

She had looked up in startlement at mention of Judea,

and he did not miss that widening and darkening of her eyes.

Pontius Pilate's small mouth smiled. He knew how to arouse her. He was not in the least in love with her. But she was the granddaughter of Augustus and had been acknowledged daughter of Tiberius before all Rome. He wished to remain in her graces, and he could remind her of favors.

"It was once my good fortune," he said in the languid tone which was the fashion, "to bear East and back again a message concerning you."

She had completely forgotten Psiloriti's brief mention of his surname when the Greek had returned to Pandataria. Beyond that she knew nothing, and she looked at him in surprise.

"Little over a year ago I was starting for Gortyna. The Cretan freedman who tutored you was at that time in Rome."

A Roman born, she thought to herself, would not bother to call him freedman. It is the speech of an outlander whose citizenship fits badly.

She said coldly: "My tutor, who is also my friend, holds both Roman citizenship and office of magistracy."

He was amused rather than pricked, for his skin was not thin.

"I shall remember his offices when next I speak his name. But the name which I was about to speak when I innocently gave you offense is that of the tribune Andrus Draco."

Her wine cup was halfway to her lips and her face half turned to him. She seemed to freeze into marble, and only her red mouth moved.

She said very softly, "He is with the Tenth Legion. One cohort is at Jerusalem, but the cavalry rides out."

He stared at her in amazement. She had no husband to tell her. Tiberius, of all men in Rome, was shut-mouthed about his troops. The young dandies like Lepidus, who were her only companions, neither knew nor cared about the disposition of armies. She was staring across the table at a painting on the wall: a painting of a Roman armored mounted troop in action. She spoke again in that slow, low voice which sounded to him like a voice from sleep.

"I dreamed it. In dream I saw—"

She stopped so short that he heard her indrawn breath; and he put out a hand and caught the cup of wine as her fingers released it.

She was staring at him, breathing hard; but the others had not noticed. He wondered if she were lying or if she had really dreamed. He believed in dreams and omens, but he took them with a pinch of salt, as he took all things. Upon the other hand, some man who knew might have told her. She was lovely enough to coax secrets; but he could not imagine her coaxing. In fact, he told himself, she was lovely enough to be liked for herself as well as cultivated because of her connections. Now her eyes were dark with distress. She begged like a child: "Do not tell what I said!"

"The Emperor's daughter," he answered, "honors me only by asking. I have already forgotten that she has dreamed in the past, and I shall remain oblivious if she dreams in the future."

5

TRY as she did to escape it, mention of Draco pursued her. It seemed to her that all Rome was talking about him. Livia knew that Tiberius was troubled about affairs in the East.

"Valerius Gratus, Procurator of Judeans, has been continually embroiled with their high priests. I advised Tiberius against appointing him. He is no diplomat, and the Jews are clever."

Lepidus, lounging nearby, laughed.

"Especially the priests, I have heard. They are very nearly *your* match in diplomacy, noble Livia."

She did not resent it; she was pleased.

"Our men would do well to take a lesson from them. The Roman with a short sword in his hand is unconquerable, so long as he drives upward and thrusts forward in his own way. But his clumsiness in Palestine grows more and more apparent."

Procla had been only half listening. But Livia's next words jolted her into full attention.

"Now Gratus has chosen as his messenger to Rome a man who is more soldier than politician. He has sent word to the Emperor that the military tribune Andrus Draco is the only one he is willing to trust as his envoy."

Lepidus laughed again.

"Livia's judgment is flawless. My friend Draco knows better how to wield a sword than a wily tongue."

"Nevertheless," said the Emperor's mother tartly, "he must be treated with respect when on the Emperor's errand. I should be as great a bungler as he, did I not hold by that. I am already planning a banquet in his honor, and I shall expect you both to show him all honor at it."

They both realized she was banqueting him in the hope of drawing him near enough to persuade him to divulge to her the secrets he brought to her son. It was bitter to her that Tiberius no longer let her sway him. As he withdrew she tried harder to keep her grip on affairs by keeping a grip on the men who were his advisers. Lepidus, although lazy, was keen. Knowing Draco, he felt sure that her banquet would be given in vain.

Procla looked forward to it with dread which amounted to horror and fear. Sometimes she thought she must scream aloud and tell them what she knew. What if she shrieked it aloud at Livia's banquet? What if Livia knew there was blood on the strong hands that she judged capable only of wielding an honest sword?—Blood of the mother of Claudia Procula, wife of Tiberius and daughter of Augustus!

They would only think her mad, of course. That was the reply to her question. Draco would deny it, and the Emperor would believe him, and Livia would cover it all with her robe of diplomacy.

The girl stayed in her own room until Psiloriti became distressed. He recognized the signs she had shown on Pandataria, and he knew that Draco was coming. All that he could conclude was that Procla loved him but had made up her mind to hate him because he had preferred her mother.

Pandataria came back to Procla in those days. She turned to it as a refuge from Rome. She thought of Yod and hoped that he had reached his homeland safely. She could not tell, because she had left the island before the Sicilian returned. She had confided in old Ennius and entrusted to him both the secret message and the pouch of coins for the smuggler. Yod, she remembered, had said that his village was Bethlehem. Psiloriti had mentioned

that some strange star stood over its roofs when a Chil\
was born. Lalibela had believed that child was the Messiah. There was hope even in the name; but she knew that
Lalibela's faith had root in old prophecies. Procla still believed in prophecies and dreams, in spite of her grandmother's skepticism. But her heart was still held by Lalibela's gentle hands. Never in all their friendship had
Lalibela been unkind.

She cast herself on her bed and wept, as she seldom did.
Pride could restrain tears of a love that was not returned
by a man. But there was no pride between her and this
gentle memory.

Procla stopped sobbing and lay quiet, thinking . . .
thinking how Lalibela had longed to see the Messiah. . . .
On Lalibela's account, even more than for herself, she . . .
Procla . . . hoped to see him someday. It was hard to believe that any god would offer love and forgiveness without desiring reward or demanding an eye for an eye and
a tooth for a tooth.

A servant roused her by drawing the curtains. "The
tribune Andrus Draco waits in your hall, lady."

She sat up, hands clenched until their nails cut the
palms.

"I will not see him!"

Then she recovered herself. "Tell him the Lady Claudia
is weary, and that he need wait no longer."

The *Claudia* would remind him from whose house she
sprang. She reserved it to stress formality. As the servant
left she jumped to her feet and paced up and down, as
Julia had been accustomed to pace in anger. Her mouth
was red and full, but there was no softness in its set. Her
eyes were black instead of gray, and they gleamed between narrowed lids. There was no longer any hint of
Lalibela's gentleness about the Roman girl who had just
wept for her.

But when she had Livia's command to the feast in honor

of Draco, she dressed herself more carefully than she had ever done before.

She chose a russet tunic that left one white shoulder bare in the latest fashion taken from Greece. Its silk was threaded with gold, and deep golden bands hemmed its floor length and bordered its neckline. Its golden girdle called attention to her slim waist. Its leaf-brown hue enhanced her white arm and her small white oval face. Her hair, repeating the color scheme, was curled and drawn up on her head and clasped by a half-wreath of jeweled and gold grapevine.

Livia placed her on Draco's left and herself reclined on his right hand. When Procla dared look at him she saw that he was even leaner and browner than she remembered. To honor his hostess he had worn full dress of a cavalry officer, with the short cloak of his order swinging from one broad shoulder. His thin mouth, naturally stern, was drawn to one side in a saturnine smile. Procla wondered whether he was trying to be agreeable or was openly laughing at the rest of them.

She was occupying herself with Lepidus who was on her left. Had he not been a man of the world, he would have fallen into the pit which has caught so many men used by women to spite other men. But he saw just what was going on, and although he did not understand what lay behind it, he smiled with amusement. Across the table Pilate watched them all with hooded eyes.

Not until near the dinner's end could Draco find his chance. He had been continually beset by other men and women, and whenever he turned to Procla she was leaning toward Lepidus. Now most of them were silly with wine, but his hard head was still clear. He turned and grasped the bare white arm and pulled her by main force around to face him.

"Is it the same one," he asked, examining its elbow, "that a fish bit long ago and that I bandaged, Procla?"

She wrenched it from his hands with a jerk that threw her left toward Lepidus. That he should dare to speak of fish! Was there anything that he would not dare?

"I have no memory," she said, "of your services—or need of them now. I was asking Lepidus—when you interrupted us—to take me some night for a ride in his chariot."

Chariots had not been mentioned, but Lepidus understood. His eyes went over Draco's set yet surprised face with lazy triumph.

"I shall be where your cypress alley ends at this hour tomorrow night," he said. "I will wear the dress of my charioteer, and you will know my white horses."

6

WHEN Procla had first seen the horses she had longed to ride behind them. Now she had lost all zest for that. She could think only of Draco. If he had stayed in the East, she might have forgotten him. She had already fought it out and had hoped and thought he was left behind. Now, just as her life seemed rearranged, he had come back to torment her. Had he no decency—no shame —no fear of punishment?

Then she reminded herself that he still thought his crime undiscovered. She could see that last swing of his cloak as he disappeared in the darkness. By the time the house was aroused he could have been down on the beach. He must have made guilty haste, for he had lost his helmet. She felt sure it had been the one too big for shriveled old Ennius' head.

She had no insight of Eastern affairs and no idea how long Tiberius might be going to keep Draco in Rome. For all she knew, he might be transferred permanently. Pontius Pilate, for some reason, was being kept close to the Emperor. Both he and Lepidus were friends to whom her thoughts now turned with relief. She could allow them both to spend more time in her company. It would be one way to shut Draco out. After having kept silence so long she could never explain her true reason for avoiding him. If she slighted him openly, Livia would demand why. Her best plan would be to pretend such interest in another man that she had no time for anyone else. Pilate was attentive but by no means ardent. She sensed the fact that he would take to wife whomsoever his Emperor bade him take. Many men did so because they were forced to do so. He would do so willingly, waiting to make his choice until he was sure of the imperial approbation.

That left Lepidus, who was ardent enough underneath the studied lightness of fashion. He was indolent. He owned frankly that he tried to curry favor from an elderly relative for whose estate he hoped. He was doing it carefully and well. He had to be careful. Sycophancy had become a profession, and the birth rate had fallen in consequence. Too many men and women preferred receiving such favors from the old to the duties of marriage and a household and children. Consequently the unmarried were taxed, and the law put obstacles in the way of such inheritance. But as Lepidus told his closer friends, somebody had to get the old man's money and he himself would at least know how to spend it gracefully.

Such impudence seemed only to make him more attractive. He dressed elaborately and drawled affectedly. Yet he could sit daylong in the arena at the games, watching men and animals fighting and dying in torture. Emotion overcame him only when the arena's stench became so unbearable that he called sharply for a slave to sprinkle perfume upon and around him.

Devotion to the games however, with its attendant disregard of pain and cruelty, was the rule rather than the exception for Romans of that day. More than one noblewoman was known to be having an affair with a popular gladiator. But that did not prevent her, with thousands of others, attending the combats in which he fought, and gloating upon each bloody detail of death.

Lepidus was if anything a little above the average. Too, he was handsome and tall and he appeared masculine in spite of an almost effeminate mode of living and manners. He is tall and slender like Draco, she thought to herself; but he lounges always, while Draco is straight as a spear.

I will not think of Draco, she thought, lying wide-eyed

and sleepless hours after she had returned from Livia's banquet.

She rose and went to her doorway, which was curtained off from the court. Above its one-story roof to west she saw a slim crescent moon. She heard the rhythmic chirping of the frogs out in her garden. Otherwise all was silence. The rest of the household slept. Her bedroom was most remote of all those opening on the court. Kitchen and eastern dining room were between her and the hall. She had moved into that bedroom from the one she first occupied because the widow Catella snored so loud that a light sleeper next to her could get no rest at all. From the time her duties released her until called for breakfast she snored. Psiloriti was now hard of hearing. Besides, even if he knew, he would reprimand but never betray her. Neither would her slaves. They would not only be afraid, they really liked her. One of Pandataria's gifts to her had been to teach her that slaves were human beings and could even be her friends.

But she had Julia's blood too, and it was running fast tonight. She was young and beautiful, and she saw what other women were doing. Even so, except for Draco she might not have done it. She knew that if Tiberius found her out he would probably treat her exactly as Augustus had treated her mother and the older sister whom she had never seen.

How could Tiberius find it out? Lepidus must feel they were safe. He loved luxury too well to risk either death or exile. He loved her too, and this was her chance to flaunt his love in Draco's face. It would not be hard to return it. There was no man she liked any better. This was her chance to throw herself into an affair with him which would keep Draco at arm's length. It would be pleasant to tell him: *"No. For Lepidus claims all my time."*

So it was Julia's daughter, with Julia's hot blood stirring, who left the house that next night.

She crossed the court and the hall and passed into the garden through the little door where the painted dog kept watch. The cypress trees were aligned like spears, steel-black against the sky. Only the frogs heard her soft steps and fell silent as she passed by.

She was wearing a short, dark-gray toga, and a cloak of the same hue that hid her hair and disguised her shape. To anyone who glanced carelessly she could be a peasant woman, or a slave whom some young nobleman had chosen to share his pleasure. She threaded the cypress alley swiftly but without haste; and as she emerged at the garden's end she saw the white horses.

The man in dress of the charioteer was standing at their heads. Without words he seized her arm and thrust her into the vehicle. As he leapt to his place beside her she smiled to herself; for he was tall, not small and muscular like Diocles.

"Lepidus," she whispered, "looks so well as a charioteer that he should drive more often."

Instead of responding he leaned forward and gave a short, hoarse cry. She gripped the rail of the chariot's guard as the steeds swung into a gallop. Not until then did she notice that they were a pair instead of the team of three which had been brought to her garden. The chariot was different too. It was not a racing car but was of that type which was privately owned and driven by men of fashion.

She was silently amused. Lepidus was choosing to treat a midnight jaunt with more seriousness than she intended to treat it. He was choosing to be strong and masterful and silent. But she had to see that he could drive. He was crossing the city at full speed and handling the powerful team with a skill she had to admire. They were more heavily built, she saw, than the horses of Diocles; their heads were larger and their legs less long and slender. It heightened her opinion of this young exquisite that he could throw his strength against theirs and guide them to his will.

They swept through the darkened city while he stood tall at her shoulder. They left the last scattered slums behind and burst free on the Appian Way. As the white horses saw open road they plunged and thrust their massive chests against the thongs that harnessed them to the center pole. They broke into a full run and the chariot swayed from side to side. The cypress tops on the hills flashed by like the spears of a cohort passing. The moon was a thin blade drawing to set in a dark sea west. The man beside her uncurled his whip and its lash flung out and forward. The wild white horses mouthed their bits and leapt into madder speed.

The hood of her cloak fell back and her hair blew out in a russet cloud. She clung with both hands to the chariot's prow, thrown hard against him and then away. He was taking her out of the world she knew, as the gods sometimes chose to take women. So must Europa once have felt . . . and perhaps Proserpina. . . .

But the cold intelligence of the soldier line bred in her told her this was no god but an idle Roman sportsman. Had he only been Draco—with her and alone—with the flying steeds and the dying moon!

He swung his horses at right angles with the ease of a trained charioteer. They were galloping up a narrow road that led off from the Via Appia. Its steepness was cutting down their pace and she heard the spent animals' gasping breath. The turn had been suddenly to the left and had thrown her hard against him. He shouted a short command to halt, and the horses stopped short as he dropped the lines. Before she could draw away, his arms were around her and she was looking up into the face which he had kept turned from her.

She struggled then. But his sinews were steel. All she could do was to strike him with her clenched fists and whisper: "I hate you! Why did you come back to torture me? I loathe your touch! Let me go!"

His mouth was hard and drawn to one side. His close grip did not slacken. He did not try to kiss her; but he stooped his head and she felt his hard cheek for a second against her tumbled hair. Then he pushed her roughly away and against the chariot's rail.

"I wish no favors that are not given willingly," he said. "If you think I brought you out for that, it is your mistake. But I have a right to know—and I command you to tell me—which of these Roman sybarites with whom you seem so congenial has set you against Draco, an honest soldier and your friend?"

7

HE had given her the very word and she swung it like a whiplash.

"Honest?" she asked, and added: "Liar and murderer!"

His hands caught her shoulders in such a grasp that, except for rage, she would have cried out. But rage held her upright and facing him, with scorn and hatred on her full red mouth.

"Murderer of a woman for whom you pretended love! Coward and sneak, who chose the night to creep out! Liar, who lured her with untrue words! You thought you had escaped all eyes, but I—*I saw you kill her!*"

"Little fool," he asked, "are you mad? Or am I? Whom did you see me kill?"

"I saw you kill my mother—Julia, wife of Tiberius and daughter of Augustus. All others think that she threw herself into the ocean for love of you."

Involuntarily she recoiled as he leaned toward her. The movement made the horses snort and paw to be off again. He flung a short word to quiet them, then turned back to her.

"Be still and do not shift your weight, or you will start them running. I'd rather you were not flung out and trampled before you explain. Do you realize the gravity of the crime with which you accuse me?"

"Do I realize it?" she countered. To her horror she heard her voice rising high. She must keep her temper to deal with him. He was as cold and bloodless and unnatural as the fierce fish.

"It is you who seem not to realize. Do you think you

can change the subject and make me forget?" Her voice was bladed with scorn. "Perhaps you are trying to hide your fear that I may expose you."

He looked at her in silence. His face was unreadable.

"Are you utterly fearless," he asked, "or only a fool? Do you not realize that a man who had killed the Emperor's daughter would certainly kill you here and now rather than let you inform on him?"

"That you dare threaten your Emperor's daughter, tribune, is but another proof of your treason. It helps me to understand how easy it was for you, thinking yourself hidden by night, to commit your crime."

"Procla," he said very softly, "by the gods, you would make a soldier! Were I sure of such courage behind me I would not hesitate to lead my men against Pluto himself in hell! With you beside me I could go far on a brave road, Procla!"

"Go," she said, "but without me. Go—back to your savage provinces. Go on your brave road, hidden by darkness, to murder helpless women!"

She seldom lost control of herself, but she was sobbing now. She was leaning as far from him as she could, bent back and over the chariot's rail. All she wished was to fling at him every taunt and word of hatred she knew. But he was hard and wicked and impervious to shame. He was not even trying to deny her accusation. How could he deny it? For she had seen him. Yet, she realized suddenly, she had had a small hope in her heart: a tiny hope that her eyes might have deceived her and that some explanation might awaken her from the nightmare.

"Why do you not kill me," she asked him, "as you killed my mother Julia? Are you not afraid I will drag you before the Senate? Are you not afraid of being disgraced and put to death?"

He shook his dark, close-cropped head, as if he were trying to clear it.

"No. You have waited too long, my dear. Your story is fantastic. You see your mother murdered by a man who is leagues away; but you keep silence and let a year pass without denouncing the murderer."

His voice grew softer, but she could detect the mockery in it.

"Can I think that you did it to spare me, Procla? Or did you dream it in loneliness—on a lonely island—with a mother who neglected you and a dotard tutor and African slaves?"

That first sentence was the last straw. Fury and pride surged through her. She would have liked to kill him. That he should dare, she thought to herself—he the murderer of my mother—to stand refusing any defense, mocking me because I spared him!

Knowledge that his taunt held truth and that she had spared him because she cared welled up in her now with the bitterness of gall. In that moment she hated him more than she had ever loved him in her lonely girlhood and her first hero-worship. She braced her body with both hands against the metal guard behind her, and the thin moon chiseled her like a huntress: slender and swift as a javelin, with long back-blown hair.

"I spared you to spare my mother's name," she said coldly and proudly. "You have disgraced both your birth and your rank; but if you have any Roman blood you should understand, tribune, the need to shield from gossip an emperor's daughter's name."

He did not reply, as he could have done, that gossip and Julia were old friends. His voice was surprised and grave.

"So you really hate me, Procla?"

The words broke her. She could not stand any more.

"No, I do not hate you; I despise you. Hatred is an honest feeling due to a foe who is worthy of it."

She closed her eyes and saw again that helpless body

falling. . . . Grief and rage overcame pride and dignity. Sobs made her speech staccato, and her right hand let go of the rail.

"If I—were a man—I would kill you! I hate—no! I loathe and despise you. I only wish I had a dagger such as yours! If you value your life you'd better kill me now. For I warn you I shall do all I can to bring you to justice."

For a long moment he looked at her with his mouth drawn crooked across his cheek. Then he drew his dagger and offered it to her, hilt first.

She put out a hand, not to take it but to ward it off.

He laughed at her then. "You complained of its lack, so I gave you the chance. I might have known that the only weapons you can wield are hard words."

In reply she raised her hand and struck him with all her strength in the face. He stood for a second frozen by surprise, gazing wordlessly at her. She could see that the blow had cut his lip against the set teeth behind it, and that a thread of dark blood ran from his mouth to his chin.

Then he leaned forward and with his left hand locked both of her arms behind her. She felt his right hand take hold of her hair and he jerked her head back savagely. He pulled her against him, and his mouth shut down on hers so hard that it hurt.

She tried to fight, but she could not move an inch from that close embrace. The wind and the night and the crescent moon were spinning strange circles around her. . . .

She had never before been kissed that way, and she felt herself going limp in his arms. She tried to resist, and she told herself that she still wished to kill him. But she was forgetting why, and was forgetting everything else. He and she seemed alone in the world . . . alone between earth and its moonset. . . .

He released her suddenly and almost violently, pushing her away and seizing his driving lines. His movements were curt and businesslike, as they had been before he kissed her.

The horses were rested, and at his touch they threw up their heads and neighed shrilly.

"Hold on!" he exclaimed impatiently, as they plunged and he wheeled them sharply. "You are now my prisoner. I intend to hold you until you have told your mad story in court. I shall take you to the magistrate who was on Pandataria when Julia's death occurred. Always I have known that cursed island was under some adverse spell, and it is small wonder you were affected by it. But you are a Roman and have charged a Roman tribune, and I'm going to make you prove it, Procla!"

8

PSILORITI was now with them in the hall. They had found him walking in the cypress alley in the twilight of early daybreak; but he had not yet asked them to explain the nocturnal ride. Draco had given him no opportunity. He had demanded at once and in the language of the law that Claudia Procula, Roman, either prove her charge against him or withdraw it and make full reparation.

This seemed like a nightmare to Procla—more so than the charge that she brought. She had lived with that for more than a year and she was convinced that Andrus Draco, military tribune attached to the Tenth Legion, had murdered an older woman to rid himself of her. She saw that Psiloriti's face was drawn with worry.

"Why did you select me to judge, tribune? I am not sure my appointment still holds, or that my judgment is allowable in Rome."

"Augustus' appointment holds until Tiberius withdraws it," said Draco. "I chose you because I hoped this matter need go no further. I still hope so. But I warn you that if you cannot resolve it, I am prepared to go before the Senate to clear my name."

"It must not go further," the old man said. "I will hear the evidence."

"*Proclamete!*" she answered him; and she gave it coldly and carefully. She had possession of herself now. Draco was striking back, and she must be wary. He was evidently sure that she could prove nothing, since he dared to force the issue. But there was one thing that he did not

111

know. There had been one piece of concrete evidence to which she had witnesses and of which he was not aware.

The eyes of both men were on her while she spoke. She had pulled her hair back carelessly and pinned it severely away from her brow. In her short, dark toga and leather shoes she looked like a thin young boy. Her face was ivory-pale and her high cheekbones stood out. Her eyes were dark and narrowed, her full mouth curved in scorn. Below one corner of it was a small stain of dried blood. Psiloriti thought she had bitten her lip; Draco knew how she had come by it.

He stared at her hard as she finished. There was pity in his heart for a girl so lonely she had to dream, and imagine dream a reality. But there was no pity on his face. His school was a hard one and he meant to teach her in it.

He turned from her to the trial judge.

"You must know, magistrate, that you have to dismiss this charge. At that day of week and month and year I was in Palestine. As an officer of the Tenth Legion I am ready and able to prove it."

Psiloriti had feared that answer. He did not know what to think. But he knew Procla better than Draco knew her, and he told himself that she had seen murder. Yet, knowing the law, he knew she could not injure a Roman soldier merely by accusation. It was likely that if the matter went as far as to reach Senate and Tiberius, he would go clear and Procla be branded a liar and punished.

"Claudia Procula," he said, "you have told your story. Never have I known you to lie, and I believe that you think it true. But against the tribune's word it proves nothing—unless you have evidence or witness."

"I have evidence, and I have witness to that evidence," she replied—and she flashed a look of hatred and triumph at Draco.

He merely folded his arms and looked back at her.

"I am waiting to hear what they are."

"Evidence is a helmet of the Equestrian Order. It was picked up by Ennius the slave at the foot of the cliff. Witness is the magistrate himself. He saw it. I call upon him to speak."

Draco wheeled upon Psiloriti. Not a muscle of his face moved, but his eyes were glittering now.

"Did you see this helmet of which she speaks? And did you recognize it?"

The Greek was even more disturbed than Draco was. Although the young tribune was stern, the old man had been sure in his heart that he would let the matter drop when Procla had told her story. But it looked now as if the girl was bent on making trouble.

"I saw the helmet," he said slowly and unwillingly. "For the fact that it was found by the cliff, I have only the word of a slave."

"Yet, magistrate," said Procla, "I think you will recall that it was you who rose early that day and saw Ennius bringing it up from the beach. I think that you, knowing Ennius, will bear witness that he is as stupid as he is honest. Did or did it not seem to you that he told a straight story?"

In spite of himself, Draco was glorying in her. He told himself that, all of his life, he had been waiting for her. He had been waiting for a woman who had all a woman's attributes of beauty and pride and passion but who lacked neither brain nor courage. He had always liked best the enemy who struck hardest. Being a Stoic, he carried his war even into his love.

But Psiloriti, like most other men, was wishing with all his heart that the gods had denied brains to women.

"Ennius told a straight story," he admitted. "The man is not only honest, he is too stupid to invent."

"I asked you," Draco repeated, "if you recognized this helmet?"

"I did. I held it in my hands. It was without question a helmet of the Equestrian Order."

"I thought this a mirage," said Draco. "But I see that it has substance. I ask permission to call a witness for my defense."

He sent for Pontius Pilate, and they waited until he came, yawning and careless, playing the exquisite awakened early. But he missed no word, and his pale eyes took in each smallest detail.

"As soon as I get to bed you rout me out again. Is the matter of such importance that I must rise at this hour?"

"It is," said Draco. "I summoned you as witness for my defense against an accusation of gravity. Will you tell the magistrate who was or was not aboard and exactly what you did when you stopped last year in my galley at Pandataria?"

"Your sailing master," said Pilate, "and I were in command. I forget the number of the crew. But I recall the date we dropped anchor, and that we lay to only that night in order to discharge your errand."

Draco looked at Psiloriti. "You may examine the witness."

"Was Andrus Draco aboard with you?"

Pilate's eyelids seldom opened wide. But they did so now, and he glanced around with startled interest. Still he made a good witness, and he answered quickly and frankly.

"The tribune Andrus Draco was not with me but in Judea. He asked me to be his messenger, since he could not leave his legion."

Procla's teeth sank into her lip until her own blood wet that dried red stain. She said, "From what I have learned in Rome a military tribune has little trouble in getting a holiday. Could not this one have secured passage upon another ship and overtaken or met you?"

Pilate smiled. He knew, as she did, that the military

tribunes were sons of important houses and darlings of
the Empire. They could more or less do as they chose, and
many of them did so. But he knew that Andrus Draco was
a soldier from sandals to helmet.

He said: "It is not impossible. But I bear witness that
this one did not do so and that no other ship was near us."

"I ask you," said Psiloriti, "to tell me what message he
sent and exactly what took place while you lay at anchor."

"You must know the message," said Pilate, "since I sent
it to you. I was told by Andrus Draco to give it only to
you or to the Ethiopian prince who was your steward. It
was he whom I sent ashore; and I bade him tell you that
a war galley was not allowed to take a woman as pas-
senger. I told him I bore dispatches from Draco to Augustus urging that the Emperor at once send his own ship
to bring Claudia Procula to Rome."

He looked around him, puzzled and determined to
know what went on.

"You must know this, magistrate. The steward must
have given you my message, since the plan was carried
through and she was brought to Rome."

Psiloriti spoke slowly. "I got that message, but not at
first. I have to ask you what message you sent from
Andrus Draco to Julia."

"Andrus Draco sent no message of any kind to Julia.
The message I sent concerned only Claudia Procula. The
galley weighed anchor and moved before the dawn of
next day."

"Something is hidden deeply here," said Psiloriti softly.
"With your help we may discover it. I ask you to be pa-
tient and to give us every detail."

Pilate was a careful witness, and he honestly wished to
help Andrus Draco. He thought intently as he tried to recall the scene.

"It is doubtless of no importance, but the steward was
difficult. I recall that it surprised me, because on the voy-

age his manners had been as smooth and his behavior as gracious as that of any patrician."

"In what way was Telke difficult?"

"I offered him gold when he came back aboard and said he had carried the message. But he drew himself up to his full height. He is tall—as tall as Draco. He said, 'In my own land I am a prince, and a prince does not take money as a gift.'"

All three of them were looking at him intently as he went on.

"I tried to placate him by telling him that in Rome I had never known anyone, even a prince, to refuse gold. But he stood with his arms folded and stared down at me proudly.

"He said, 'In my land, from prince to prince the gift is some token or garment that has been worn by the giver and that will be worn in friendship by the one who accepts it.' He said, 'The gift I ask of you, a nobleman of Rome, is your helmet, Roman, and your equestrian cloak.'"

9

FOR long seconds Draco's eyes held Psiloriti's across the room. Then the soldier spoke quietly and curtly.

"I ask you, magistrate, to dismiss the case. I am satisfied that my own innocence has been proven. On the other hand, I am satisfied that my accuser had reason for accusation and did not act maliciously."

But she cried out: "No! No! For I must understand this thing!"

"What good will it do to understand?" the old Greek asked her. "Julia is dead. Let me close the case. The tribune is wise, as well as kind."

She turned then and looked at him. She was brave enough to take defeat.

"I thank you. I ask your pardon—and your mercy, Andrus Draco."

He held himself the more stiffly because he longed to take her in his arms and comfort her and shield her from what had been and what was to come. She looked slender and pale and desolate, but more beautiful in his eyes than she had looked at the feast with gold leaves in her hair. She threw back her shoulders and lifted her chin, and he watched the long lovely line of her throat.

"I must know what you know. I am not afraid. My nature is such that I must have the truth. I believe what Pilate has witnessed. I must own that in the night I could have mistaken the steward for Draco. But both Telke and his wife were my friends. What reason could he have had to kill my mother?"

117

In that silence she looked from face to face. She pleaded: "Psiloriti, tell me!"

He sighed, but he told her. "Because of Lalibela."

Her eyes went wide with horror. "Do you mean—?"

"I mean that of all the household you were the only one who believed Lalibela's death to be accidental."

She was holding her face between her hands. "Why did you not tell me? I had the right to know."

"We were trying to spare you," he said, "as the tribune tried to spare you."

She wheeled on Draco then. "How could you know?"

"I did not know. But I guessed as soon as Pilate told of the helmet and cloak. That sounded as if the man who asked them wished a disguise. He was a hostage in parole to Julia, and"—he finished bluntly—"I knew Julia."

"I feared that he might take revenge," Psiloriti said sadly. "I was thankful that he was not on the island when his wife's death occurred. I hoped that time would make the slaves forget their dreadful suspicions."

She shook her head. "His name means *he remembers*. If he believed Julia had caused Lalibela's death, nothing could have prevented his carrying out to the letter his Mosaic law of *an eye for an eye and a tooth for a tooth*."

"Call her women," said Draco sharply. "Have them take her to her room and rub her body with oil and give her a draft to make her sleep."

But she disregarded him and asked Psiloriti: "Did Yod know what you have told me? Was that why he was determined to get away?"

"I think so," he told her simply. "And now, will you not go and rest?"

She bowed, and raised her hand in a gesture of farewell. Draco watched her leave, holding her tousled head high as she walked between two women servants.

Then he looked at the other two. "I say that this matter

ends here and now. If I hear a word of it elsewhere I shall know whom to blame."

Psiloriti nodded his white head. "It is too late to help Julia. Procla will be best helped by silence."

They looked then at the third man and saw that his eyes were bright with calculation.

Suddenly Draco was sorry that he had called him to witness. He wondered why he had not rested his case upon mere denial. His word against Procla's would have held in any court. But he had been overanxious to stand clear in Procla's eyes. He frowned and repeated angrily: "I say that the matter ends here."

Pilate said nothing. Psiloriti, more intuitive than Draco, was even more apprehensive than Draco. But he only said suavely, "Since the case is closed and you have dismissed the charge, tribune, public talk about it could be branded calumny."

Draco went out through the door with Pontius Pilate following on his heels.

They found the white horses waiting with a slave at the head of each, and Pilate smiled as he looked them over.

"The latest gossip in Rome," he said, "is that Lepidus got drunk enough last night to quarrel with his charioteer."

Draco looked at him in silence.

"Half of the sportsmen in Rome would be glad to hire Diocles." He smiled and ran a strong, square hand along the cropped manes. "So all Rome is asking why he gives up his source of income by quarreling with and discharging Rome's leading charioteer."

Draco still stared at him coldly. "Is that all you have to say?"

Pilate stepped back as the near horse swung its head round and bared its long teeth.

"Only this: that except for the fact that one of yours is

dangerous, his team and yours might well be mistaken for each other."

"Danger is present," said Draco; "but it is not in the horse. I remind you that Lepidus drives three. I do not race, and I drive a pair from Mauritania, not from Spain."

"A horseman would notice the difference. But do you think that, in the night, it would appear to a woman—or even the average man?"

Insinuation always angered Draco. He said: "I do not care enough to give you my opinion."

"Neither do I care," said Pilate. "But Rome is asking the question. For some reason young Lepidus, after his quarrel with Diocles, drove alone and recklessly through the streets in the darkness. He cracked an axle and overturned just in front of the house of old Flavius Maro's daughter."

Both of them knew the little lame girl who was heir to all Maro's wealth: balsam gardens in the East, plantations of palm and cedar, in addition to the palace on the Capitoline Hill. She was the same age as Procla, but she seemed a child by comparison. For she lived alone with her guardian and seldom appeared in public.

"I have heard," said Draco warningly, "that the lady of whom you speak is learned in many languages and is known for her good deeds."

"So have I heard," agreed Pilate. "But it was neither her learning nor her charity that drew the young man to her house last night. The servants who carried him into it thought that he was dead. But he is recovering; and all that now troubles the gossips is whom he was seeking when he used Rome's streets for a chariot race. He was seeking someone; for it is said that he blamed Diocles for tardiness in bringing his team from the stables."

Draco thought of the soldier paid to intercept and delay Diocles, but he felt neither remorse nor regret. So without replying he sprang over his chariot's rail and signaled his horses to start.

And Pontius Pilate stood smiling and watched them on their way down the long north slope and across the temple area.

10

FROM Draco, Procla learned now of a Rome greater than the one she knew.

Livia had regaled her with scraps of political gossip. Lepidus had revealed the life of the lazy and rich patricians. From old Paulus Lexus and his like she had caught a glimpse of dark and twisted ugliness which was also a part of the whole.

But Draco's Rome meant an empire flung northwest to Druid Britain and south from Mauritania to Egypt's ancient river. It meant Spain and Gaul and Belgium and Germany and the snowy passes of what is Switzerland. It meant the beat of the legions' feet to Armenia and Assyria, across the torn lands of Palestine where he had been soldiering.

Tiberius still kept him in Rome; and for once the young soldier did not itch to be back in desert camps or out on cavalry forays. He courted Procla openly and in his direct fashion, and she was happier than she had ever been before. Psiloriti approved, and neither Livia nor the Emperor showed disapproval. It seemed to the girl too lovely to last. Young as she was, she had learned to mistrust happiness. As they walked with his arm around her in the dark green ilex shade, she asked him anxiously: "When must you go back to Judea?"

"Ask your father that, my own love. He is my only master; and only Rome has a claim prior to yours and can take me away from you."

She had guessed that already, and her voice was troubled. "Are not wives forbidden to go to the provinces?"

"They are—unless their husbands hold equestrian rank."

"I will go with you wherever you go," she told him. "But of all places in the world, I long to go to Judea."

"Why so?" he asked her in surprise. For he was thinking in terms of the red dust and the difficult terrain for marching and the turbulent mobs that gathered on every pretext.

"Because I had a childhood friend on the island—a Jewish goatherd called Yod—who came from the village of Bethlehem where the Messiah was born."

He withdrew his arm and faced her. "What did you hear? Who told you of a Messiah?"

"An Ethiopian hostage, the wife of a prince. It was of her death Psiloriti spoke. She told me the prophets had foretold that a Messiah would come, and she thought that this child born in Bethlehem was the long-awaited Savior."

Draco had heard of course that many thought this Jesus was the Messiah, but he paid no attention to rumor. He said: "The house of Herod is corrupt and perverted, the populace rowdy and vociferous. I have heard of a young Nazarene whose words have astonished all those who have encountered him. Some even believe that he may be the Messiah. But his influence is too small to mean anything. It is as if a small shoot of green tried to push up on a stony plain under the feet of restless Jews and the march of legionaries."

It was Lalibela's simile. She cried out: "Lalibela said that a blade of grass or a tendril of vine could sooner or later push its way through sun-parched earth, or even split solid rock."

He laughed as he drew her closer. "Many men have claimed to be saviors—what the Jews call Messiahs. Some were schemers for power, and some were merely mad."

She lay still against him, recalling that Yod had said the same thing. How then could one judge truth from falsehood? Perhaps by the strength of the blade of green. If rooted in something stronger than the force that trampled it, perhaps it would blossom and scatter seed for centuries to come. . . .

"The surest savior," said Draco, with his hard cheek against hers, "is a cohort of foot soldiers or a body of horsemen. This country where you imagine a Messiah has been born is so lawless that its own people appealed to Rome for government. If you saw them yelling and throwing stones and trampling each other, you would soon realize no blade of grass could grow beneath their feet. You are a Roman, Procla, and the wife-to-be of a Roman soldier. Remember that the Roman eagles go at the head of the legions from where the blue-painted Britons fight to the red dust of Judea."

So she lay in his arms and listened while he told her of campaigns against the fair-haired barbarians. "It is a land of black forests and of deep, onrushing rivers which are pent between high, rocky banks. I did not go very far into it. Germanicus' expedition was punitive."

"Livia says that a triumph is being planned for the great general upon his return."

Draco did not consider Germanicus great. He was a braggart who had risked the lives of his soldiers when there was no need for risk. But his very bluster gained him popularity with the people. He agreed: "A triumph will be given Germanicus."

She lifted her head and her eyes flashed. "Will you take me to see it? I have heard of Roman triumphs . . . of the victors crowned . . . and the vanquished. . . ."

"I shall probably be obliged to ride in it," he told her. "But I shall see that you watch it from Livia's box, and that the eagles of my command are dipped to you as we pass."

He had hoped to escape it by being transferred to the East; but since he was in Rome he knew he would be involved. However, he could not regret his recall since it had given him Procla: long-limbed, slender Procla, with her red mouth and grave gray eyes. . . .

He released her reluctantly. It was unfair, he thought, that her curved lips should promise all things, but her gray eyes set a limit. Now she held him at arm's length and they fixed thoughtfully on his face. "You do not approve this triumph?"

He would have preferred just making love to her on that marble bench under the cypresses; but he saw that her huntress eyes had captured for the moment the mood from her Venus mouth. "No real soldier could approve a triumph, my own love. It is a spectacle given only to please the public. It is for them a holiday when they are fed free and may gloat over captives against whom they did not fight. But a soldier remembers those captives as a brave foe beaten to earth. He is more deeply shamed than they as they walk at his chariot wheel."

She considered that, with her slim hands still braced against his shoulders. Underneath the cloth of his toga his muscles felt like knots of wood. She closed her eyes for a second as she thought, He could hold me and crush me. . . .

He did so at once. When she pulled away she begged: "Will you listen to me?"

"I will if your heart is set on it. But I'd rather kiss you."

"We have the rest of our lives for that. But it has always been my fault that I am unhappy if I do not understand."

"It is a good fault," he told her. "What do you not understand?"

"So many things! But most of all this strange difference of gods. The god of the ruler Solomon is one god and a jealous god."

"A god," he reminded her, "who exacts an eye for an eye and a tooth for a tooth—a savage god, to suit a savage people."

Psiloriti had told her somewhat the same thing. Telke had kept that savage code; but Lalibela had been good and gentle beyond the teaching of Roman or Hebrew gods. If a god of wrath was the answer to a wrathful people, must there not be an answer to loving and for-giving? Could there not be a Messiah such as Lalibela dreamed? If the gods of Rome and Greece were only the embodiments of men's physical desire and their fury for war and hunger for harvest in the fields, could a Messiah not be the actual embodiment of that spark of something good which burned more or less clearly in everyone? Of Lalibela's gentle faith, of Draco's courage, of her own yearning that was sometimes as sharp as thirst in her mouth?

Draco was thinking his own thoughts; for he believed neither in the god of Solomon nor the worn-out gods of Rome. All he believed in was the long line of the legions stamping time to their marching songs as they carried the eagles to conquest. They were tough fellows who drank and brawled and were always after women. They made up obscene songs about their officers, and sang them loudly and rudely around the campfires at night. If they were not paid they mutinied as they had done on the Rhine. But give them pay in their pouches and meat in their bellies and a short sword in their hand and a man who knew how to lead them! He knew how to handle them. He merely laughed at their songs about him; but he never let discipline down and he punished default se-verely. They had never yet failed to follow him or broken beside him in battle.

He must soon go back. He was only a servant of the Empire. He must go where sent: to the deserts east or the forests and rivers north or the hot, high plateaus of Spain and Africa. But when he went his equestrian rank would allow him to take his wife with him. He would take this girl with her level eyes and her skin so white that the blue veins showed in the temples above her high cheek-bones and under her dark red hair. She was the wife for a soldier, with her courage, intelligence, honesty. He cradled her in a hard fighting arm and looked down into her wide gray eyes.

And then, with his other hand he closed the white lids across them, so that they could ask no more questions about gods of foreign lands. On the bench in the cypress garden he forgot Rome and her legions while he held a slim girl hard to him with his mouth on her red, sweet mouth. . . .

11

THE triumph of Germanicus, although begrudged, was elaborate. Hundreds left their homes before dawn to walk out to the Campus Martius, from which point the parade would start and where its units were forming. Dust hung over the immense field, and from it came squealing of horses, shouts of command, blows of whips, and oaths of impatient officers. To this uproar the gathering onlookers contributed laughter and comment, bawling of sleepy children and barking of dogs.

The tribune Andrus Draco was in its midst and was in such a bad temper that his men eyed him with respect. As an officer of distinction who happened to be in Rome, he had been assigned to the mounted guard of honor which would follow the chariot of the triumphator. He did not appreciate the compliment, and he disliked leading men whom he had not himself trained. To his mind the whole affair was a joke and a sorry one. Germanicus had brought no war to an end and extended no boundaries. He had not even brought home captives and trophies sufficient to furnish an imposing display. Rome's prisons were being emptied to fill in the necessary miles of prisoners. Weak from confinement, they stumbled as they were lashed into line. The ones who were still able to stand at the end of the march would be sent into the arena against mangy lions and aged bears in the games which followed the triumph.

Draco's face was dark beneath the bright crest of his helmet. He wheeled to face his cavalry. "You sit like old women riding home from farm work on harnessed bul-

locks! Eyes front and heels down and in and shoulders
back! By Mars, I'd rather lead dancing bears! Unless you
pass in faultless review when we reach the Capitol, I'll
make it so hot for you that you'll beg Vulcan to cool you
on his forge!"

That was language they understood, and they grinned
and took firmer knee grip as they reined their horses into
rank after rank behind him. Already the head of the long
procession was miles away and approaching the Capitoline Hill. In Livia's box, which was next to that of the
Emperor, sat a girl waiting to see a young tribune pass.
She was flushed with excitement, for she saw only the
glory and strength of Rome in this exhibition for which
Rome's great men had gathered. She saw the wide streets
arched and looped with garlands of laurel and rose and
bay. The cheering of the people and the grind of chariot
wheels drowned in their noise the cries of pain and curses
from captives dragged forward and flogged. She saw the
spectacle as it was in its inception meant to be: acknowl-
edgment of duty done and deeds of bravery by soldiers
like the soldier she loved. It was the thought of him that
flushed her to such beauty that Pilate, whose chair was
behind hers, leaned forward and whispered to her. But
she did not hear or answer him, and he sat back with
folded arms, glancing aside at Lepidus and Flavia Maro,
who were Livia's other guests and sat upon her other side.

Livia's hard black eyes missed nothing that went on in
her box or in that of Tiberius. She knew that he both disliked and feared her grandson Germanicus. But the people favored him, Tiberius was thinking. He heard them in
the distance roaring their applause. His thin mouth drew
thinner as the ovation swelled. They loved a brawler and
blusterer as loud-mouthed as themselves.

He thought with nostalgia of Rhodes and the high ob-
servatory's roof and the calm, tall Egyptian who had
taught him to read the stars. The stars had foretold a

Messiah who would be both king and martyr, somewhere
off on those high Asian coasts where he had gazed night
after night. If he could only have stayed there or gone
farther east for his studies. If he could have forgotten
Rome and Augustus' harlot daughter! Although dead she
came back to haunt him with memories of her lewdness.
Pontius Pilate had just informed him that the tribune
Andrus Draco had been one of her intimates during her
exile.

Draco had brought him reports from Valerius Gratus
and he had been considering replacing Gratus with Draco.
Duty on the fringe of the Empire was as good as banishment. Augustus would have dared to make an issue of it
and send for the proclamator to publish his displeasure.
Tiberius had the soul of an anchorite, and scandal of this
kind was to him a whip of scorpions. He had acknowledged this girl who sat in his mother's box in order that
scandal might not be awakened. But Pilate had hinted at
an affair between her and the tribune Draco, the very
man charged with having been her mother's lover. He
would soon put an end to that by dismissing Draco from
Rome and marrying her to somebody else.

Between the green garlands and flower festoons he saw
the first chariots coming. In those leading chariots rode
the senators and magistrates. Most of them were elderly
men, many of them were obese and bald. The horses that
drew their cars had been chosen for steadiness; but even
at that slow pace, togas fluttered and gold-leaf coronets
stood at odd angles above perspiring, dusty faces. With
words and gestures they greeted their constituents along
the line of march. Behind them a unit of trumpeters proclaimed the advance and burst into a paean as they
sighted the Emperor's box.

After the trumpeters, commenced the long array of
loot: captured ensigns and weapons and armor, statuettes
of alien gods and miniature representations of alien

temples, baggage wagons upon which were built the towns captured and the battles won by Rome. Afoot and on wheels their bearers passed, showing the citizens into what strange lands their heroes had gone and what they had brought back.

The sacrificial animals followed that mile-long display of spoil. There were doves in gilded cages carried or drawn in cars, and yoke after yoke of white oxen with spreading gilded horns.

Next came the prisoners, chained either together or to the chariot rails. A few of them were shaggy, blond barbarians who tried to glare, but cowered. The rest had merely been spewed from the city prisons to fill in. Some of them could hardly walk, and there were women among them. But the crowd yelled as ferociously at sight of them as if they had been an enemy marching upon Rome.

On the heels of the captives, slaves led the animals which some of the captives would have to fight. They led chained bears and wolves that growled and snapped and leapt against their chains and were forced back into line by other slaves with tridents. Three cars bore cages carrying a tiger, a lion and a crocodile, to reassure the audience that there would be bigger game.

A roar of applause from the onlookers greeted the next unit. It was a squad of gladiators dressed for the arena. They were young, magnificent athletes, with sandals strapped high on muscular legs; and the short swords they carried were twined with bay and myrtle.

Procla was watching with parted lips. She did not see the cruelty and sordid evil underneath the pagan pomp of the trumpets. A soldier was returning to Rome, and Rome was giving him her thanks for victories that he had won for her. She knew that Draco was leading the escort of Germanicus. He too was a soldier and might come home someday to a triumph of his own.

The chariot of the triumphator was approaching at last.

It was drawn by four black horses and was twined with laurel from heavy wheel spokes to the guardrail where he stood. The people were throwing before it green branches and blossoms. He waved the laurel in his right hand and called back to them in the comradely ease they loved. Procla saw that he was dressed all in purple and gold. A slave stood behind him and held a crown just above his head. Germanicus' bold eyes singled out Livia's box and fixed themselves on Procla's face. As he came abreast of them he raised the eagle scepter in his left hand and saluted his grandmother.

But Procla's eyes had deserted him for the mounted guard which followed. Draco, in battle dress, was riding straight as a spear. He did not turn his head, but his eyes met hers and adored her. Out of the corner of his mouth he barked at the men behind him: "Keep your rumps down and your swords up and salute Livia's box, or I'll have your unwashed hides, you sons of Cerberus!"

Their swords flashed up and they yelled hoarsely and in unison: "*Io triumphe!* Hail the triumphator!"

12

SO it had passed, in a roar of salute and a hail of thrown flowers and a trampling of horses and a cloud of following dust. Lepidus coughed and leaned to fan the sweet-faced crippled girl who sat beside him and looked at him as if he were the triumphator. Livia smiled, pleased at the recognition she had received. Procla, oblivious of them all, turned her head and gazed after the horsemen who were winding their way on to the temple of Jupiter. Pilate sat still and watched her with expressionless eyes.

At the games which followed she sat in Livia's box again. Draco was released from duty, and was beside her. Neither of them was watching the arena below where two gaunt barbarians stood back to back, and armed each with sword and dagger, tried to hold off three hungry lions.

Draco leaned closer and caught her bare arm against him and under his cavalry cloak. She felt his fingers turning the armlet of red-gold which she always wore above her right elbow. "This is no Roman bracelet," he whispered in her ear. "I can tell by their feel that the symbols carved on it are strange."

"It is the mate to one that Lalibela gave me," she said. "Before I left the island I went up to her room and took it out of her box of scented wood. I had reason to know that she would wish me to wear it."

She did not tell him about the one that she had given to Yod. She kept silence partly from loyalty to Yod and partly because she feared that Draco might disapprove. Although she loved him passionately and completely, she realized there was ground upon which he and she could not meet.

Looking up at his straight profile she saw the shadow of a frown. Lalibela's name had reminded him of Pandataria. He wished with all his heart to forget that ill-starred island and his brief friendship with the evil woman upon it. He thanked the gods he had got this girl safely away.

He knew exactly why Tiberius had acknowledged her. The hard man had shown her no tenderness and would be glad to have her leave Rome. Draco's family was great enough and old enough to receive a Julio-Claudian. He himself had made a brilliant army record, and Tiberius had received him well. He felt that his power in Rome and his favor in the Emperor's eyes made it sure that he would be given the ruler's unwanted daughter. Unwanted? The very word angered him. For he wanted her more than he had wanted anything else in his life. He tightened his grip on the slim arm and he felt its soft, quick pulsebeats. . . .

Above and around the box the crowd burst into a roar which made the imperial party look down in the arena. One of the tall prisoners had been brought down by a lion, and man and beast were rolling in a death grip on the ground. As Draco looked, the other two animals closed in on the man who was still standing. He felt Procla shudder against his side, and he pulled her closer under the hiding cape.

"It is quicker than crucifixion and a braver way to die."

"I wish that I had not come," she said. "Can we not go away?"

He glanced around and met Livia's eyes. He knew she would be affronted if he left her party so early in the games.

"After a little while," he said. "Soon they will be so enthralled in the show that they will not notice our departure."

She heard a shriek, and shuddered again and looked down over the barrier which protected them from the wild beasts. A horse with dragging trace chains was already being brought in, and the hooks on those traces were being attached to what lay in the arena. Men with whips and tridents drove the lions from their meal and lashed them back again into their cages. Slaves ran forward with sand and straw to cover the red slime which overlay and colored the damp earth. Dry footing was being arranged for the next victims. The crowd had no objection to seeing men die horribly; but it would have shouted down the chief official in his box above the triumphal arch had its pleasure been shortened by the slip of a fighter's foot in blood.

The official was now standing, and the crowd fell silent in hope of some novelty to come. Through the gate, marching two and two, came six young and brawny women. They were dark of skin and were dressed in short, coarse togas of red or saffron yellow. Each one carried in her left hand a large scarf as red as blood and in her right a thin glittering sword.

Pilate leaned forward, and Procla felt his breath on the back of her neck. "This is the event of the circus," he informed her and Draco. "I am happy to say that it was I who suggested it."

Draco said low but sharply: "Women in the arena are not my idea of sport."

"They are Iberian prisoners and were to be sold as slaves. I have campaigned in that peninsula, and I know that its people have a liking for games with bulls. I told the chief official, and he ordered that the six strongest of the Spanish women be brought to him. He gave them their choice between the slavery which was their sentence and fighting a bull to the death before the Roman people. They chose at once to fight the bull, although only one of them knows anything of the sport. She has been instructing the others and I hear that they have learned well."

He folded his arms and leaned back in his chair. "I am sure that we will enjoy it."

The six Spanish women were below the podium now and were saluting the Emperor with outheld swords. Their voices were strangely musical, mournful and yet staccato, as they cried the Latin they had been taught: *"Morituri te salutant!"* They were swarthy, muscular peasant girls, with broad cheekbones and coarse black hair. One of them walked to the middle of the arena. The others fanned out in a semicircle behind her. She raised her sword and it flashed in the signal of an arc, and the attendants raised the steel-barred gate that she faced.

Through it burst the most enormous and most furious bull that Procla could have imagined in nightmare. It was sorrel coated, and its long horns pointed directly forward. Their narrowing points had been filed to make them even sharper than nature had made them. Tortured by that and by spear pricks to make its entrance imposing, it rushed directly forward—then stopped so suddenly that its cloven hooves tore long furrows in the ground. With them it now pawed threateningly, while it raised its huge head and glared around. Procla could see its small, vicious eyes like two red coals that were burning with hate.

She felt Draco pull at her hand and heard him curse under his breath. But she was frozen with fascination and horror and with the pervading mob excitement. The mob was stilled by the novelty. In that silence she heard the fighting bull blow out his breath like a gust of wind. He dropped to his knees, and turning his head from side to side, he gored long ruts in the hard-packed earth to ease his rage and his pain.

The chief official signaled then, and a thrown spear struck him in the flank. The audience gave vent to a howl like a wolf pack as he leapt to his feet. The girl who stood in center was walking slowly toward him. She walked on her toes like a dancer but was coiled as tense as a spring. She unfurled the brilliant square of cloth and waved it toward the monster.

With a bellow he plunged toward her. She stood still and vibrated the scarf. As the swordlike horns almost reached her she spun on her toes and away. The bull drove on and crashed into the barrier. He rose to his feet amid splintered wood and looked around for his next charge.

The girl who had dodged him was calling to the others to beware. She knew that the bull was even more dangerous now, but she knew that she could at least tire him and enrage him beyond caution if he continued to charge her. She wished to keep him away from her unskilled companions until the danger was blunted and all could close for the kill. Her words were lost in the yells of the crowd, delighted to see something new. Pontius Pilate was looking around, proud of his innovation's success. Draco was swearing softly and trying to pull Procla to her feet. The bull stood facing the woman who enticed him with the red flag. He pawed the ground with long strokes and lowered his head for the rush.

But he too had cunning. From the corner of one red eye he saw another figure not far to right of him. He plunged directly forward—then swerved in a sharp turn that brought him directly down upon the other girl.

She forgot all that she had been taught, in the terror of that approach. She screamed and dropped sword and scarf and started running, instead of waiting to make the sidestep that would have saved her life. Draco saw the leader dart to intercept, but it was too late. The bull had struck his victim down and was trampling her.

This time Draco did more than pull, he jerked Procla to her feet. As he dragged her toward the exit he threw back at Pilate a word more in use with the legions than with the patricians.

Pilate did not resent it. His expression did not change. He appeared quite pleased with himself and somewhat thoughtful as he glanced from their retreating backs to the place where Tiberius sat.

13

A TERRIBLE excitement was pounding at Procla's temples. She was Roman and she had just been steeped in an orgy of cruelty. The experience had stirred the instincts that it was meant to stir. Flushed and throbbing from head to foot, she leaned against Draco's shoulder as he guided his team through the city. She did not know where they were going and she did not care, until she saw the silhouette of a fort on the crest above them. It was the citadel on the north peak of the Capitoline Hill. The horses passed it in a walk and carried them down into the small valley adjacent to it and to the sacred grove. She had never been to Draco's house, but she knew they were near it; Draco's house of which she would be mistress when she was Draco's wife.

It was not his way to ask. He said, "The games will last until midnight. I am going to take you home with me. Do not be afraid, my darling. All is planned and my steward has his orders. He will give us the evening meal just as if we were man and wife—which we are soon to be. You will cross my threshold for the first time, and I shall have the joy of seeing you at my table. Then I will take you home while the streets are still deserted and before the citizens begin to leave the games."

She caught his bare arm tighter and laid her cheek against it. She was not by nature overamorous, and he felt the excitement in her touch. But he loved her so well that it awakened only tenderness. She was so young to have come unscathed through a mire of corruption. He knew all the abuses of Roman society and was not himself above reproach, but he gloried in the fact that this girl was different. When he looked at her he thought of one of the tall white lilies that the flowersellers hawked on the temple steps in Jerusalem. In spite of the dust and the heat and the bargaining of their sale, they still held their heads at the day's end high and white and untouched. He would keep her always so. No man except himself should touch her. And he loved her so truly that he could wait.

The white horses carried them slowly through the wooded dell and skirted Jupiter's grove. Draco's house stood on the south slope and they were approaching it.

Slaves ran to take the team, and the steward bowed before them. The master of the place was doing nothing clandestine. He was informing his household that this slender, bright-haired girl was to be his wife and their mistress. He handed her up the low marble steps and through the door. Two enormous boar hounds chained to a pillar rose and stretched and wagged their tails and yelped with joy as they saw him. He left her and stepped across and released them. They walked stiff-legged to Procla while he watched in amusement. Then they sniffed her from sandals to girdle. She let them investigate in their own way, making no hurried gesture which they might have taken for threat. Then she put out her hands gently and stroked their big, bristly heads.

"I think they know just who you are," he told her in all seriousness. "I have found that animals take in simply and quickly things which have to be explained laboriously to human beings."

Then he clapped his hands, and two Greek women came in and led her to a small room where the basin of a fountain was set at about the height of her waist. They placed a stool beside it for her, and they unlaced her sandals and bathed her face and hands and feet. All around the basin's rim life-sized marble geese spouted water from their beaks into it. The walls were a frieze of pictures telling the popular story of how Rome had been saved by the alarm of those birds.

The older of the two slaves smiled as she saw that Procla's eyes were following it.

"This was the Lord Draco's playroom and bath when he was a little boy. He used to climb up on the backs of the geese. See where he has broken the tails off of two? He liked to ride on them and play, but he refused to be washed. Had I not been younger then, I could never have caught him. Day after day I chased him all over the sacred grove, and brought him back yelling and held him by force while I scrubbed him and changed his linen and tunic."

Procla was enchanted by this youthful picture of Draco. She sat laughing while they served her, dressed her hair anew and perfumed her neck and arms from onyx jars and tiny golden vials. Then she went out in the hall where Draco was waiting for her, and the two hounds were gnawing at bones on the floor.

He had removed helmet and cloak and the bronze guards from his legs. He wore the same short toga with leather battle belt, and house sandals strapped high with leather thongs. From their soles to his close-cropped head he looked scrupulously clean. Procla stopped short and burst into a peal of laughter.

He frowned back at her. "Why do you stare? Are you laughing at me?"

"I was looking," she told him through her mirth, "to see if Kelaine had caught you and washed your knees."

He pulled her close and laughed with her. "So Kelaine has been telling tales? She loves to torture little boys by scraping their knees raw and turning their ears inside out for a grain of dirt." His arms tightened suddenly and hard. "She shall have other little boys to wash; shall she not, my own love?"

She raised her hands and drew his head down. "For that

I shall pray to Demeter: for small sons who will be like my husband."

He was not even angry when the steward walked in on them standing wrapped in each others' arms in the open hall, with the hounds at their feet growling softly and tearing at their food. He wished them all to realize, as his hunting dogs had realized, that this was the woman to be his wife and to rule his house and them.

Procla sat on her couch at his side in a daze of joy. The steward had chosen the banquet well. He stood to one side and directed the slaves. She was young and strong and hungry, but she hardly knew whether she was eating honied dates or some strange fish brought in kegs of oil from Sicily and cooked with rare and precious condiments. She was watching Draco and thinking, My life will be like this. It is why I was born and why I ran free on a windy, rocky island. It is why Draco was brought there by his friends. He was meant to find me and we were meant to be always together. I shall be married to him and come here to his house in the red veil of a Roman bride. I shall be with him always and sit each day at his table. I shall be so happy that I will try to make him and all his household happy. And little sons will be born to us, to play on the geese by the fountain. . . .

Draco was under the same spell, but he was more practical. He was watching the water clock that stood at the long room's end. The slow drip of the water into the marble dish below was counting away the hours, and he must take her home. But soon his house would be her home; he would have her always with him.

He rose to his feet and drew her up and stood with his arms around her. She asked childishly: "Is it time to go? Must you take me away now?"

"I must take you back, my darling, much as I want to keep you. This parting is not a real parting, only a few hours apart. We have too much happiness at stake and cannot afford to risk the imperial displeasure. Tomorrow I will see Livia and ask her help in our behalf, and I will also go directly to Tiberius."

His mouth went down to her mouth, and they stood in a long embrace. For them both it had all the passion of that first kiss on the stolen ride on the Appian Way. But now it had tenderness as well . . . and the promise of fulfillment. . . .

Only a sudden clash of metal at the entrance to the hall at length caused Draco to look up.

As he raised his head he was facing the door. Through its arch he saw that the big room appeared to be full of soldiers. In that first glance he recognized the Emperor's own body guard.

He saw the centurion at their head step forward and stand at attention. In a kind of frozen awareness he recognized the gesture and it recalled to him another scene. He had once been present when another centurion had taken into custody a superior officer. He had seen it all happen before. But—could it happen to him?

The centurion answered that question. He spoke reluctantly, for he knew whom he was facing; but he spoke the dreaded order word for word.

"By command of Tiberius, Emperor of Rome, I put under arrest the tribune Andrus Draco and the lady Claudia Procula."

14

PROCLA stood now with Draco where she and Psiloriti
had stood to await the Emperor on the night of her
arrival. She was a little dazed and terribly angry. It was
this righteous anger which had so far crowded from her
heart the cold fear that had hold on Draco. She knew that
she had done no wrong, and she would tell the Emperor
so. Her head went higher and two red spots stained the
set whiteness of her face. How dared he, Emperor or not,
have her brought through the streets under guard? How
dared he so insult her and a man of noble birth—an officer
of his legions—who loved her honorably and intended to
marry her?

Draco knew all that; but he knew Rome and Tiberius
too. He was thinking of other men fallen from high rank
and happiness. He had seen it happen to them, and he
recognized the pattern. This was disaster's dark web, and
he and she were caught in it. The fact that they were
innocent meant nothing; that they were under arrest
meant that Tiberius had already lent ear to some informer.
False as the information might be, there was no defense
against it if the Emperor believed it. He realized that it
probably meant death for him, and the gods only knew
what fate for Procla. And he was utterly helpless to save
either her or himself.

The centurion barked an order, and the guards at the
door clashed their weapons. They moved apart in two
files, and Tiberius entered between them. Procla's heart
skipped a beat as she saw that Pilate was following him.
Here is a friend, she told herself. Once he had witnessed

well for Draco. He will bear witness now for us both, and we shall be set free.

Her eyes sought his face eagerly, but Pilate's eyes did not meet them. He stopped just within the door, and he gazed without expression at the opposite wall.

But Tiberius came forward with slow steps and a bleak face.

"So it is true," he said to the girl, his harsh voice harsher than ever. "You are your mother's own daughter. I should have sent you away."

She blazed at him then. "Why should you? I have done no wrong. I demand of you, in the presence of these other Romans, why you have done this to me and the man whom I love? Am I not your daughter, and the grand-daughter of Augustus?"

Draco heard a rustle of steel and a gasp of surprise and interest from the legionaries, as they stirred to see. But the Emperor ignored her and spoke to the centurion.

"Conduct the tribune to the prisons," he ordered. "I will deal with the Lady Claudia Procula."

She moved away from Draco then and toward Tiberius, and she was far more imperial than he was.

"We have done no wrong," she repeated. "Pontius Pilate is our friend, and he will speak for us. He will tell you that my Lord Draco loves me and intends to ask you to give me to him for wife."

Tiberius lowered his head in the way that the bull had done at the games. But the thwarted lust and twisted hate in his eyes shone more red than the eyes of the beast. Why should the stars have doomed him, he wondered in his dark mind—doomed a man who hated his flesh and feared his natural instincts—to be tormented first by a wanton for wife and then by her wanton daughter? He could not endure the sight of her. He turned from her on the man.

"I have my informers," he said, and each word seemed to grate on his teeth as he spoke. "You have been watched and were seen to take this woman to your house. Not even an officer of the Legion can with safety flaunt an Emperor's granddaughter as his mistress."

Procla saw Draco's dagger in his hand; but the expression on his face alarmed her even more.

"Who calls her that is a liar," he said. "Tell me who informed you?"

Tiberius spoke slowly. He enjoyed this part of it.

"I shall not tell you who informed me. But I tell you I believe it of her, and I too call her that."

Draco, goaded, lost his head. Dagger in hand he jumped for Tiberius, sadist and dreamer and tyrant, and Emperor of Rome.

The huge room broke into turmoil. Tiberius stood his ground. But Procla saw the centurion's sword as it flashed out and up. She was next to him, and she had just time to throw herself between its descending point and Draco's unguarded back.

Then there was only a shock like a blow . . . and a slow, deep, drowning darkness. . . .

15

IT was lonely on the marble bench in the dark shade of the cypresses. Not only was she forbidden to go beyond her own garden, she was too weak and listless even to wish to go. She longed for Psiloriti and his calm wisdom; but Psiloriti had died in his sleep one night while she was ill. That was the advantage of old age, she told herself. Old age could escape; but youth must stay and suffer—as she was suffering.

Looking back she realized that all her life she had been more lonely than other women. In all her life only three people had come close enough for love: an Ethiopian princess, an old Greek philosopher, and a young Roman soldier. Death had taken the first two. Silence had hold on the third. Whenever she—Procla—mentioned his name, the widow Catella threw up her hands and went into hysterics. She was a sycophant and feared to incline one way or the other until she knew how her patroness Livia inclined.

Livia had visited her granddaughter daily during that time of fever and pain. There had never been any danger that Procla would not recover. The centurion had seen her in time to check his blow to some extent. But the wound and the shock had caused a high fever. For part of the time she had been delirious; but she remembered Livia's voice giving orders and Livia's cold, composed face bending above her.

Livia, like Catella, awaited another decision. She had liked the girl; but liking and love were two different things. She had learned long since to forego the indulgence of her emotions and subordinate them to her ambition. She reminded herself that Procla was only a few years younger than she herself had been when she went from her sons' father to Augustus. She could still recall the time when she thought she loved that older Tiberius. But she could smile now at remembrance of love. And she was determined to teach Procla to smile at it too. All she wanted was decision from that strange and indecisive man, her son, who was Emperor of the Romans.

So she gave Procla no sympathy, and only told her shortly that she should and would abide by the Emperor's decree. Draco was still in prison. That was all she knew, and she refused to discuss him. But a word of advice: his case as well as Procla's own case might be helped by Procla's submission and obedience to orders.

Procla saw the dowager then for exactly what she was: a sycophant of high rank, with dyed hair, hard eyes, and harder heart.

But Livia was her only link with the world in which Draco still lived, although he lived in a dungeon of the political prison. She made up her mind to use Livia as Livia had used her: coldly, carefully and unhindered by conscience. She owed nothing to Rome or the Julio-Claudian house. She owed nothing to Mars or Venus or their greedy companion gods. They had done nothing for her or her soldier lover. She had learned that they were faulty and cruel—as cruel as Telke's Jehovah who demanded an eye for an eye.

Of many who had pretended to be her friends, Lepidus was the only one who dared to visit her. He came through the cypress walk, as exquisitely dressed as ever, and she rose eagerly at sight of him.

"You are kind—and brave—to come. I thank you, Lepidus."

"I am both," he agreed ironically as he arranged his toga's folds and seated himself beside her. "Frankly, I think I am foolish too. But Flavia made me come."

Procla's heart warmed with gratitude to the lame girl.

"I did not think there was anyone in Rome who cared. You are lucky, Lepidus, if she loves you."

He nodded, and she saw his eyes light behind his supercilious mask.

"I know that I am lucky, and I know that she loves me. You may find it hard to believe, but when I take her for wife I shall be marrying for love and not for money."

"I do believe you, Lepidus."

She saw the delicate face and the dark curly hair. She was touched by the girl's goodness, and she wished good fortune for these two who seemed her only friends. But their happiness only made her own prospects look darker. Lepidus watched her long lashes droop darkly on her pale cheeks.

"I bring you a message from Draco."

She cried out at that. "Oh, have you seen him?"

"No. I am not so silly as that. I bribed the centurion— the same one who put him under arrest and wounded you by accident."

"But what of Draco?" she begged. "How is he? What was his message?"

"His health is good but his temper bad. The centurion told me that he was a privileged prisoner and was allowed to do as he pleased within bounds. The guards are old legionaries, and they know his fighting record."

She shook her head. "You are trying to comfort me. I am thankful that he is treated well, but I know he is in danger."

Lepidus frowned. "No one can tell what Tiberius may do. Draco sends you word not to worry about him, but—" Lepidus paused and added slowly—"*to do whatever the Emperor orders you to do.*"

The words of that message told her how serious Draco knew their plight to be. Chilled to her finger tips she sat, staring down at her sandals.

"Lepidus—could the Emperor—would he put Draco to death?"

"He could; but I do not think he will. I think that Draco's sentence will be at the worst banishment. His friends are hoping that he will be let off with foreign duty somewhere far from Rome and—" he stopped and looked away—"far from *you.*"

So I was right, she thought, to mistrust happiness. I shall not have it, not even if Draco is allowed to live. But he must live and he shall live, even at that cost. I am warned now, and the warning has armed me for what is to come. I have no time to waste in weeping for our lost happiness. I must concentrate every thought of my mind and every nerve of my body to save him by any means I can. I will do what the Emperor tells me if he will spare Draco's life; but I will drive a bargain as hard as the one he drives. And I shall remember all my life what they have done to me; and I shall only bide my time to hurt them as deeply.

Lepidus lifted her clasped hands and opened their fingers one by one. He knew what she was thinking, and he smoothed gently the palms where her nails had cut grooves in the soft flesh.

"I wish I could help you, my dear. The fact that I am a coward in no way keeps me from recognizing bravery in others."

"You and Flavia are brave to do what you have done. No one else has dared to do as much."

She steadied her voice and went on. "You have shown me what course to take. I had still hoped to argue my case with the Emperor and persuade him to set us both free and allow us to be married."

"For Draco's sake," he said quickly, "do not try that. It would probably cause Tiberius to have him put to death."

"But why?" she implored, in a last attempt. "Why

should we be kept apart when our love is honest? Surely you do not believe otherwise?"

He shrugged. "I had not even given a thought to that. I believe whatever you tell me. But what does it matter? Tiberius is enraged and has made up his mind to punish you both. Nothing you say or do can make him let you marry Draco or even see him again. He will be escaping lightly if he is allowed to live. After all, he tried to kill the Emperor."

Procla, watching his face, saw his eyebrows lift derisively.

"Others may wish to do that, but not many do it and live. So bend all your efforts to placating your judge. If you antagonize him, he will be more severe—and Draco will suffer even more than you do. I advise you to think of that when the Emperor summons you."

"I will remember," she said slowly. She went on as if to herself. "I shall waste no time in pleading, since you tell me it would be useless. I shall put Draco's love behind me and work to save Draco's life."

He looked at her in pity as he rose to leave. But he told her honestly: "I shall not come again."

"It is better that you should not," she agreed, and her voice was level now. "Again I thank both you and Flavia. I ask you to tell her that if ever the time comes when I can do some kindness for her, I will not fail her."

16

ONLY a few days later the Emperor sent an escort of Praetorians to the little stone house in the dark green garden. Surrounded by that escort, which was really a guard, Procla's litter and that of Livia were carried swiftly and quietly to the imperial palace. But before they left the little house Livia had instructed her.

"I have known the Emperor longer than you have. For your own sake I advise you to ask his pardon for what you have done, and to agree without protest to whatever he tells you to do."

"I have done nothing," said Procla, "for which I need ask pardon of him or anyone else."

Livia echoed Lepidus. "That matters not at all. You have offended him and incurred his anger."

Procla lifted her head, and her pale cheeks flushed carmine. "I think I offend him merely by being Julia's daughter. If you ask me, that is my only crime."

"I do not ask you," said Livia sharply. "I merely remind you that the fate of Andrus Draco has not yet been decided. My opinion is that it will be settled by this interview."

Procla remembered that while she waited for Tiberius. It was her third interview with the man who had acknowledged her as daughter. She had never felt any love for him; now she felt both fear and hatred. She recalled the night when she and Psiloriti had arrived . . . and the night when the Praetorians had led her and Draco to the palace like a pair of criminals. . . .

Upon the first occasion Tiberius had faced a child

152

brought up in clean loneliness on an island far from Rome.
Upon the second he had taken unawares a girl deeply and
innocently in love. Now he dealt with a woman, cold and
angry and wary.

He strode into the hall, his face furrowed with anger,
disregarded Livia and stopped in front of Procla. For
minutes he stared at her wordlessly. His mouth was so
thin that it appeared to be lipless, and the pupils of his
eyes were contracted to pin points of light.

"I have not yet decided your punishment," he told her,
"or whether your partner in harlotry shall be put to death
or not."

Both words and tone took her by surprise. Her talk with
Lepidus had prepared her to beg mercy for Draco's attack on Tiberius. She had planned to say that the fact that
he had lost his always-steady head proved the respect
and tenderness in which he held her. But if she was
branded a harlot that argument lost its force. And she was
frightened even more by the furtive eagerness in his voice.
He is enjoying this, she thought. He likes to look upon
torture. He hates others to be happy. He is even more
angry with Draco and me for loving and wishing to marry
each other than he is with Draco for trying to kill him.

But she held herself straight before him, almost as tall
as he, too slender of body now and too white of skin. She
tilted her chin upward so as to meet his look bravely, and
she tried to clasp her hands loosely instead of clenching
them.

"I ask the Emperor's pardon for any offense I have
given. Perhaps I was wrong to go to Draco's villa. But I
went in innocence with the man I intended to marry, and
he and his servants treated me with every respect."

"Do not lie," said Tiberius. "You were caught there in
his arms. Confession and repentance will help you more
than lying."

He hopes, she thought, that I will confess. He would

gloat over confession. But I will die and let Draco die before I'll confess to a falsehood.

To her surprise she was hampered by no agitation. She was cold with hard anger and deadly fear, but she was thinking clearly. She had not expected this senseless and useless torment. She had expected fury and personal abuse, but he was more dangerous than she had known. Only a dark perversion could cause anyone to prolong and enjoy watching pain. Livia had warned her that she had known him longer. Lepidus had risked bringing her Draco's message. Draco himself had sent her word to obey.

But this man who judged her had as yet issued no order. He was keeping her in the arena, with wild beasts snarling and tearing at her brain and her heart. He was taking pleasure in the sight of her torment, withholding his decision of mercy or death.

She fixed her eyes upon his with a desperate insistence. "I beg you to believe," she told him earnestly, "that I have regard for my name and for your high place, my father. I ask you not to take the word of an informer who could lie against the word of your own daughter."

"You are not my daughter," he shouted. "If you were I would disown you!"

Involuntarily she stepped back and away from him. His burst of rage and the shock of his words confused her for a second. Then her brain cleared and her head went up, and she felt a cool wash of relief. She was glad—glad with all her heart—to know he was not her father. She was glad no drop of his blood was running in her veins.

His expression was demoniac and his mouth was twisted with passion. He followed her and thrust his face close to hers.

"I acknowledged you as my daughter only to silence scandal. The Dowager Empress—" he stopped and glared at Livia on her couch— "is responsible for that mistake. I should not have listened to her. I should have known your inheritance from the courtesan who destroyed my home. Now you have brought upon me and Rome a shame as great as that which your shameless mother brought on her father Augustus."

Procla stood as still as one of the statues that lined the walls. She dared not speak. Her words appeared only to feed his anger as fuel cast into a fire makes it blaze more high.

His eyes were fixed on her face. He breathed as fast and as loudly as if he had been running.

"You loved the tribune Andrus Draco enough to cause your own disgrace and to endanger his life by going alone at night to his house."

She knew that he wished no answer and that it was useless to answer. He was pausing and smiling, slowly and cruelly.

"I intend to find out now whether you still love him enough to save his life by becoming the wife of another man, and leaving Rome for a far-off province."

It surprised her so that she could not at first reply. She had expected exile alone, or imprisonment. But this. . . .

He took her silence for objection. He said: "I can force you to do it. But that will cause more gossip. I wish this affair forgotten. Talk will soon cease if you, of your own will, marry another man and go with him to his station. Andrus Draco, with another woman for wife, will then be allowed to rejoin his legion."

Before Procla could speak he added: "Unless you do it, your lover dies."

In the half second before she spoke she saw it all with clarity. She saw that she dealt with a twisted brain, and that he only spared them because he hoped they would suffer more alive than dead. But she made her plan in that brief time. Only death could keep her and Draco apart. Alive, he would find her and take her from a husband she did not love. Tiberius had accused and convicted her when she was innocent. His sentence gave her the chance to use the husband he thrust on her merely as a means of rejoining Draco. She would do so without a thought of that husband or of this tyrant. Her only regret was that she could not now laugh in his face and tell him he was forcing her to do in the future what he had accused her of, and of which she was still innocent. Draco would leave any wife for her. He would come and take her to live with him in some place where Rome could not reach them.

She looked Tiberius in the face and her voice was steady. "I agree to the bargain you offer. I will marry whomever you choose."

PART THREE
Judea

1

THE long journey was drawing to a close. Standing on the deck of the galley, which made its way steadily through soft winds and under bright skies, Procla reviewed the time she had spent with this man who was her husband, and forced herself to realize his good qualities. She recalled that journey to his first post on which they had set out the day after their marriage. From the beginning he had been considerate in every way to her, and she told herself she was fortunate that he had been the Emperor's choice. Gradually she had roused from her grief and listlessness and had forced herself to take an interest in her new life. I must waste no time in sorrow for the past, she had told herself, and remember that each day takes me nearer Draco now. It may be days or months or years, but he will come to me when he can.

All she knew was that he had been sent to Syria, and would rejoin his legion when his errand there was done. So anxious was Tiberius to get him out of Rome that he had ordered the tribune to leave directly from his wedding for Damascus.

The knowledge that he was safe and free had given her strength to carry out her part of the agreement. Her own wedding had been private, but all formalities had to be observed. Then the man whose wife she was had taken her in her red veil to his house nearby the Temple of Vesta.

She was fair-minded. She told herself that it was not his fault and that she must not allow herself either to blame or dislike him. She reminded herself that he had

been Draco's friend as well as her own. Had he been
given the chance, he might have interceded for them that
night at the imperial palace. He had to obey the Emperor,
as she and Draco had to obey.

He had not made the mistake of being too ardent a
bridegroom. He had been very gentle with her, and re-
spectful and attentive. He knew well enough that, although he was her husband, all her thoughts and her love
belonged to another man. So he had tried to be kind, for
her sake as well as his own. He had comforted her and
cheered her and anticipated her wishes, and she had found
herself liking him better every day.

Now they were journeying to Judea. Because land
travel was easy and that by sea inconvenient, he had
taken her south to Brundusium by the Appian Way and
embarked for the East from that seaport. The South
Italian inns seemed to her luxurious. The prospect of a
new land quickened her interest. Changing scenes, she
found, made the days pass more quickly.

Pilate was amused by her interest in Judea and the
Jews; but seeing she wished to hear of them, he told her
all he knew.

"You are the only woman I have ever met who can talk
of anything besides love and food."

"What of your patroness Livia?" she challenged him
promptly.

He laughed and shook his large head. "Livia's world is
only political. She tried hard to rule it, but she failed at
last. When that happened she had nothing left. But I think
you love all beauty, Claudia."

"Psiloriti taught me that," she said.

Since their marriage he had called her only Claudia,
and she realized his reason for doing so. It said without
other words: My wife is of the Julio-Claudian line. She
was glad; for *Procla* belonged to Draco and Psiloriti and
a life that was entirely apart from this new life. She had

to live this new life, and she would do her best with it.
But she would keep it separate from the love that was past
—and the love that was to come. . . .

She looked at the blue waves parting at the galley's
slow curved prow. Crete had been their midway stop, for
water and fresh food. She had stood upon stone and earth
of Psiloriti's birthplace; and she had felt him standing
there beside her. He had exerted more influence on her
life than anyone else. But he was gone now. She held him
only in memory. She knew his gods and the gods of Rome
as mere reflections of human thought. She could do without gods, she told herself. Rome's idols were for the ignorant. And Judah's Jehovah was invented to rule the
weak through fear.

Psiloriti had taught her that fear was a destroyer. Yet,
she wondered, must not fear be the other side of the
shield of love? Except for a few childish alarms caused by
the shark or the ram goat, she had not known real fear
until she knew real love. Fear for Draco's life had caused
her to do what she had done. Where was he now? Was he
thinking of her? What woman had Tiberius forced him to
take as wife?

She saw in review the women whom she had met in
Rome, at banquet tables, in boxes at games or theaters.
They had meant nothing in her life then. Which one of
them meant something now? Tullia Aventina was handsome and provocative; but Draco had once commented
she was too fat for his taste. Servia Marcia was sharp of
tongue and older than she pretended to be. Lucretia was
not pretty, but her hair was pale gold. . . .

Caesarea of Palestine rose in one blue noon. It soared
from blue sea into bluer sky, in terraces of snow-white
stone. A circular quay was built around the harbor. Upon
it were walkways and housed bridges. Beyond this,
wharves and streets and temples and homes and theaters
rose in tier after tier to the glory of Herod the Builder.

The galley was rowed slowly into the stone-locked haven. Gradually the mass of buildings ashore seemed to separate, each one taking on its individual life. Procla could now see their difference from the buildings of Rome. Sunlight behind her slanted on rounded domes and long arcades with awnings. As they moored to one of the many wharves she heard the strange cries in Hebrew. She saw striped turbans and long eastern robes. She saw the palm trunks with their feathery crowns lining the broad, hot streets.

Then she spied the cohort sent to meet the new governor. They were footmen, not cavalry, but her heart leapt at the sight. They were drawn up at the dockside in stiff array, with eagle-eyed centurions watching for any defection. As she stepped from the galley's deck she stepped between their two files of steel.

With their short swords they struck their shields and stood at rigid attention for the landing of Pontius Pilate, fifth Procurator of the province of Judea, and of his lady, the noble Claudia Procula.

2

THE deposed Herod had been the last to enjoy the royal palace at Caesarea. It was now the official residence of the Roman governor. While not so magnificent as the palace at Jerusalem, its exotic beauty and immense size took Procla's breath away. It looked out on the main square or gathering place of the city. Between the blue and crimson hangings of her apartment she watched the colorful movement of citizens and sailors and visitors from the plains and mountains east. Robed men tore through on horses with streaming manes and tails. Overladen camels swayed by with long, pacing steps. Sometimes fights broke out between seamen and civilians, and there was knife play and yelling, and flight with the guards in pursuit.

Procla had brought no serving-woman. Livia was determined that no whispers about Draco's love should follow Pilate's wife. The steward brought a girl to her the day after arrival: a girl of about her own age, with high, full breasts and rounded hips and warm brown eyes. Procla liked her at first sight.

"Who are you?" she asked. "Do you wish to serve me?"

"I am Talitha, the niece of Mary Mark of Jerusalem. Since the death of her husband, I must earn my own living."

The steward translated the soft words. They were harsher in Latin and in his voice. Procla was already beginning to understand a few words in Hebrew. She repeated the lovely name.

163

"Talitha! Has she other family here in Caesarea? Who recommended her to you, Servius?"

"Her older brother Zebulun brought her from Jerusalem, hoping to find work for her in the seaport. Zebulun is a mariner and a respectable man. The girl's aunt married a Greek and was widowed some months ago. I am sure the girl will serve you faithfully, lady."

Talitha served her faithfully and became a friend as well as a servant. From Talitha Procla began to learn both the speech and the customs of the country. Pilate, hearing her bargain in Hebrew with a traveling merchant of shawls, reproved her afterward with a kind of amused contempt.

"Why do you stoop to meet them on their own ground? I never dispense with my official interpreter. It preserves formality and keeps the Jews at a distance." She saw the hint of a smile on his lips. "Also I find it convenient at times to know more than they think I know."

"Could you not rule them better if you got closer to them and tried to understand their ways?" she asked earnestly.

He flushed with anger. "I know how to administer my office. It has never been Rome's policy to make concessions to the ways of an inferior people. So long as they pay their taxes and keep peace I shall leave them alone."

"I did not mean to offend you," she told him, vaguely troubled. For it was her first experience of his fierce temper, and her first suspicion of his deep dislike of the Jews.

Yet he was flattered and pleased when a messenger from Tiberius brought him word that Herod Antipas, the Tetrarch of Galilee and Perea, asked permission to visit him and pay his respects to Rome.

One wing of the palace was made ready for the visit. Procla questioned Talitha in faulty but eager phrases, and the girl replied:

"Antipas named his capital in honor of your father Tiberius, the Emperor of Rome. He built it where Rakkath used to stand, and old graves lie beneath it. It is because of that, Lady Claudia, that orthodox Jews refuse to live in the city. He has tempted them with fine dwelling houses. His palace is a tall fortress that looks down on the Sea of Galilee."

Talitha was still shy and did not talk unless questioned, but the interest of the governor's wife drew her out. The girl moved and spoke with modest composure, and her dark eyes burned with an inner radiance which puzzled the restless, imperious Roman woman.

Talitha dressed Procla with loving care for the royal visitor's banquet. Together they had looked out between the window draperies upon his arrival a few hours before. What they could see of the litter was of blood-red lacquer ornamented heavily with a motif in gold leaf. Its curtains were royal purple bordered with gold. Two attendants drew them apart and Herod Antipas stepped out, while his bearers prostrated themselves, and his guard of mounted Gauls flashed their swords in salute.

He had not brought his wife Herodias. But his first request to Pilate was that the Lady Claudia should sit at table with them.

Pontius Pilate himself brought her the message.

"I am glad," she said, "for Talitha has been dressing me for hours. Both she and I would have been disappointed not to display the result."

He smiled back at her, but his eyes were appraising her.

"You are very beautiful—and what is better, regal. This half-breed who licks the hand of Rome will be impressed by my choice of a wife."

She looked at him in surprise. Choice? she thought. I was forced upon you, as you were forced upon me. But although frank in speech, she could not say that aloud in the hearing of a third person.

"If you have any advice or instructions for me, I am glad to listen," she told him.

He asked quickly: "Advice as to what?"

"As to my conduct at this banquet for three. I had expected to converse with the wife of the tetrarch while you discussed affairs of state with him."

"I discuss no affairs with him," said the procurator. "He has no power in Judea, and he comes on my sufferance. The fact that he asked to come shows that he knows that."

He frowned as he added, "I shall make no concession to his religion or his race. The banquet will be in Roman style and you will behave like a Roman. To do otherwise on a Jew's account would be demeaning yourself."

Perhaps he is right, she thought. He must know Rome's policy as to the province he governs. But a spark of resentment had kindled when he said "behave like a Roman." She was Roman born and of Rome's imperial line, although she knew now that like Pilate she had only her mother's name.

"I will try to do as you wish," she assured him.

Then she went with him through the long corridors with their mosaic paving to the banqueting room. She had only time to see that it was arranged as if for a banquet in Rome and to settle herself on her couch, when the steward announced the guest from the door.

He came preceded by the youth who was his cupbearer, a slender Grecian boy with a scarlet mouth and a wreath of scarlet poppies in his fair curls.

She had seen his like before, and her eyes left him for his master: Antipas, son of the Herods, heir no longer to their throne but doomed to all their evil inheritance.

He looked kingly as he crossed the floor. His robes of embroidered purple touched and trailed it. His thickening body was girdled with a wide belt flashing with gems. She could see the glitter of rings on his dark, spatulate fingers.

He was now close enough for a good view of the face underneath his elaborate headdress.

She saw first that his beard was dressed in seven curls. Their smooth, oily cylinders accentuated the length of his face and the droop of its sagging muscles. Sinister green-violet shadows enlarged his eye sockets and called attention to his small glittering eyes. They seemed to have no depths beyond that artificial gleam. Beneath them spread a thick, flat nose and a coarse, sensual mouth.

As she raised her hand in greeting the loose mouth moved to speak, and the shallow shifting eyes fastened on her with the intensity of a focused burning glass.

3

STILL, he was an easy guest to entertain. He sat on the
right of the procurator, across the narrow table from
her, and his loose mouth seemed to utter whatever came
into his head. It sounded unstudied; but once when she
looked at her husband and suddenly back at her guest,
she caught him observing her with a speculative expression in his green-shadowed eyes.

Alongside of him Pilate looked sturdy and manly and
clean. She checked it up to his credit; for in her, Augustus'
conscience warred with the strength of will which the Emperor had also bequeathed her. Until Draco came for her,
she must be kind to this man she did not love. He had
been kind to her, and she must help him all she could in
her role of a Roman governor's wife.

Her thoughts went out to Draco, as they did upon any
excuse. Was he yet back from Syria? When would she see
him? Whom had he been forced to marry? Had he brought
his wife to the East? But no matter what was the answer
to any and all of these questions, she would go with him
whenever he was ready and wherever he took her.

Herod was leaning toward her. "My wife Herodias and
her daughter Salome are eager to entertain you. We would
esteem it an honor if you and the procurator came to visit
us at Tiberias."

"Not now," said Pilate shortly. "I have other affairs more
pressing."

He showed no resentment of the slight. "It shall be at
your convenience. I will have my wife's daughter dance

for you. Her skill at dancing is unsurpassed. I hope it will
give you pleasure."

"I like to see dancing. I have seen some at banquets
and theaters in Rome. But—" there was surprise in Procla's voice—"my grandfather Augustus forbade those of
equestrian rank to dance. It interests me to know that here
a princess may do it."

"She does it better than any slave from Africa or the
East."

Herod drained his cup of wine. His eyes were glittering
and his baggy cheeks suffused with reddish-purple. The
tip of his tongue crept slowly around his wet, parted lips.

"It is as if she had no bones." His voice rose with excitement. "Her limbs writhe and her body twists and contorts
itself. She is a spotted leopard at play . . . she is a coiled
viper waiting to strike and kill. . . ."

Procla, listening in disgust, saw a slight scuffle behind
him. Servius, following Pilate's orders, had stepped forward to refill the tetrarch's cup. But Herod's cupbearer,
unused to the Roman service, was trying to take the
pitcher from him. His voice was high and clear as a child's,
and Procla understood the Greek.

"I, alone, pour my master's wine," he protested to the
steward.

Without changing his expression, Herod threw up his
right hand in a gesture of careless annoyance. The gesture
appeared to be careless, but Procla saw the back of that
hand encrusted with rings strike the boy in the face.

"Back to your quarters," said Antipas. "I will deal with
you later. When I feast with Rome, I prefer to do as Rome
does."

He turned to Pilate. "I have tried to give my people the
benefit of customs brought from Greece, as well as from
your country. But their nationalism is so strong that they
will not give up their own ways."

Then how they must have hated your house, Procla was

thinking, since they begged Rome to depose your brother and send them a foreign governor.

"They keep their own ways," said the tetrarch. "Any interference inflames them and incites them to riots. My brother tried to subdue them. My nature is gentler than his, and I have so far avoided violence."

Procla had heard that the brother had been savage and brutal. She believed that in his way—in his indirect, vulpine way—Antipas could be just as cruel.

"There is unrest through Palestine," said Antipas. He looked troubled. "But it is not as bad in Judea as it is in Galilee."

Pilate merely looked at him; but he needed no spur to continue.

"Not only is Galilee breeding place of the rebel sect of Judas the Galilean, but I am plagued by a firebrand who incites the people against me."

Procla's eyes went wide. "Is it he whom they call the Messiah?"

He shook his head, and the jewels that hung from his earlobes flickered.

"He whom they call their Messiah is the carpenter Jesus."

Procla's voice was eager. "Long ago I heard of a child who was born in Bethlehem. There were prophecies about him. Is this man that child grown up?"

"He is," Herod replied.

Again he drained the large winecup, and the steward refilled it.

"This Jesus of Nazareth works at his trade and bids his followers work and pay their taxes. But John the Baptist is a wild man who claims to be a prophet. He calls me names which enrage Herodias. I have nothing against the carpenter. He has done me no wrong."

Pilate, replete with food, leaned back on his couch and observed his guest.

"Yet I have heard that he alludes to you as 'that fox.'"

Procla, startled, looked from Pilate to Herod. It describes him perfectly, she told herself. I have been stumbling to find comparison. The man who called him that must know all about human nature. He *is* a fox, swift of foot and wary to hide from one stronger than he, never brutal but cold of heart, subtly cruel to all the weak.

Herod appeared to be amused.

"It is evident that the procurator has knowledge of all that takes place, although he has not yet spent much time in Judea." He smiled and raised his cup. "I drink to expectation of long tenure in office for you!"

Pilate and Procla inclined their heads. Pilate was telling himself: It is well that I set this savage in his place at once. Procla was wondering what lay behind that painted smile.

"Although not so learned," said the tetrarch, "in Roman customs as you appear to be in news of Galilee, I have every reason to hope for the fulfillment of my toast. For I understand that my friend Tiberius has expressed his approval of long governorships in the provinces."

He turned his golden cup in his hands as his eyes slid from one to the other.

"I have been told that the Emperor says his governors enrich themselves as soon as they take office in a foreign land. Therefore he reasons—with logic although with cynicism—that both Rome and her provinces will lose less if a man who has already achieved his object remains in office than if another succeeds him and robs both Rome and the province again."

Pilate scowled but did not speak. Procla told herself that Herod Antipas had not been as amused as he appeared to be when reminded that he was called a fox.

She tried to relieve the awkward pause. "Will you tell me something of the so-called Messiah?"

"There is actually little to tell. That is the strange part. For the people talk always of him."

"Is he a rabbi? Does he preach?"

"He is not a rabbi and he does not preach. Once while still a child he talked with the doctors and rabbis and startled them by his learning. Now he works in his father's shop at his father's trade. Many go there to ask him questions, some believing in him and others trying to trip him. From what I have heard in regard to his answers, I judge him kind and wise but unorthodox."

Antipas frowned and tapped the board with his broad-tipped fingers.

"Even though he does not preach, his sayings are discussed all through Galilee. Some recall that story of a star standing over his birth, and they say that he is preparing himself for a mission."

Procla's voice was eager. "Is he young? What of his looks?"

"Yes, he is young. My sandalmaker describes him as straight and slender of body, with a noble expression of face, deep blue eyes and a fair beard."

Antipas stopped short, as if ashamed of his interest.

"I will tell you only what I hear from servants who hear it from rabble. The Nazarene does me no harm, but this John the Baptist reviles me for marrying Herodias while she reviles me for not silencing him."

"Why do you not silence him?" Pilate asked.

"His following is strong and violent. Any act against him might turn his faction against me."

Procla saw fear on his face as he leaned toward Pilate.

"If I could take him secretly, I would do so," he whispered. "I would do him no injury, but I would keep him deep in my fortress where no one could hear him. But which way, I ask you, is the more dangerous: to let him arouse the people against me as he is doing, or to anger the people by having him seized?"

He spread his hands palm upward in a gesture of appeal. But Procla saw that Pilate had only scorn for him.

Herod Antipas saw it too. His small eyes glittered greenly.

"You do not understand or care for my predicament. But perhaps, Procurator, you may before you leave Palestine find yourself caught in some such cleft fork of politics."

4

WINTER had come again, and its winds blew bleakly on Caesarea. The waves broke in icy spray on the quay and the great jetty. Herod's engineers had builded well, but his choice of a site had been unfortunate. The outthrust of the coast left it exposed to the full fury of the sea and the sweep of its storms. Braziers burned night and day in the palace, and Talitha spread additional rugs in her mistress' bedroom and hung double curtains across its windows. But sleet rattled against them, and the damp cold driven by sea wind was more bitter than any cold Procla had felt in Italy.

She had heard Pilate say that the army was going into winter quarters at Jerusalem.

"Are we going too?" she asked him.

"Not this year; but I hope to change headquarters to that city. Its climate is better, and living there will be less crude than in this savage seaport."

It did not matter to her whether they lived in Jerusalem or Caesarea. Talitha was her only friend in all Judea, and for all her life she had been accustomed to loneliness. So she asked no more and thought no more about it. But the next morning as she waited at the breakfast table for Pilate to join her, she heard his voice raised in anger at the door.

"Tell your commander, centurion, that I have given my orders. I will not change them, no matter what the delegation sent to him says. The Emperor's ensigns are to be carried in Jerusalem exactly as elsewhere. Tell him my orders are to march at once, and to march with the Legion's standards high."

She saw that he was disturbed as he came into the room, and he did not wait for her to question him.

"I'll show these Jews who is master! Their insolent priests demand that I lower the Emperor's ensigns when the Legion enters their city."

Phrased that way it sounded unreasonable. She thought about it before telling Talitha. The girl's dark eyes showed distress, but no surprise.

"Your standards carry the effigy of your Emperor, lady. Our commandments forbid all graven images. To carry them into the holy city would profane it. Our leaders have hoped and begged that it might not be done."

Procla's thoughts went back to Yod. He had turned his face away from her little clay figures. She was distressed.

"If the governor understood, I am sure he would change his orders. I will go to him at once and beg him to send a messenger to overtake the Legion."

"It would be useless," the girl told her. "Appeal after appeal has been made to the governor, but he does not understand my people. Even the officer in charge of the legionaries warned him."

Procla remembered the ragged scrap of talk she had heard from the door. By this time she knew Pilate well enough to know his obstinacy. But she still knew little of Judea, though more than he did. She wondered whether he was inflicting upon the nation he governed a senseless insult which was bound to inflame them, or whether they were a crafty and insolent people trying to use their religion to lower Rome's prestige.

"You said that the officer in command had warned the governor. Who is this officer? Has he been in your country long enough and had enough experience for his judgment to be sound?"

"Both my brother Zebulun and your steward Servius say that he is a hard man, but a just one and to be trusted.

He has served with the Roman cavalry in Syria and Judea.
They speak of him as the tribune Andrus Draco."

Procla whispered, "Andrus Draco? He is here—now—in
Caesarea?"

"Not now, Lady Claudia. He is now on the march to
Jerusalem. But for the last days of the month he has been
at the barracks here, and he has come to the palace every
day for a conference with the governor."

He had come to Caesarea—and gone—and she had not
even known it. Desolation swept over her. Why had he
not seen her? Why had he not stayed in the palace? The
commanding officer of the Legion in Judea ranked second
only to the governor. Had he refused to be their guest? Or
had Pilate kept him away and kept the knowledge from
her?

"Lady Claudia," begged Talitha, "you are cold and
your hands are shaking. Let me wrap you in this woolen
shawl and bring you a cup of hot wine."

Procla drank it and tried to warm her cold hands at her
brazier. She reviewed the days when Draco must have
been in Caesarea. Pilate had seemed to be busy, she recalled. Several times he had sent her word that he could
not meet her at a meal. At such times she and Talitha had
eaten in her apartment. She had thought nothing of it
then. She tried to discount it now. Perhaps it was all accidental. If Draco had suddenly arrived to take over the
Legion's command, he and the governor would have had
many plans to make in the few days before he marched.
At any rate she was now helpless to do anything about it.
But had Pilate done it on purpose? The question haunted
her.

He sent for her that night to dine with him. He did not
come to her room for her, as he had done in their first year
of marriage. He met her in the dining room, his face
flushed and his voice loud. She saw that he had been
drinking; and during the meal he continued to drink

steadily. None of the dishes suited him, and he sent several back to the kitchen. Finally he dismissed the steward.

She watched him in silence. As soon as they were alone she asked quietly: "What troubles you?"

He thrust his face almost into hers, and his voice rose. "I am not troubled! Do you imagine that I allow a few noisy Jews to frighten me?"

"You need not shout," she said in disdain. "If the Jews cannot frighten you, even less can you frighten me."

He stared for a second, then broke into drunken laughter.

"It is a pity Augustus died before he saw you. He would have recognized himself in you. He would have liked you as much as Tiberius dislikes you. That is why I chose you for wife: because no man can frighten you. When other men see you—whether they be Galilean tetrarchs or Roman officers—they must see that the Procurator of Judea has an empress for his wife."

She raised her brows. "For the second time now you have said that you *chose* me. You have been good to me. I have no complaint. But need we deceive ourselves and say that we chose each other?"

A look of sly amusement crept over his face. He laughed again, and glanced around to make sure they were alone.

"So," he said, "you did not guess that I had planned it all? I am clever—much more clever than some who despised me in Rome."

He is drunk, she thought. He does not know what he is saying.

He was drunk, but he went on. "I made up my mind to have you for wife. You are Augustus' granddaughter, although you were reared among barbarians on an island so remote that in loneliness you imagined yourself in love with your mother's lover."

"Stop!" she said. "It is you who are a barbarian. I will not listen!"

"If I am a barbarian, I am a suitable husband for you. Do you still fool yourself that Draco wants you, now that he knows Tiberius has scorned you?"

She rose to her feet, cold with fury, but his next words held her. "Did not Draco tell you to agree to marry me?"

"He did it to save my life."

"And his own," Pilate sneered. "I gave witness for him in Rome concerning Julia's death. For all you know he may have bribed the Ethiopian to kill her because she had some hold on him."

Procla left him; but as she went she heard him muttering, "I am clever in politics as in love. I am clever enough to outwit these Jews. I ordered the standards carried high."

She tried to submerge her own misery in thinking of the Jews. She told herself: Draco loves me. He was never Julia's lover and he did not kill her. I will not doubt him. All I can do is to make the best of my life until he is able to take me away from Pilate.

She dreamed of the ensigns that night. Tiberius' grim face, graven upon each and multiplied by their numbers, seemed to glare out of the darkness upon her. Even in dream she kept telling herself that she should not see them in darkness. A Roman Legion entered a city by day, she knew. Its officers were instructed to make a display of its strength. The standards should go through Jerusalem with sunlight flashing upon them.

When she awoke she saw Talitha staring out of the window. She sat up in bed, but the girl did not even turn. She was completely lost in something that she was watching.

"What is it?" Procla demanded. "What are you looking at?"

The girl turned a frightened face. "At the people in the square. They have been gathering all night, and there must be hundreds of them now."

Procla ran to the window. The space below the palace

was filled with men, and other men were arriving with every moment. She could tell by their dress that they were Jews. Beyond them and across the big open place, foreign seamen and Syrians and eastern tribesmen gathered in groups and watched curiously. No soldiers were in sight. The departure of the Legion had left only a few companies in the barracks. There was no disorder. The dark-clad figures merely stood there, looking up at the walls of the governor's palace.

Hour by hour their numbers increased, until at midday they filled the square. Talitha brought Procla bulletins of news which she got from Servius, and which he in turn had from the palace guards.

"They are coming from cities and plains and valleys all over the country to protest the desecration of their holy city by the Roman images. They are priests and merchants and farmers and fishermen, moneylenders and beggars and scribes. The governor has at last agreed to allow them to pick three men and send them in to him to state their case."

The Jewish girl was eager with hope that Jewry's case would be judged kindly. But shortly after that message the two women heard heavy steps approaching through the hall. Talitha ran to open the door and admitted Servius. The steward looked grave.

"My lady, a man of this mob has been caught with an ornament stolen from you."

"That is impossible," she said. "I have lost nothing, and none of those people could get into my apartment."

"This thief either managed to get in or else he has an accomplice inside. He is one of the three chosen to talk with the governor. When the guards at the palace door searched him and his fellows for knives, they found in this man's moneybag a golden ornament which I have seen you wear."

"Who is the man?" she asked. "Is he a robber?"

"No; he is a clerk by name of Nathan Bar-Jonas. His people say that he stands well, and they are making a great outcry."

She looked at Servius, puzzled. "What is it of mine that he has?"

"He has in the purse in his belt your golden bracelet, my lady."

For just a second her heart seemed to stop. She ran her left hand up her right arm and felt the heavy band of gold that encircled it.

"Bring him in to me," she said. "Let the guards remain in the hall."

He came through the door with Servius: a short man, heavily built, holding himself with dignity. He wore the robes and head covering of the Judean merchant. He was angry, not in the least afraid. She saw the same proud disdain on his face that she remembered on the face of a young, ragged goatherd.

But he stopped in his tracks as he saw her. Slowly his expression changed. Surprise—and wonder—and unbelief played over his mobile features.

"Yod," she said, her voice shaky with tears. "Yod—you got safe to your homeland!"

5

HE looked back at her, as shaken as she.

"Procla from Pandataria! You are the wife of the procurator?"

She nodded, trying to steady her voice. "But still Procla to—to my first friend."

"As I am Yod to you, even though since my return I bear my true name Nathan Bar-Jonas." He paused. "I did not guess it might be you, although I knew that Mary Mark's niece served Pontius Pilate's lady."

"Then you know Talitha and Talitha's people?"

"It was her uncle, the Greek named Mark, who got me employment with the bankers for whom I clerk. Mary has made her house my home since I came up from Bethlehem, and Talitha has been like a young sister to me."

Procla waited; for his eyes shone and his lips parted to tell her more.

"When I was lonely and newly arrived in Jerusalem, they took me with them to the wedding of a friend in Galilee. It was there I met the daughter of a blind man of Bethsaida, the girl who has since become my wife. Oh, Procla, I have much to tell you! But time is short. I must go."

"Yod," she said, "I thank the gods that you are safe and happy."

"There is but one God," he said sharply. "I told you that long ago. But Procla, I have seen his Son—Lalibela's Messiah."

The light in his eyes had transfigured his face. It was no longer closed and watchful and hard, as she remembered the face of the slave boy on Pandataria. He had forgotten where he was and the errand that called him there. She too forgot all else at mention of Lalibela.

"Is it the same Child?" she begged. "Have you really seen him? Tell me what Lalibela's Messiah is like?"

"He is young and slenderly built and of medium height; but I have seen him tower over evildoers. His face is austere yet gentle. He wears a fair beard. His eyes are dark and deep with love, but they can flash with lightnings."

He stopped as Servius appeared between the doorway hangings. But Procla waved the Roman steward away. "Tell me how you got to Judea and Jerusalem."

"I worked my way on a coastwise trading ship that was bound for Ascalon. Until I reached that port I had not spent a coin of the money you gave me. At Ascalon I exchanged it for food and articles of trade, and with a pack on my back I started east for my home in Bethlehem. But there I found that my parents had died since I was taken away."

She stood, looking at him and trying not to weep.

"Those coins you gave me under the ilex set me up in business as a traveling merchant. But I wished to go into banking. A friend of my father, in Bethlehem, gave me a letter to his friend the Greek banker Mark in Jerusalem."

He paused and drew her armlet from the pouch in his girdle.

"I never sold your armlet. I kept it to bring me luck."

"Keep it still," she begged. "It is a link between us."

He shook his stubborn head. "Its work is done. My greatest luck has been in finding you. You may be able to help us. The crowd out there has increased to a mob. They chose me as one of their envoys to put their case before the procurator. Can you not persuade your husband to spare my people this insult?"

She had tried; but Pilate was adamant. On the fifth day, after long conference with the officer in command of the

auxilia, he ordered the portable judgment seat of his office to be carried out in the square. It raised Procla's
hopes.

"Talitha, I think he is yielding at last. I think that he
will confer with the people and they will make him understand."

But Talitha had heard from the guards rumors which
she dared not repeat. She leaned from the window, gazing
down at the unarmed, helpless crowd of her countrymen.
And Pilate's wife leaned with her, just as troubled but less
apprehensive.

They saw the judgment seat set down, and they saw
the governor take his place. Except for a dozen Gauls in
the Legion's armor who stood at attention behind him, he
sat alone and in the midst of more than a thousand Jews.
Procla told herself that it was at least courageous of him.
Although the Jews were unarmed they were excited. Some
of them were crying out and trying to get closer to him.
But others held them back, and only the leaders approached to speak.

The parleying continued; and Procla was so intent upon
it that Talitha had to press her hand to attract her attention.

"Look, my lady," she said. "Look and tell me who are
those men now coming from every side into the square!"

Procla looked. In groups of two or three, men were
coming steadily from the streets that led into the place.
Their dress was nondescript; but she saw that they held
themselves stiffly and strode with long steps, as if accustomed to distances. With a purpose which could not be
mistaken they infiltrated the mass of civilians, stopping at
positions which were spaced and encircling them in unbroken lines. As one group of them deployed beneath the
palace walls, the women above could see their features
plainly.

Talitha was wringing her hands. "Those men are not

Jews, lady! The rumor that I heard was true. Nathan Bar-Jonas told me."

Procla caught her breath. Her window was not high from the ground. She had plainly seen the keen blue eyes of the men grouped beneath it, eyes cold and yet bright with the eagerness of a hawk that waits to strike. They were taller too, by inches, than the Judeans.

"They are Gauls," she said in a sharp whisper. "They must be the auxilia. But why are they not in the Legion's dress, and why do they mingle in this way with the crowd?"

Her husband gave her the answer. Just then he raised his hand, and one of the soldiers behind him blew upon a trumpet the call which preceded any proclamation.

Slowly the crowd fell silent, except for rustlings and the soft shuffle of sandals as those on its edges pushed nearer. Upon the faces that Procla could see there was a strained intensity, as they waited for the answer of the Roman who governed them.

The proclamator had stepped forward, and Pilate motioned to him to speak. He was chosen for his powerful voice, and it rang out like the trumpet.

"By order of Pontius Pilate, Procurator of Judea, this gathering is dispersed. He refuses to parley further. The Emperor's ensigns will be kept in Jerusalem and paraded there as elsewhere. During this judgment you have been surrounded and infiltrated by Roman soldiers in civilian dress. They are armed, and instructed to strike to kill unless you obey this order. Return at once to your homes, under pain of death!"

As he stopped there was dead silence. Procla now saw bared swords in the hands of the Gauls. Now that she could distinguish them better by the weapons, she saw how numerous they were. Some merely stood with the steel in hand. Others made threatening gestures and began to herd the Jews toward outlets from the square.

Then she heard what seemed at first a faint vibration of the air. It increased into a moan, deep and low but rising. It rose into a terrible wail for the trampled hopes of thousands. Instead of departing, the Jews stood their ground, crying out and rending their garments. The leaders who were near Pilate threw themselves flat on the ground, and the others began to follow suit.

In vain the officers shouted orders to their soldiers. In vain the soldiers struck with clubs or the flat of swords. Many were by this time wounded. Few remained on their feet. But none had left the square. They fell to the ground and lay prostrate, making no resistance but baring necks and chests to the weapons of the baffled Gauls.

Procla heard Talitha say softly, "They have sworn they would rather die than see the holy city profaned."

Pilate was on his feet and shouting orders. The trumpets began to blow. The governor and the governor's portable judgment seat were escorted back into the palace in undignified retreat. In the square officers argued, commanded and sweated. The auxiliaries sheathed their swords sullenly. Passive resistance was a defense against which they had no method of penetration, and the governor, as he made his hasty departure, had ordered them not to butcher these unarmed opponents who lay flat, beating their heads and moaning.

The scene remained unchanged until night came on. Torches were lighted on standards along the front of the palace. Their red light moved weirdly on all in its radius.

Talitha crept downstairs to question Servius. She brought back word that the governor had dispatched another messenger and given him orders to ride fast.

"He sent one yesterday and one the day before." She stopped to wring her hands. "Oh, my lady, do you think he is recalling the Legion to wipe out my countrymen in one quick massacre?"

"I am sure that he would not do such a thing. Besides, the auxilia could have killed them just now. Where is the governor?"

Thought of Yod out there among them sharpened her anxiety.

"He is in his apartment, conferring with the officer in command at the barracks."

When she knew that the officer had left her husband, Procla sent him a message to ask if he would see her. But Pilate sent back a blunt refusal. She could only wait and, sitting at her window, watch the torchlight on the strange drama outside.

More than a thousand men still lay flat upon the ground. Among them stood and moved the Gallic auxiliaries, some puzzled and some disappointed at the turn affairs had taken.

Before midnight Servius informed Talitha that a small squad of cavalry had ridden into the courtyard at the back, and that their commander had been taken straight to Pilate.

They could only speculate. Who was the officer? Why had he been summoned? What instructions was the governor giving him? From time immemorial cavalry had been used to disperse mobs by riding them down. But Procla had never before heard of a mob that lay on its face. To charge those prostrate hundreds with horses would be just as cruel as to kill them with swords where they lay.

It was hours later that Talitha ran to the door at Servius' low call. The steward's voice was hurried and frightened.

"It is a visitor for the Lady Claudia."

He had hardly finished speaking when Draco pushed by him and into the room.

He looked at her, his mouth hard but his eyes both tender and hungry. His face was lined with weariness and his dark cape gray with dust. He had his helmet under an arm and his thumbs in his leather belt. He spoke curtly to Talitha.

"Wait outside, and warn your mistress if anyone comes."

As she went he dropped the helmet on a couch and took a long step toward Procla.

"I have only a moment, love," he said as he took her in his arms.

6

BUT the moment was prolonged, while Talitha and Servius watched outside.

"Oh, my darling," he said again, "it has been so long!"

"Why did you not see me when you stopped in Caesarea? I did not even know you were here until you had come and gone."

"Because you were ill. I asked for you and was told that the sea winds made you ill."

She dropped her lashes quickly to hide her eyes from him. She wished to waste no precious time in telling him the suspicions of her husband which troubled her.

"It is true that I suffer from the cold. But I was heartsick when I heard that you had gone on to Jerusalem. Are you going back there now? You said that your time was short."

He held her at arm's length, frowning.

"I go back as soon as this mob has broken up and started on its way out of the city."

"You will not use force on them?" she begged unhappily.

"Certainly not. To do so would make martyrs of them. I have just told the governor that."

"Then he has agreed to their demands?"

"Yes. The proclamator is now telling them. I am supposed to be out there and in charge, but I turned the job over to the commander of the auxiliary troops. It was my only chance of seeing you."

She heard the trumpets then. Even in her personal joy

she had time to be glad for that. She told him so. He frowned again.

"I am thinking of Rome, not of the Jews. It is unwise to press a small point like this on a people whom we are trying to rule."

"It is not small to them. It is desecration of their shrine."

"That means nothing to me. I am thinking only of how best to hold them for Rome. If we antagonize them about a matter which does us no harm, we will find them harder to handle in more important matters."

Even with me in his arms, she thought, he is thinking still of Rome.

He was looking down in her eyes, and he read her thought. But it did not change him.

"Against the Empire, Procla, what does one person weigh?"

She gave a cry of protest and clung more tightly to him.

"Darling, I do not mean you. I mean myself, as a soldier. No matter what the Emperor or the governor does to me, I am still an officer of the Roman Legions. My promotion is overdue, but I am still a tribune."

"You commanded the Legion," she said. "You took it down to Jerusalem. Are you not now a legate?"

He tried to smile, but she saw his eyes.

"I am not a legate, although I have been for some months performing the duties of one. The procurator sent for me and gave me the command at a time when he anticipated trouble. I reminded him that other governors saw fit to leave off the Emperor's likeness from Roman money coined for Judea. But he refused to capitulate. He ordered me to carry the ensigns through Jerusalem."

As he spoke she was remembering a dream. . . .

"Knowing that it would be an affront to the orthodox and would cause an uprising, I waited and entered the city by night. But they were waiting too, and watching. You have seen what occurred in consequence."

So that was why she had seen them in darkness in her dream. She wondered how much he knew about her husband, and just how far in loyalty his love for Rome would carry him. So far as she was concerned, she would go with him there and then . . . wherever he chose to take her. . . .

Again he seemed to read her mind. He seized her shoulders with both hands and shook her roughly.

"Make no mistake about this, Procla! I serve Rome, but I hate both the Emperor and Pilate. To them I owe nothing —and neither do you. But I am a Roman officer in command of troops in a Roman province which is on the edge of rebellion. To leave now would be desertion from duty."

"I know," she said. "I know—and I will wait until you can come."

He caught her closer. "But I cannot live without you! You belong to me, and not to him. I can make opportunities for us to be together."

"I will do whatever you say. You have only to send me word. You can trust the girl who serves me."

"And we can trust the steward," he said. "He rode in my command in Gaul. It was my first campaign, but Servius was a veteran."

"Send me word soon," she begged him. "I shall be waiting."

He held her with both arms and rocked her gently to and fro.

"If I could only keep you now! If I could stay with you! But the prefect knows I am in the palace. He thinks I am still with the governor, and he is waiting outside for me."

Rome was taking him from her. Rome had taken him before, and would take him again as long as he wore Roman battle dress. She knew there was no use to plead, but she pleaded: "Come back to me soon!"

He kissed her hard and released her. She must give him up to Rome; but—a pang of jealousy tore her body and mind—she could not and would not give him up to any other woman. In Rome she had been forced to do so—or else give him up to death. But warm from his arms, she could not! Who was now waiting for him? Whom had he married at Tiberius' orders?

She clutched at his sleeve as he turned away. "Tell me, Draco, who is the woman—"

But he interrupted her curtly as he picked up his helmet.

"No woman matters to me except you. I told you the prefect was waiting."

Then he was gone, without even a backward look.

Talitha found her standing, straight and pale, and she let the girl undress her and get her to bed. Through her own heartache, Procla remembered what had transpired.

"I am glad for you and your people, Talitha. You must sleep well tonight. You have kept a long vigil."

"I shall sleep well, my lady; but first I shall give thanks to God. In my prayers I shall ask for your peace of mind."

She drew the curtains and dimmed the lamp, and Procla lay alone, thinking. . . .

How could she have the peace of mind which Talitha was asking for her? She knew now that Pilate had kept Draco away with his talk of sea winds. Only weak fools wasted their time crying to gods which were not. If only she might find a god who stood for justice and strength and love—a god who would show her what to do while she was torn between a lover she worshiped and a husband whom she could no longer either trust or honor.

But she had not yet found that god, and she saw no escape. She was trapped. Even if Draco were willing to desert, he would be unable to escape with the governor's wife. She tried to tell herself that the time must come when some friend of Draco would be in power. Tiberius was a man sick in mind and body. His successor would only be following precedent if he demoted or destroyed all whom Tiberius favored and looked with favor on those whom Tiberius punished.

She knew that her husband could be left to destroy himself slowly but surely. Why should she be loyal to him when she knew now he had schemed and lied? He had been brutal with the Jews, yet too weak to enforce his orders. Wine was his answer to all problems. Sooner or later he must fall from the high place his scheming had won. Then he would be able to hold her no longer.

She heard the slow and steady shuffle of hundreds of retreating sandals, as the great crowd out in the night withdrew. They went contented and orderly, thanks to a Roman tribune.

Then she heard a quick command in a voice she recognized, and the clatter of hoofs as the squad rode off to the barracks.

She turned and buried her face in the scented head cushions, and her strong, slender fingers tore at the silken sheets.

He had brushed her question aside . . . but *what woman was now his wife?*

7

THE governor's wife, as time stretched out behind her, at length accustomed herself to the foreign port. In her litter she was carried through its streets and arcades. With the governor she attended spectacles in its amphitheater and hippodrome. But they two were alone. They had no friends. The higher ranking Roman officers were in Jerusalem. Pilate was anxious to establish his headquarters there. He told her about it. Since the incident of the ensigns he had not been drinking to excess, and he had been kind and considerate.

"I have discovered that Caiaphas, the High Priest of the Jews, is the most influential man in the province. I think I would do well to make an alliance with him."

She agreed, for it sounded reasonable. Besides, her heart leapt at the thought of going to Jerusalem. Draco, she knew, was still there. Every few months, since that brief meeting that now seemed an aeon ago, letters had come from him. Servius received them in some way and gave them to Talitha. She had had two letters recently, both brief and businesslike. They told her not to answer and simply to wait. "I will know when the opportunity comes and will find you then," he wrote.

Her emotions were mixed when Pilate informed her that Herod Antipas had sent a messenger with a formal invitation to them both to visit him at Tiberias, and that he felt they should accept. She frowned as she recalled the tetrarch's appearance and conversation. She had hoped never to see him again. More important than that was the fact that Draco would be sure to know of the governor's journey. If she stayed in Caesarea, it might give him the opportunity which they both awaited.

"I dislike and despise the tetrarch, my lord. From stories I have heard, I do not think I would like his wife any better. Unless you command my attendance, I shall remain here."

He looked at her shrewdly. "Is dislike of the Herods your true reason for not going?"

She smiled. "It is a true reason, but only one of two. The second is the weather. As you know—and as I know you have said—the cold and the sea winds of this coast make me ill. I prefer to stay indoors at this season."

He turned before she could see his face. "I do not command you. But you do not help me to friendship with the people I rule when you refuse to visit their tetrarch with me."

She knew that he did not rule Galilee, but she did not argue. She made up her mind not to go, but the next day brought a letter which changed it. Draco wrote that he was riding to Galilee to arrange reinforcement for guards at Herod's palace. "Herod Antipas holds an important prisoner," he wrote, "and lives in terror that the man's friends will attack the palace. Come with the procurator, so that we may see each other."

Oh, to see him again! she thought. To feel his arms around me. And to make him tell me who is the woman he married!

So she told Pilate: "I have reconsidered, my lord," and he only stared at her and made no comment.

Talitha rode with her in a large, chairlike vehicle. The girl was excited and talked more than she usually did. Procla questioned her as they were carried northeast, across the low hills of Carmel and the great plain of Esdraelon.

"You seem to be well informed and well educated,

Talitha. You tell me many things of interest about your country."

"Both my aunt Mary Mark and her husband were educated. They sent me and their young son John to the school of the synagogue."

"Do you like to travel? Are you pleased to go on this journey with me?"

"I am happy to go anywhere with you. But—" the girl leaned forward with her eyes shining like stars— "I am even happier because we are going into *his* country."

Procla looked back at her, not understanding the words. She had been long absorbed in her own troubles. She was fighting with all her resources to save her own happiness, asking no favors of anyone else's gods.

But the radiance in Talitha's eyes had blazed into a flame. "Did you not know that his home is in Nazareth?" she asked.

Then Procla remembered the carpenter who was said to be the Messiah. She had forgotten him in all that had occurred. She had had no room for him in her life. The thought of him had been crowded out by things which seemed to her more important. She recalled now that Herod had called him "the Nazarene." She knew that the village of Nazareth was on the road between Caesarea and Tiberias. Even Yod—hard-headed, practical Yod—had said—

"The governor said that Nazareth would be our last stop on the way. Do you expect to see this man, Talitha?"

"I do not know. I have seen him once. If you could see him, my lady, you would know that he is the Messiah. But he goes where he is needed. He is ready for any call. He is not always at home in the shop of Joseph of Nazareth."

"I remember that Antipas Herod said this man had done him no harm, but that John called the Baptist abused him and plagued him."

"John is a prophet who came not long before Jesus Christ. He is not gentle like Jesus. He strikes with a sword of flame. He says that he was sent to clear the way for the Messiah. He is a great man, and good and brave, but he is not divine. I have seen them both, my lady. I tell you I saw the difference!"

Procla was interested. As the bearers carried them slowly she questioned Talitha about John and Jesus.

"They are kinsmen, my lady, both of the House of David. Jesus was baptized by John in the river Jordan. John protested that he was not worthy to lace Jesus' sandals. But Jesus had the humility to beg him for baptism."

It was hard for Augustus' granddaughter to understand humility.

"Could he not do more good if he were not so humble? Is not such humility a sign of weakness?"

The Jewish girl shook her head. "What is strength, my lady? A man or a nation is only strong until an opponent still stronger appears. Palestine was strong against weaker client countries. You must know well that she is not strong against Rome. Rome had the stronger weapons, so Palestine is weak. But what weapon can avail against meekness and humility? How would your legionaries go about a conquest of unselfishness and self-abnegation?"

With their short swords, thought Procla. Those are their only weapons and they know no other fashion of warfare. Yet they are the world's conquerors. She thought of the Empire's limits. Draco had told her all about that. What empire could this Jesus boast, although they called him "Christ the king?"

They spent their last night of travel at an inn in Nazareth. When Talitha brought the evening meal, Procla saw sadness on her face.

"Have you heard that Jesus the carpenter is not now at home? I am sorry for your disappointment."

"He is away," said Talitha, "on one of his missions of

preaching. I am sad that I will not see him; but that is my own selfish grievance."

She turned from the bed she was spreading with the silken sheets that were carried for the governor's wife.

"The innkeeper told me something that is of greater importance than my own disappointment. He said that Herod Antipas had sent soldiers to seize John the Baptist. He said that the tetrarch now holds Jesus' kinsman, the prophet, imprisoned deep in the dungeons of his fortress."

8

THE village of Nazareth was so near to Herod's capital that the train of the Governor of Judea arrived next day at Tiberias. Procla looked up at the dark, sheer walls of the fortress-palace of Antipas and remembered the fear she had seen in Antipas' green-shadowed eyes.

Her rooms commanded a sheet of blue lake that rippled farther than she could see. Talitha leaned from the window and gazed enraptured upon it.

"It is the Sea of Galilee! All my life I have longed to look on it. This is the heart, Lady Claudia, of the Galilean country, and the country of Galilee is the heart of Palestine."

But although Tiberias stood in the heart of Galilee, the house of Herod Antipas was as mongrel as his ancestry. Procla saw at first glance that it had been built for defense. It was taller than any other building she had seen in Palestine. Armored guards with shields and swords were patrolling its parapet. She noticed the thickness of its walls as she entered the great door. The columns of its long corridors were lost in dusk overhead. As she made her way through its rooms and halls she realized that its decoration was an elaborate mixture of the culture of many races.

Now, in her overcrowded and ornate apartment, she looked around and wondered what was ahead for her. Where was Draco? How could she pretend friendship for the women of Herod's dynasty when she had only scorn and contempt for Herod?

Her thoughts were interrupted by an Egyptian slave with a message. The Princess Salome sent to ask the Ro-

man governor's wife to drink wine and eat poppy cakes
with her on the roof of the palace.

An escort of two palace guards waited to conduct her
up the narrow, turning stairway of stone. As she followed
them she was comparing in her mind the decent dress of
Talitha with that of the princess' handmaiden. The Egyptian girl was small, with sharp features but thick lips, and
her complexion was dark and sallow. Only her eyes were
beautiful—except for their expression. They were long and
large, but they were as fixed and baleful as the eyes of a
snake. From waist to ankles she wore a metallic, close-
fitting skirt which outlined every muscle of her body as
she walked. Her feet were bare below wide golden anklets. Above the waist she was unclothed, except for a
golden collar with a mass of twisted tassels that hung between her breasts. Her hair was cut in bangs across her
low forehead and fell like a straight, coarse black mane
around her head.

As they came out on the flat roof Procla saw the sentries
at its corner turrets. Then she saw the woman on the
crimson-draped divan and the group of Roman and Jewish officers surrounding her. She saw Draco detach himself
and start to meet her. As he reached her Talitha stepped
aside and out of hearing; but the Egyptian girl stood
close, staring with her evil eyes.

Draco turned on her and uttered the one word "Go!"

By the way she cringed Procla feared that she was accustomed to abuse. She glided over by Talitha but looked
back with hate in her eyes.

He lost no time. "I have been here before. When this
night's banquet is half over neither Herod nor Pilate will
be in condition to know who is still present. Watch me,
Procla, and follow me when I leave the table."

She had come to this place to meet him, yet she hesitated now. He said sharply: "Will you do as I say?"

What is holding me back? she wondered. I love him

more than ever. Yet something was holding her. She felt it like a strong hand. Could it be what a Jewish handmaid had told her of the life and precepts of a Nazarene carpenter?

Before she could speak the woman on the divan sat up and beckoned to them. The gesture seemed to give her whole body a sensuous pleasure. It vibrated from shoulders to heels with a snaky movement. It even rippled the crimson fringe of the silk on which she lay.

But Procla saw as they approached that Salome was not young. She had expected a slim girl—this daughter of Herodias was at least thirty. She was small-boned and thin, with skin the color of dark gold. Procla could judge well of it, for the upper part of her costume consisted only of a pair of jeweled breastplates. Like the maid she wore a long skirt; but it was so diaphanous that her thin yet shapely legs were plainly visible. Her anklets were set with jewels and there were gems on her toes. Her hennaed hair was cut shoulder length and stood out from her small head. Her mouth was wide and mobile but her other features more delicate. Now her gilded eyelids lifted, and her black eyes fixed themselves on the tall, fair Roman girl.

"My greetings and welcome to the wife of the Governor of Judea," she said. Her voice was warm and husky and entirely at variance with her appearance.

Procla bowed gravely and lifted her hand. "And my thanks and my greeting to the Princess Salome."

"The tetrarch tells me that in Rome you are forbidden to dance. What is the reason for that? Does dancing offend you?"

"It is merely a custom," said Procla. "I enjoy watching the dance. I have been told that the Princess Salome excels in the art."

"I do!" she cried loudly. She threw herself back on her couch and extended a jeweled arm toward the officers who stood behind her. "Does not the Princess Salome excel, O

Lucius Julius? Have you seen in the East any better than she, Sholem Saul and Meraioth?"

They cried denials and compliments, but she was insatiate. She turned with her snakelike movement and called to the guard on the wall. "Have you brought into barracks or seen on the street a dancing girl who could surpass your princess, young Philip Jocundus of Perea?"

The boy turned, startled and flushing from collar to headpiece. They could all see his embarrassment, but she held out her arms to him.

"How handsome you are, young Philip! You shall see me dance again. I will tell the tetrarch I wish you nearby to catch my veils as I throw them. The tetrarch cannot refuse me any request when I dance."

Procla saw the faces of the officers reflect a gamut of expression which ran from excitement to disapproval. She felt Draco's hand on her arm, and she let him draw her aside. The young sentry had turned away, but Salome was calling after him: "Herod will think I am dancing for him, while I dance for *you*, Philip Jocundus!"

Draco muttered, "More than once I've had to send a squad to clear the city streets of just such prostitutes!"

"She is not even young," said Procla.

He shook his head. "She has been married twice and is the mother of two almost-grown children. She does not know the meaning of restraint or dignity, but she is not cruel like Herodias. All she asks is to be allowed to dance and to fondle some young lover."

He scowled at Procla and changed the subject abruptly. "You have not yet told me you will come."

"Draco," she pleaded, "I love you. But I am still Pilate's wife. You have a wife, although you have not yet told—"

There they were interrupted again. He had only time to whisper, "You will do as I say."

She had hoped to be seated by him at the banquet. But she and Pilate were placed upon either side of Antipas, while almost directly across from her Draco was between Herodias and her daughter. He made no attempt to converse with them but devoted himself to the meal. Procla wondered if that neglect had displeased the two women, for they were exchanging low and apparently unfriendly words across him in their own tongue. Salome's expression was in repose both vacant and lascivious; but she seemed more than once to be on the verge of angry tears. Her mother the queen showed signs of once-voluptuous beauty, but her face was just as sensual and even harder than the face of the younger woman. She seemed to be urging something which her daughter refused. The latter once shook her head until her frizzed red hair flew out. Her thick lips set sullenly; but later Procla saw her glance sideways at her mother with a look of fear. Procla wondered why fear should dwell in the strongest fortress in Galilee, in the eyes of the ruling family and in the movements of their slaves.

Antipas paid every courtesy to the Roman governor's wife, but she saw that he was watching his stepdaughter. Procla knew she was blood kin to him, as well as connected by his marriage to her mother, a woman much older than he and once his brother's wife. What tangled desires and terrors are loose at this table? she wondered. What is Pilate thinking? He has drunk as much wine as Antipas, but he keeps his dignity. What do the younger officers at the lower end of the table really think about the Princess Salome? Their laughter is growing too loud. When is the princess going to dance? Why is she afraid of her mother?

Herod Antipas clapped his hands, and laughter and talk were silenced. His head nodded unsteadily on his neck as he leaned forward.

"For our own joy and for the joy of our noble guests," he said, "I beg our daughter the Princess Salome to dance as she alone in the world can dance!"

9

SALOME played with her winecup. Her eyes slid from him to her mother.

Draco folded his arms and sat back. As he did so Herodias leaned across him and spoke low but sharply to her daughter. Salome shrank as if she had been struck. Her thick lips pouted more sullenly.

"I do not wish to do it," she said hoarsely and loudly.

Procla was startled by the remark; but she was even more startled by what she saw now looking naked from Antipas' face. He had drunk enough to lose all pretense. His loose lips worked and his fingers curled.

"Dance for me," he implored her. "I will give you whatever you ask!"

She laughed at him. "What if I ask for your guardsman, young Philip of Perea?"

His face contracted as if with a sudden spasm of pain. Draco's eyes were on him, cold and contemptuous. Pilate was watching with a not-too-sober amusement. In the pause Procla heard Herodias' thin whisper.

"Little fool, I command you! Dance—then do as I say."

Salome rose slowly and reluctantly, while the young officers below the salt clapped and cheered. Even when reluctant, Procla noticed, she moved with the effortless and fluid grace of water. Excited in spite of herself, Procla watched carefully. The slender figure was almost lost in the shadows between the great pillars. Then it emerged in the torchlight, for a second poised and still.

The first movement was pure beauty: rippling water and swaying poppy stems. It was poetry and music, and

Procla, watching it, even forgot Draco for that brief time. It was a shock when the dancer stopped in a mist of rainbow veils.

There was no sound in the banquet hall as she approached through the pillars. They paid her the tribute of silent applause. Salome drew slowly nearer, with a fixed look in her eyes. Her head was thrown back and her gilded lids hid all except that thin gleam. She was near enough now for Procla to see that her feet were broad and ugly. All their ornaments could not hide spatulate toes, and ankles thick from muscular strain. But they touched the floor so lightly that the figure they bore seemed to float. It floated forward—then stopped suddenly. A shudder seized it and shook it. As if mastered by something more powerful than her thin, plain body, Salome went into the second phase of her dance.

One by one she discarded her veils. She was dancing in her breastplates and only a jeweled loincloth when Procla started at the touch of Draco's hand on her shoulder. She looked up at him in entreaty and shook her head. But his fingers closed more tightly, and he leaned and whispered: "Do you prefer this swinishness to coming with me?"

She followed his eyes then. Salome was prone on the floor. She was coiled like a snake, and her limbs seemed to writhe.

Procla looked up. But Draco had gone. He was as sure of her as that. And he was right, she told herself in reassurance. His love was clean and strong and natural, while this . . .

She rose to follow and pushed her way through the crowd at the door, unnoticed. Guards and servants had crowded there to watch the princess dance. As she emerged in the great dusky hall Draco stepped free of a pillar, and she went to him. He drew her farther along the lane between tall columns and into a small recess behind two of them.

"Procla, I could not have waited another hour or minute! To see you across the table while that cursed Cyprian danced!"

He felt her shiver and press closer to him.

"Forget it," he muttered, his lips following the line from her chin to her throat.

"I cannot ever forget it! At first it was beautiful. Then it changed to something as dark and as awful as death."

She heard him swearing softly.

"I can see no beauty in degeneracy. Beauty must be both clean and strong. That is your beauty, my own love. You keep it proud and unspoiled."

She clung to him even more closely.

"But the waiting will break me, Draco! I want to be with you! I fear delay. Why can you not take me away tonight?"

"I would do it, my own love, if I could—if I could do it without desertion and dishonor."

"What honor is there in guarding a creature like this Herod Antipas? Why must you protect him?"

"I would like to see him thrown from his walls for the dogs in the street below to eat. But Pilate rules Judea for Rome, and that allies Rome with Galilee. Procla, do you not love me enough to understand that I am a soldier? Do you not love me enough to wait while I do my duty?"

"I love you enough for anything," she told him very softly.

"Then we have tonight at least."

His voice was low but exultant. He lifted her and held her, as he had held her long ago in the garden on Pandataria.

Her arms were both around his neck, and she did not lift her head from his heart as she felt him carrying her. This is where I belong, she thought. It is as right for me to be here as it is wrong for me to be with Pilate. Yet she tried once more—and for the last time—to protest.

"Draco, you know how I love you! But what of the others? I know we belong to each other. But, will they not miss us and seek us? Besides, you have not yet told me of your wife."

"Their wine and their dancing will keep them. Tonight is for you and me, Procla."

He was walking through the half-lit hall, carrying her as easily as if she had been a child instead of a tall young woman. At the foot of the stair which led to her rooms he turned and began to ascend.

"I can trust my handmaid," she whispered. "But what if the governor comes?"

He stopped short on the dark stairway and gripped her so tightly he hurt her. His voice was no longer composed: in it were fury and agony. "If the governor comes tonight, I will kill him," he told her.

He carried her on to the next level and along a narrower corridor. At its door he set her down, and she called in a whisper: "Talitha!"

The girl came at once. She had been waiting in the ante-room which led from corridor to suite. She looked with wide, startled eyes from her mistress to Draco.

It was hard for Procla to meet that look.

"You may go now, Talitha, down to the maids' quarters. They are having a feast in the servants' wing of the palace. You need not return until morning."

The girl's eyes went darker with distress, but she stepped aside. "I will do whatever you bid me, my lady."

Procla took one step—and stopped with a gold sandal still on the threshold.

For a terrible clangor of beaten shields burst out on the walls above. She saw Draco stiffen, and withdraw his foot from the sill.

All along the parapet ran the brazen noise of alarm. Halls and stairways suddenly rang with the heavy sound of running feet. Beneath the window a mutter of many voices was growing louder and being raised in cries and imprecations.

Instinctively she turned and clutched the man she loved, trying to hold him from whatever danger it was. "What is it?" she implored him. "What is happening?"

"I do not know," he said slowly.

He was a soldier, not a lover now. His voice was level and he kept his arms at his sides.

She heard somebody running then up the stair by which they had come, and she moved and stood with Talitha behind the doorway curtains. From there she saw the young Roman, Lucius Julius, break from the stairhead, and saw Draco step quickly to meet him.

"Tribune," he gasped, "I was seeking you! There is mutiny in the palace and a mob forming outside!"

Draco's voice was quick and cold. "What happened to cause this?"

"The princess caused it," gasped the young underofficer. "The princess demanded of Herod the head of the prisoner as her reward for dancing. The drunken butcher gave it to her! He ordered the man beheaded."

Talitha gave a low, anguished cry. Procla reached out and caught her hand. She heard Lucius Julius still stammering, and she heard Draco's voice cut like a whiplash through his incoherent words.

"Was the prisoner whom Herod killed the man called John the Baptist?"

"He was—and the people are maddened. He was the people's prophet. When they saw his head, the servants rushed from the palace and told of it. A mob already surrounds us, and they are yelling for vengeance. I hurried—to find you—and to ask your orders, tribune."

Behind the curtains the Roman and the Jewish woman clung to each other in dumb horror and misery.

But Draco's voice came to them, harsh and decisive, above the rising cries and shouts outside and the threatening clash of shields on the roof and the confused calls and movement below.

"By all the gods," he told Julius, "I would like to open the doors and let the mob in on these Herods and watch them at their work!"

He stopped, and when he spoke again his voice was bitter as well as hard.

"But, instead, we'll protect them! Order the squad of horse to arm and meet in the court. I will speak with the governor, then be with you by the time you are ready."

And Procla, still clinging to Talitha, heard their quick footsteps departing, loudly at first on the stone of the stair—then lost in confusion below.

10

BACK in the gloomy, wind-lashed palace at Caesarea
a month later, Procla and Talitha talked alone. Pilate
had left for Jerusalem.

He had not even invited his wife to go on this journey
with him; and whether that was from design or haste she
could not be sure. She knew that he was in correspondence
with Caiaphas, and that he hoped to please the High
Priest by restoring to use some aqueduct.

They had not yet recovered from the horror at Tiberias.
Talitha wept at mention of it. Servius had told her that
all Galilee was in a state of uprising; revolution was kept
down only by the borrowed Roman guard. He had also
told her that Herod, in drunken fury and remorse, had
commanded the palace guard to slay his stepdaughter.
They had recoiled at the awful order. But one soldier, a
young Perean named Philip, had stepped forward and
killed her with his sword.

Procla shivered at the memory of it all. She thought
back upon her refusal to go with Pilate. Only the hope of
seeing Draco had taken her to the fortress by the Galilean
Sea. Then that strange and tragic train of events had torn
them apart once more. This prophet of the Messiah had in
his death come between them.

Talitha told her one day that a cousin had come from
Jerusalem.

"He is John Mark, the son of my aunt. He has come not
only to see me but to hear from my lips the story of the
execution of John the Baptist."

"Was he a follower of the Baptist, Talitha?"

"He knew the prophet only by name, but he too is a follower of Jesus of Nazareth. The house of my aunt Mary Mark in Jerusalem is a meeting place for those who believe in him."

Procla saw again that flame leap like a beacon in the dark eyes.

"Oh, my lady, if you could but see him and hear him!"

Procla shook her head. "My own gods have failed me. It will serve me best, I think, to learn to fight my own way through life. I do not find it easy, but I ask help of none."

"My lady," asked Talitha, "will you allow my cousin John Mark to visit me here?"

"Of course," said Procla. "Let him come, and anyone else you wish."

When the slender youth, half Jewish and half Grecian, arrived, he brought with him the friend Bar-Jonas, whom Procla knew as Yod.

Talitha asked hesitantly and formally: "Lady Claudia, will you do us the honor to stay and talk with Nathan and my cousin and me?"

It was just what Procla longed to do. Rain fell outside and the sea wind blew and the corridors were drafty and damp. She said eagerly, "I would like to stay. Light another brazier, and tell the steward to send us date cakes and wine. Perhaps your cousin will explain to me about the aqueducts through which the procurator hopes to carry water to the city of Jerusalem."

Mark knew their history. He spoke modestly, yet with assurance about his subject.

"The Pools of Solomon are six miles south and west of the city, and the springs which feed them flow from rock on a higher level. Long ago some builder constructed masonry channels from these pools to Jerusalem. It is known that King Solomon used to go to the place called Etham to enjoy its flowers and its flowing waters."

"My Greek tutor taught me," she said musingly, "that although people died, ideas were indestructible. A princess from Ethiopia was my beloved friend in childhood, and she told me about your King Solomon. Yod knew her too. Although she is dead, her thoughts did not go from me with her. They keep coming back to me from the lips of others."

"I am half Greek," said John Mark. "I know what your tutor told you. Following beauty, Greece strayed from the true road."

Yod broke in. "What he means is that Jesus Christ has shown us a beauty greater than any Psiloriti showed you. Jesus Christ has shown us that people, as well as ideas, do not die."

"What has changed you?" she demanded of him. "On the island you told me you thought this Messiah another impostor. I was surprised by the way you spoke of him when we last met, but I had then no time to question you. I was surprised by the change in you. You were always stubborn and hard to convince."

"I am still hard to convince," he said. "I was not convinced until I saw. With my own eyes I saw him change water into wine."

She was startled. "Could it not have been a trick?"

"No; for I was one who oversaw the water drawn. Mark had taken me with him to the marriage of one of his friends. They were poor people and the wine gave out. I know what poverty is, and I saw the family's embarrassment. When a young man who was a guest from Nazareth ordered water drawn and brought, I hurried the servants who were staring dumbly at him."

He paused and added: "Not only Mark, but his mother and Talitha were there."

Mark said: "I was there and drank of the wine. I did not, like Nathan Bar-Jonas, see the water drawn. But without seeing I can believe."

"I cannot," said Yod. "I must have proof. But Jesus has given it to me. At this wedding in Cana of Galilee was a maiden from Bethsaida. I was impressed by the kindness she showed her blind father. Although unable to see, he had expressed a wish to attend the wedding because he was related to the bridegroom. His daughter Leah never left his side to enjoy herself with other young people. When I carried wine to the corner where she sat with him, I found her lovely as well as kind."

"Did you not tell me you married her?" Procla asked.

"I loved her at once and wished to marry her. But she refused to leave her helpless father. It was as much in order to release her as to regain his sight that this blind man of Bethsaida appealed to Jesus to heal him."

Procla shook her head. "It sounds incredible."

"It was incredible to me until I saw him do it. I would not have believed had I not seen it."

It was John Mark's turn to break in. "Why should it be incredible? If you believe in any god, is not that divinity stronger than, and able to command, mortality?"

Procla looked searchingly around at the three other faces. Outside the window the sea wind drove the rain across the square. Figures with soiled robes thrown over their heads hurried by. Small donkeys trotted faster as boys urged them on with their loads. But within, the charcoal braziers threw a warm, rosy light. It flushed Talitha's smooth cheeks and made her big eyes softer. It showed the marks of work and suffering on Yod's strong, determined features. He was older than the two girls, but John Mark was even younger. His face was thin and eager, his eyes burned with hope and with dreams.

Procla addressed him directly. "Why would you believe without yourself seeing proof?"

"Because there is in every mortal a spark of immortality. With some it is only a flickering spark, with others a leaping flame. Jesus Christ is the Son of God, divinity in man's body. With him that immortal spark that God has given to each of us flames so strongly that it can command mortality."

She thought about that. It seemed credible from a common-sense point of view.

"If that is true it is purer and more beautiful than any other teaching I have heard. But only a few believe it. Are not your more prominent men, your priests and rulers, opposed to him?"

"They are, because of the fact that they fear his rule threatens theirs. Although his kingdom is of God rather than of man, it is bound to expose and overthrow tyranny and hypocrisy. He is meek and humble but utterly fearless. He cast aside his meekness when he threw by force from the Temple men who used it for selling and short-changing their buyers. Hypocrisy is the one sin with which he has not been gentle. And hypocrisy, I regret to say, is a sin in which our rulers and priests indulge."

Procla remembered that Antipas had said this man would sooner or later run afoul of the priests.

"Hypocrisy is a double sin, and most contemptible of sins. But he must be fearless to offend the powerful."

"Some of the powerful are with him in heart but dare not say so openly. He has warned us that his way is not an easy way. He tells us to forgive others if we wish to be forgiven. He tells us that any man who puts other things before his service cannot be his follower."

"He must be brave and strong and kind and wise and good. I have never before heard of such a doctrine," she said.

"Never before has there been such. He gives his life and risks his death to bring it."

She shook her head. "You who accept it are so few, and you have neither wealth nor power. The end of his ministry may be his death and the death of you who follow."

"Not the end!" cried John Mark.

As if his own cry had aroused him, he leapt to his feet and stared in alarm at the water clock set in a niche.

"Forgive me, my lady! I forget time when I talk of Jesus the Christ. But let me tell you before I go what he himself told us of what you fear. We are few and we are poor and we have powerful enemies. But he gives us faith as immortal as the seed that grows while we sleep. We do not understand how its shell holds that immortality; but we know that it springs and grows and ripens and bears fruit."

The flame in his eyes was hypnotic. She thought: I have heard this before.

"This is the way the Master explained his ministry," said young Mark. "His own words were: *First the blade, then the ear, after that the full corn in the ear.*'

"Do you not see," he cried—and his voice was triumphant now—"that this religion taught by Jesus Christ can never die? Do you not see it growing like corn through the world and the years? Do you not see that whatever his enemies do to us, we are blest who witness that springing of *first the blade?*"

11

THAT conversation stayed vivid in Procla's memory. She contrasted the two young men: Mark in whom the spirit flamed recklessly, and Yod who was logical and demanded tangible proof. Yet both were as sure as Talitha that Jesus was divine.

Procla had time to ponder it, for the aqueducts were keeping Pilate occupied. He made journeys to confer with Caiaphas. Engineers came to consult at Caesarea. He was busy and interested, and she saw that he took a justifiable pride in his rise to popularity. He told her about the work.

"My engineers find the lower conduit in better repair than the upper. We are restoring the lower so that it may carry its flow to cisterns under the Temple."

"It is a fine thing to do," she replied. "You will get back for Rome more than the money's worth of good will by putting the people's taxes on a public benefit."

"The taxes?" he exclaimed. "Do you imagine that I am spending Rome's income on this project?"

"What other fund is there for it?" she asked.

"The Temple money. Jewry has always been wealthy, and their priests have a hoard." His eyes narrowed. "But the Procurator of Judea is master of its finance. I'll make their priests disgorge for their aqueduct."

She said no more. Although she now knew that he had got her by trickery, she knew she was helpless until Draco took her away. Since she had to stay with Pilate, she had made up her mind to try to live peacefully with him until that time came. Since the visit of young Mark she had another interest too. She kept questioning Talitha for news of Jesus Christ and everything that he said or did.

Talitha seemed to be always informed. "For the first time since John's death he is preaching outside of Galilee. He hurried into that country as soon as he heard about John, in order both to quiet the populace and to see that those who believed in the Baptist should not lose heart and scatter."

"Does he travel by horse or litter?"

"He travels afoot with a few of the men who love and follow him. He goes where he is needed, at a moment's notice. Homes are always open to him and arms held out in welcome. But—" a look of trouble creased her smooth forehead— "my brother and Servius tell me that his enemies are conspiring to stop his work and even to take his life."

"Does Servius mean the Romans?" Procla asked her unhappily.

"Oh, no, lady! The Romans have said openly that he does no harm. Servius says that the tribune of horse at Tiberias told Herod to his face that Jesus Christ did more for peace in Galilee than the Roman cavalry did. Many Romans, like Servius, believe him to be the Messiah."

"Servius?" cried Procla.

She visioned the hard-faced veteran of wars in Spain and Gaul. Could he have been won to a creed of unselfishness and meekness?

"Before you came to Judea, when Servius was in barracks, my brother took him to a meeting of Jesus' followers. Ever since that your steward has believed in him and loved him."

So that was the bond between her steward and her handmaiden. She learned from the former that many Roman legionaries as well as auxiliary soldiers had been enough impressed by Jesus to accept him as the Messiah and join his following. Their officers had no objections. As a whole they considered his influence good. His following among the Jews was growing fast; but in proportion to its growth opposition from the priests and politicians grew. Several plots to destroy him were discovered before they succeeded. But the preacher of peace refused to take vengeance and, although it was openly said that the assassins were hired by the priests, the instigators were never uncovered.

There were other plots all through the land. Judea boiled with revolution: with resentment of the Romans and with hatred of its own leaders. And wherever the red-hot brew ran over the sides of the kettle, the tribune Andrus Draco was sent with his cavalry. He did not come to Caesarea, and for long months he did not write. Pilate was obsessed with his aqueducts and inspected every mile of them. In the palace at Caesarea his wife and a Jewish girl talked. Day by day it became of greater importance to Procla that she know what the Nazarene carpenter had last said and whom he had healed. She did not herself realize how his influence was filling her life; but she felt that she would take any risk to see him and hear him preach.

It was a strange position for Augustus' granddaughter. Behind her lay long centuries of morals at variance with the morals taught by Christ. She was deeply and truly in love with one man. No other even tempted her. According to all her standards they had every right to each other if they could bring enough influence to break former bonds and marry. She knew that she and Draco had done nothing to justify their enforced separation. She knew, moreover, that Tiberius would have overlooked the very offense with which he had charged them, except for his morbid and unnatural fear of scandal. All her pagan philosophy stood strong behind her. Nothing in it was at variance with her determination to go to the man she loved as soon as she could go.

But Rome, that pagan teacher who had schooled her youth, was keeping that man away. Rome had at least taught him duty: a harsh and soulless duty, but a duty that he put even higher than his love. The woman he loved was left alone in the governor's palace, with servants who unfolded to her a teaching of love and beauty and gentle strength. It did not take her by storm, like the clash of Roman swords or the striking of Hebrew shields. It sank into her troubled, resentful heart as soft water from Solomon's Pools sank into the garden at Etham. Once again began that first great miracle: the birth and growth of an idea or a child or a blade of grain.

So when Talitha came, starry-eyed, to tell her that Jesus of Nazareth was coming to Caesarea, her own gray eyes blazed as brightly as the brown ones.

"In whose house will he lodge? Do you think I could hear and see him?"

"My brother is honored, my lady. The Master will go to his home. If you wish to be there, my sister-in-law Milcah will welcome you."

They spent a week talking about it and making plans. Procla was excited and eager, Talitha calm yet joyful. They were ready to start in the early dusk, when Servius came to her door with a letter in his hand.

"The soldier who brought it has ridden away. He said, my lady, that there was no need for an answer."

No need for an answer! Draco knew what her answer would always be. With her heart beating far up in her throat, she took his message to the window and read it by the last of the twilight: *I am only ten leagues away from you and will ride in alone before midnight. Tell Servius to wait for me at the north courtyard's entrance.*

As she folded it and pushed it into the folds of her girdle, she felt her heart's wild pulsing of joy against her fingers. She had Talitha call the steward, and she gave him the instructions. Like her, he was bred to a pagan code. Although he accepted and admired the Jewish Messiah, he saw nothing incongruous in the making of such plans on the eve of such a meeting. Like her, he was willing to give up everything else at the beck of a Roman tribune's imperious finger.

Talitha had stood by with her eyes clouded by distress. She had been telling herself: Perhaps, after my lady sees the Master and hears his words, she will have strength to send away this Roman lover.

"We will be back long before midnight," she said in her low, rich voice. "Zebulun said that the Master would start on his way at next daybreak. We are asked to arrive early, so that he may have time for rest and sleep after the meeting. He never thinks of himself; but my sister-in-law made that request."

But Procla shook her head.

"I will not go. I shall stay here, and so must Servius. Perhaps I can hear Jesus another time."

She saw the look on the Jewish girl's face—and misunderstood it.

"But you may go, Talitha. Servius shall take you now, and return at once to me. You may spend the night at your brother's house."

"It is not that," said Talitha. "It is that 'another time' may never come."

The very fact that she knew herself to be in the wrong made Procla's anger rise at the implied reproach.

"It is I who decide what shall and shall not be done. Do not forget your place, Talitha. Do as I tell you, and go at once. Stay the night with your brother and his wife. I shall not expect to see you until tomorrow. And when I do see you again, I shall expect you to remember that *I* give the orders."

The maid went without words; but the mistress was left without comfort. A strange uneasiness and self-reproach clouded her joy at the prospect of seeing Draco. She kept recalling Talitha's words: *". . . another time may never come."*

Servius reported to her when he returned. The little group of followers had already gathered; but they had reason to fear that Jesus might not arrive. They had rumors of a riot of the Judas-of-Galileans somewhere along the Nazareth-Caesarea road. Roman cavalry was there, and was said to have blocked the way to keep the fight from spreading. It was Jesus' rule, said Servius, to comply with law and order. He would turn aside from his own errand rather than incite the mob further by his presence.

So I might not have heard him had I gone, Procla reassured herself.

But she was not reassured through that long night of waiting.

She had forbidden Talitha to return. Servius stood at the north gate, as eager as she was. Alone in her apartment she tried to relax on her couch; but she kept rising restlessly and going to the windows, or watching the slow clock spill time with water drops.

With every hour she felt more sure that Draco was not coming. Although she had denied Jesus to wait here for her lover, she had a strange certainty that the Nazarene was exerting an influence over her life. Could he, like the Roman gods, be revenging himself for an insult? Or was he, by the same events which might be detaining him, teaching her to keep a law which was both Rome's law and his own?

She did not know. She was wondering still when the desolate dawn came up. All she knew was that she was still alone and comfortless. She had chosen love and kept her vigil in vain. Events more important than she and her love had disposed of the night. The Man of Peace had stepped aside to avoid inciting the rioters. The man of wrath had stayed to do his duty as he saw it.

The governor's wife still wore the dark robe in which she had dressed for the meeting, when she heard feet crossing the square.

Surely Draco would not come by day?

But she ran to the window.

The governor was arriving, with his escort afoot and ahorse.

12

EVEN before he told her, she knew that something had gone wrong. His nervousness and anger always took the form of aggressiveness. He shouted that his bearers had been stumbling and slow. He criticized the guard at the gate for having removed his helmet. He stamped into the main hall, demanding more light and wine and hot food.

Servius was not flustered or even hurried by it. He gave his orders to the staff with expressionless calm. Pilate's approval or disapproval meant nothing to him; but the very thought of Draco straightened his old shoulders. He was contrasting the two men now, and remembering a boyish officer who had led his first charge by the Rhenish marshes. He recalled that the following night, as they counted their survivors, he had gone to this young commander and told him the men were uneasy because they heard they must ride next day by the place where Varus' ghost was seen. The boy had frowned sternly at him.

"Tell them for me, Servius Brutus of Latium, that they should know me better than to think a ghost story can turn me aside. But—" he had paused and grinned crookedly— "mention that I had already planned to lead them around by the longer road."

That was an officer for you! He kept hard discipline, but he had sense enough to concede a small point rather than risk a panic among the stupid and fearful. He knew his men individually; and he let them know he knew them by the subtle compliment of using full name and province when he spoke to them.

Servius longed for those old days as he crossed the room
to refill an already-emptied wine pitcher. Living here in
the palace was fat, but he had been happier riding in Gaul.
The governor treated them well enough, but he lacked
the qualities to command. His wife was growing thinner
and her eyes bigger and darker, although her hair was
still the hue of oak leaves in the autumn. When his duties
permitted, he whiled away the hours with Talitha and
Zebulun. He preferred them and their friends to the
men of the auxilia, who were after all merely barbarians
romanized. He knew that the governor was not Roman-
born, although he was in command of men of Latium. He,
Servius, could recall sturdier, cleaner days. There was
something sturdy and clean about this carpenter's teaching. He scorned to preach one thing and practice another.
He did not try to fool people with false promises. He told
you that his way was hard. If it was true that he was a
god, he was a braver god than any Servius had yet heard
about. He was the kind of god that the governor's lady
should serve—and the tribune Andrus Draco, if he ever
served a god. Those two had in them a streak of steel
that the governor lacked.

She was saying now to the governor: "I hope all goes
well for you, my lord?"

Pontius Pilate set his wine cup down with a thud.

"All has gone wrong! I knew the Jews were tricky and
avaricious." He had drunk enough to speak his thoughts.
"I have always hated them."

She knew it was better to keep silence. His voice rose.

"They are greedy, and they have no gratitude. Their
high priest planned with me restoration of the aqueduct.
I mentioned the Temple money—in an indirect way, of
course. But he knew in his scheming heart that I intended
to use it."

He paused while Servius filled his cup. She thought:
So it is the money.

"But when I take it he disclaims all knowledge of my intention and throws me to the people—as a captive is thrown to the lions! The populace rose and rioted, as they rioted over the ensigns."

"How did you calm them?" she asked. She was thinking of Draco, wondering if he had been there.

"I did not try to calm them. This time I beat them into submission. Had I done so at Caesarea they would not have risen again. I was ill advised then to spare them. But I've taught them a lesson now."

He beckoned to Servius. "My cup is empty, steward."

"What did you do?" she asked him.

She was remembering the Judeans lying unarmed and helpless in the square.

"Draco with his cavalry is in Galilee, so I sent footmen with weapons, and orders to strike to kill. Many of the insurgents were killed, and many more were wounded. After this they will have respect for me."

She was giving silent thanks that Draco had not been his instrument. It was over now, and there was nothing that she could do. To censure him would not help; it would only enrage him. But one thing he had said still gnawed at her troubled mind. If the high priest knew of the governor's intention to use the Temple money, why had he kept silence? Why had he not warned the Roman that the people would rise and protest? Was he trying, as other high priests had tried, to jockey a procurator into a position where he would be recalled by the Emperor? If so, this Caiaphas must be crafty and cruel and dangerous; for he had paid with the lives of his people to injure the foreigner.

She did not question him further for she knew it would only inflame him more. For weeks he kept indoors, writing letters and sending them to Jerusalem by riders and to Rome by ship. Then he informed her that he was going to visit and appraise a plantation of precious woods between Esdraelon and Jordan. He asked her, a little humbly, if she would go with him.

It was in her character not to pretend that she did it solely on his account.

"I will be glad to go, my lord. I would like to see the plantations, and I have found it dreary waiting in the palace here."

His eyes contracted to pin points and fixed themselves on her face. "For whom have you been waiting in dreariness, Claudia?"

She looked back at him haughtily, and her voice was icy. "For whom should the governor's wife wait except for the governor?"

But he tried to make himself pleasant on this journey. He rode in the same litter with her and explained the places as they passed by. He told her the uses of balsam and palm and the revenue brought by their sale. At the plantations she walked for miles between the alignment of fragrant trunks, over a carpet of fallen balsam needles. She tasted dates fresh from the mother palms, and Talitha fanned her with plaited fronds. She slept on balsam pillows in which was caught the resinous scent from outside.

The color began to come back to her cheeks and the old swing to her step. Talitha joyed to see it. Her husband watched her and smiled.

She was still talking about it as they approached Caesarea. "It has taken me back to my childhood, although that scene was different."

He lay back on the litter cushions and watched her, and there was expectancy in his smile.

"I am glad you enjoyed this journey, although alone with me. Perhaps you will enjoy the journey even more when I take you to the Jewish feast of the Passover and you see Jerusalem and the Roman officers there."

She felt her face flushing hotly, but she kept her voice

cold and controlled. "I shall enjoy Jerusalem. I have often longed to see it. But I have enjoyed this visit to the plantations too."

She stopped and sought for words with which to turn his thoughts from Roman officers.

"All my life I have heard of gardens of balsam and palm; but until you informed me I did not know how immense is their value. The owner of those we have seen must be incredibly wealthy."

"She is," he said, "one of the wealthiest women in the Roman Empire."

Procla's eyes widened in surprise, and she asked the question he waited for.

"*She?* Are they owned by a woman? Who is she?"

"She is an old friend of yours. She is Flavia Maro, the little crippled heiress who was married to Andrus Draco."

13

THINKING back on the rest of that journey, Procla could feel the litter sway, and feel her mind sway with it. Flavia Maro—the lame girl with the sweet face and the brave heart. Flavia who loved Lepidus but had sent him, at undeniable risk to them both, to take Draco's message to Procla.

She saw herself back in the garden in Rome and she heard herself saying: *". . . tell her if ever the time comes when I can do some kindness for her, I will not fail her."*

Yet she was determined now—and had been determined for several years—to take Flavia's husband from her.

She bolted Talitha out, and all the night she walked her room. She could and would have left Pilate. He had got her by unfair means, and she could strike back with any weapons she had. But how could she strike at Flavia's gentleness and goodness?

She stood still and slowly unclenched her hands. The nails were cutting into the flesh as they did when she was in stress. Had not Talitha asked how one could go about conquering meekness? It had seemed only rhetorical then, but she was facing its fact now. Had it not been the teaching of that strange teacher called Jesus, who seemed to know all secrets of the human heart?

But why should she listen to teaching, from him or from anyone else? She must have Draco. He belonged to her—to no one else—not even to the woman who was his wife.

Yet why should his wife, of all women in the great

Roman Empire, be the one woman who had been kind—
the only one to whom she owed kindness in return?

She moved in a daze of wretchedness as she made her
preparations to go down to Jerusalem to the Jewish feast
of Passover. When the governor went alone he stayed at
the military headquarters; but he and she would reside
in state in the Herodian palace. Talitha told her it was
by far more gorgeous than this one in Caesarea. Talitha
was overjoyed, not at the idea of seeing the palace but
of seeing again the quiet house of the aunt who had
mothered her.

Now as they journeyed, Procla tried to keep her
thoughts on the things of which Talitha spoke, but her
turmoil of mind and heart obscured all else. She realized
that Pilate had deliberately made the revelation about
Draco's wife because he knew she was going soon to see
Draco. He had heard her express for Flavia admiration
and gratitude. In his opinion the knowledge that she was
Draco's wife would make Procla reject any overtures from
Draco. But Pilate's machinations were less important than
her fears about the effect of this marriage on Draco. Why
had he evaded telling her that the woman was Flavia?
Could it be that Flavia's beautiful character, and the
gentle helplessness of her crippled body, had so appealed
to him that he did not wish to divorce her? That fact
could well explain his reluctance to name her to Procla.

So as the governor's train ascended the Judean hills
the governor's wife sat silent and pale behind her litter
curtains. She spoke only to give necessary orders. Talitha
looked in anguish at the lovely, haughty face. She loved
this woman and wished to help, but she knew that grief
is a lonely thing. So they sat without words while the road
wound on to Jerusalem and Gethsemane.

This road was by far more beautiful than the road to
Galilee. It was spring, and the field flowers were in bloom.
The Syrian poppies grew like tares in the young green

of the planted ground. It was the sight of Talitha peeping wistfully out between the curtains that finally roused Procla.

"You may open them wide," she said.

Always upward wound the long way to the plateau. Time and again the bearers stopped to rest on chalky ledges which rose like terraces on the sides of the graded road. Then Talitha cried out and pointed ahead. Against the white clouds, like a mirage, Procla saw the fort Antonia and the Temple's dome.

She knew that the Roman garrison kept the fortress. Somewhere in its walls was Draco, and he must know she was coming. She tried to drag her mind back and listen to Talitha.

"You can also see the three towers on the west hill, my lady. Herod named them Mariamne—for the wife he loved best and killed—Phasaelus, and Hippicus. They are strongholds of protection for the palace where you will stay."

Procla looked at them without enthusiasm and remembering that they were of recent construction. For two thousand years men had besieged and destroyed and restored this city which the Jews called holy.

She was trying to busy her mind with such thoughts as her bearers carried her through one of the four gates in the north wall, and on through narrow streets bordered by flat-roofed houses. As they set her down in the courtyard she heard water running, and she smelled the fragrance of flowers. But it was night, and they hurried her obsequiously indoors. There her first impression was of lavish magnificence combined with an immense and tragic loneliness. One wing of the structure was enough to house the governor's party. The rest of Herod's palace lay dark, empty and unused.

She was too tired to dine, so Talitha brought her food to her room. The girl's voice was wistful.

"My cousin John Mark has already left a message with the guard in the court. He will return in an hour to see me."

"You may go with him and visit your aunt. I shall not need you again tonight. I am going to bed at once."

The girl had gone, and Procla stood at a window when Pilate came. There were lines of worry on his face, but he smiled when he saw her there.

"You are looking the wrong way, Claudia. Antonia lies to west."

As he came closer she smelled the wine on his breath. If he touches me now I shall kill him, she thought. She drew herself up and away from him, her eyes as black as ice.

"I was not looking at the fortress but at the road which we traveled."

He moved to a place beside her and gazed north with her. The country lay in darkness beyond the city walls. He could only vision, as she was visioning, that long road climbing up . . . and steeply on. . . .

But he had something to tell her, and he wished to observe its effect.

"A message has come from the fortress that the commander will call within the hour to pay his formal respects to the Procurator of Judea and the procurator's wife."

Her eyes were still ice in shadow. "Is it Andrus Draco?"

"It is our old friend Draco—too old a friend to be slighted. He must be received and welcomed, Claudia."

"I agree with you. When you meet and welcome him, you may excuse your wife's absence by mentioning that she is weary."

" I regret that you are weary. It is you who must receive him. I shall appear later. But one of the High Priests is awaiting me now."

She did not wish to argue. This should be cold and clean-cut. She knew he was playing on her nerves like

a harpist on harpstrings, in order to know exactly the
response each touch evoked. She was already quivering
at the thought of seeing Draco. Only to see him! Even
though she must send him away this time. . . .

"My maid has been dismissed for the night. I intended
to retire."

"Can you not dress yourself, Claudia? You are by no
means a helpless woman."

"I can. But are you suggesting that, in your absence,
I receive our friend unattended?"

His voice was amused. "By no means. All is arranged
as it should be. There are musicians and lights in the lily
garden of the south court. There are also Roman guards
stationed at close intervals. It was Draco's idea to double
the guard when we came. I have not been popular since
the matter of the Temple money."

She saw now just what he intended and had arranged:
a meeting for her and the man she loved in a brilliantly
lighted court and under the eyes of strangers. A Roman
officer would never relax his dignity with the legionaries
gazing down from the walls. That strain would tell on him
as well as on her. That straw's weight might break her
after the news of his marriage to Flavia.

She recognized it as a challenge she had to accept.

"If you will leave me now, I will make myself ready."

"You are clever," he said admiringly—and she knew he
was not referring to her skill in arranging garments or
hair.

But Pilate did not go at once. He stared out of the
window, across the hills to north. "It is a long, steep climb
to Jerusalem," he said. "For some reason it seemed this
time longer and steeper than ever. It was almost as if I
approached something monstrous and threatening."

She did not know that it was Caiaphas awaiting him,
and that he too was beset by a decision—a decision that
dwarfed her heartbreak. She was aching in mind and

body, and she had no sympathy for him at that moment. She thought, He is purposely forcing me to this decision at the wrong time, while he goes off to wrangle with the priests over Temple money. But, if he will only go, and let me see Draco for this last time!

She sighed. "I will be glad to leave Jerusalem, and Herod's dark and almost-empty palace. But however steep was the road in ascent, we shall find descent even steeper."

14

UNDER the ornate arch that led out to the south court, Procla paused and looked left between the red-and-gold pillars. An even redder gold than they, the full moon was rising out of the Arabian desert. Sounds of strange music filled the garden. She heard the high, sad wail of a pipe against the strings of a sackbut. Even in the clash of the cymbals there was warning rather than joy.

Draco saw her standing there, too slender in her long white robes. The only color about her was her golden girdle and the golden fire that the red moon lit in her hair. He came up the steps to meet her, with his cape flung back from his shoulders. His helmet was under an arm and he scowled in unloverlike fashion.

"The governor will come later," she said. "He has business with the priests."

"I know," he answered. "Better for him if he had no business with them. I have no love for Jewish politics or Jewish music."

He was guiding her along a walk that descended by terraced steps. The ripple of strings behind them now seemed almost the ripple of water. She realized that upon either side of them the hollowed stone of the coping served as a trough for the overflow of fountains on higher levels. They were leaving the musicians, but the water ran with them; and like the music it sang of old sorrows of Israel.

I will not listen to the sorrows of anyone else, she

233

thought. I have sorrow enough of my own. I will shut my heart to all others.

She did not know this garden or where he was taking her. She reminded him formally: "The governor will come later."

"It is nothing to me if the governor never comes," he answered shortly.

On every side of them lamps were swung, and painted cages of thrushes and doves. The mallowlike roses of Sharon bloomed from red to palest pastels. The night was full of the fragrance of tall white lilies. They bordered every path and were massed along the garden walls. Draco led her on between them and the channels of running water. He stopped in a pool of shadow thrown by a blossoming pomegranate. On the parapet above she saw a Roman sentry in silhouette.

But Draco's arms were around her.

"Procla, I have served my time here. After the Feast of the Passover I am free. There is always danger of trouble at these Jewish holidays, so I am on duty until this one is over."

He felt her trying to pull away, but he held her tighter.

"For the next ten days I shall probably be too busy even to see you. But another tribune is being sent out. I can go—and take you with me."

"Draco," she said. "Draco—"

The sentry was pacing nearer, but he would not release her. "What is it, Procla?" he asked her softly.

"It is Flavia Maro, your wife. I knew nothing of her and you. She dared to do us a kindness in Rome. When you were in prison she sent Lepidus to me. You know Lepidus as well as I do. He is neither brave nor unselfish. But—but Flavia is both. She made him bring your message."

"Go on," he said. He held her still, but he did not draw her closer.

"I thanked Lepidus, for I knew that his daring to come endangered them both. I told him then to tell Flavia that if ever I had the chance, I would not fail her."

In that silence the boughs of the pomegranate stirred and they heard the sentry's feet as he paced. The lute and shawn mourned faintly, and the doves seemed to be sobbing.

"Draco, do you not understand that this changes all? She is your wife."

"She is not my wife," he said. His voice was slow and deliberate.

"Pontius Pilate said that you had been made to marry her. I do not pretend to love him, but I do not think he would lie."

"He does not lie, but he plays with truth. I married Flavia. She loves me no more than I love her. Her heart belongs to Lepidus."

Her voice was cold with hopelessness. "But you married her?"

"By all the Roman ritual, I married her—and then left her. Tiberius hurried me out of Rome. The marriage was only a form."

Her voice was still hopeless. "Why did Tiberius choose her, of all women?"

"Because of her wealth, of the tax from her plantations. He thought by marrying her to a Roman officer to assure her residence in Rome and the continued revenue from balsam and palm for the Empire."

"I do not understand," she said. Her eyes ached with tears, but she would not weep. "Pilate took me not long ago to see the plantations. He told me they belonged to her—and that she was married to you."

"Our marriage was never a real marriage. I took care that it should not be. I have not yet lifted from Flavia's face the red veil of a bride."

"But she must love you, Draco, and be waiting for you to come back to her."

She felt his arms tighten, although he laughed at her.

"Thank you, my darling, for the subtle compliment. But Flavia does not love me and is not waiting for me. Tiberius has gained even more than he hoped from her wealth; but he has not made her my wife or me her husband."

He felt her trembling in his arms, and his heart contracted. It was not his way to be soft, not even in his wooing; and she had never resorted to tears or fears to move him. He knew that she was suffering more than she let him know, and he loved her more for her gallantry. She did not ask for quarter now. She said, "I do not know what you mean. If you are married to Flavia, whether or not she is your wife, I cannot shame her by taking you. I told her I would not fail her."

"What I mean, Procla, is that Pilate told you a half-truth. It is his fashion so to toy with things which are too big for his grasp. I suspect that his visit to Flavia's groves was to appraise their value for Tiberius."

"He spoke of appraising them. What has that to do with us?"

"It has this to do with us. Flavia Maro, whom I married but who was never my wife, has had the courage to leave Rome with the man she loves."

"With Lepidus? I am glad. But I did not know he was brave enough."

"He is not. He draws what bravery he needs from the little lame girl whom he really loves. I have just heard this news. Not long ago an old cousin died and left Lepidus a small fortune. He took it and he and Flavia fled to Athens. May all the Greek gods prosper them! It has set me completely free. Since my marriage to Flavia had never been consummated, Tiberius has annulled it and confiscated her wealth."

The strings of the sackbut and viol grew loud and their melody filled all the garden. A caged thrush, awakened by it, began to sing. The moonlight was honey-colored and thick with the lilies' scent. He did not after all belong to Flavia. Flavia had chosen her love. Draco was free now to take her—Procla—and she was free to go with him.

He was thinking the same thing. He said, "What is there now to keep us apart?"

"Nothing," she said. "Nothing, my love." And he felt her press closer to him. "It was only Rome that held you, and she cannot hold you now."

"And if Rome cannot hold us apart, my love," he asked her exultantly, "what power in all the world is there with strength enough to do it?"

15

DRACO and Procla did not even notice the fact that Pontius Pilate never joined them that evening. She went back to her apartment discreetly early, and in such a transport of happiness that it never occurred to her that only a matter of moment could have kept her husband away.

Talitha had returned and was waiting to attend her.

"My lady, the Master has come up for the Passover. He came to my aunt's house tonight."

But Procla had forgotten him too—had forgotten all except Draco. She listened to Talitha's story. Jesus Christ and his disciples were in Jerusalem for observance of the feast, and he had visited Mary Mark that evening.

"He did not stay long, and he looked strangely sad. Mark told me that he had said one of his twelve disciples was possessed of a devil."

Procla had no delusions about human nature. "That sounds likely. It would be hard to pick twelve men in Rome or Judea without picking one devil among them. But why should it trouble Jesus? Can he not cast devils out?"

"He can do whatever he wishes, but he does what he thinks is best. It may be he knows it is best for those who love him, and for all the world, to let this man do as his devil prompts and let consequences teach those who are hard of heart."

She went on eagerly. "The Master did not say that he would return, but he may. Will you go with me tomorrow night to the home of my aunt, my lady? She is eager to see you and thank you for your kindness. She says you must be good indeed, to be so kind to me."

Procla promised, and she fell asleep feeling strangely humble at being called *good* by Mary Mark. At any rate I shall be honest, she reassured herself. Before I go to the house which this Messiah visits, I shall at least have told Pilate that I am leaving him. . . . For she intended to tell him as soon as she saw him. In Judea his power extended only through matters of finance and the final decision of life or death in the courts. She knew that he could not prevent her departure or the departure of a man who had his discharge from the Legion.

But the next long day wore to an end and still the governor did not visit his wife. Talitha questioned Servius, who had come to direct the household. He knew only that Pilate had been besieged ever since his arrival in Jerusalem with messengers from the priests. Caiaphas and Annas had both talked with him. Even now he was in conference with them.

"Who is Annas?" Procla demanded.

"The father-in-law of Caiaphas. He was once himself high priest and he still has authority in high places. He owned the concession for sales in the Temple, and he lost a large income when Jesus drove out the sellers."

Still she suspected nothing of what was happening. She thought there might be afoot some adjustment about the aqueduct. She truly hoped that the governor would have a chance to reinstate himself by correcting that blunder. Perhaps he was arranging to return the Temple money.

He had not yet come to her when she left that evening, carried in the litter with Talitha and accompanied by the steward on foot.

Until they were caught in the crowd on the streets neither the two women nor Servius realized what was happening. Throngs were pouring into the city through its gates from east and south and north. They were

turbulent throngs, uneasy with the yeast of revolution.
The authorities had reason to fear them. The supreme
court had called on Rome for additional soldiery. Legionaries guarded the gates, and legionaries patrolled the
streets. More than once Procla's litter was blocked in
some lane, while a squad went by with cleated sandals
striking on stone. At the first such encounter Servius
raised his hand to proclaim her rank, but she called
quickly to him to stand aside. She had not been able to
tell Pilate where she was going, so could not know
whether he approved or disapproved. At least, she decided, she would not cause him embarrassment by revealing the fact that his wife had been abroad in this milling
mob. For she now realized that she had done an unwise
thing.

The litter bearers were stopping again. Overtaking them
in a run came a squad of a dozen or more men of the
cohort. One of them jerked the curtains apart and faces
appeared and grinned at them: hard young faces with
reckless eyes, and noses that had a Roman curve. They
stared at the soft, warm Jewish girl and the slim, fair
woman with autumnal hair. One of them whistled, and
one of them laughed. A centurion barked an order to go.

The little house of Mark was strangely peaceful and
gracious. Talitha's aunt thanked Procla with courtesy and
yet with uncompromising self-respect. Nobody else was
there; but within the hour Yod arrived to join them.

But although it was peaceful in the house, they could
hear in the street outside feet trampling more and more
heavily and louder shouts and imprecations.

"Yod," she asked, "have you always this excitement
at your religious feasts?"

He shook his head. "There are often clashes between
the different factions. But something is in the air tonight
—something like the storm in the east. On my way here
I saw lightning over the desert."

She talked with him, and he told her about his wife and small son. "Leah wished to come with me tonight, but she had to stay with the baby."

"Did you come, as I did, hoping to see the Messiah?"

His voice was troubled. "I hardly hoped that he would return here. I understand that he said he wished to be with his disciples tonight. We who love him wish that he had not come to Jerusalem just now. There is hatred of him in high places. We would like to get him away, but he will not consider himself."

He gave her a scowl. For the moment he looked like the herdboy on the island again. His speech was still just as blunt.

"You Romans are doing nothing to help us. Lawlessness is increasing all over Judea. You execute offenders, but you do not lessen offense."

She did not resent it, for she knew he was right. Servius told her anxiously that he thought they should return soon to the palace.

So Mary Mark and Nathan Bar-Jonas repeated for them the prayers that Jesus had taught them. Procla listened to the low, earnest voices.

"Let not your heart be troubled. . . ."

How can I not be troubled, she thought, about this thing I am doing? This Messiah must be a god in truth if he can show me the way to peace.

"If ye love me keep my commandments."

Looking back she suddenly saw that only the affairs of Jesus Christ and his terrible kinsman John had intervened to keep her from breaking them.

Mary Mark's voice was sure and sweet.

"I will not leave you comfortless."

Even in his absence, the very thought of him seemed to comfort those who believed in him. She realized now that she longed to believe in him. She had wanted to see him, to hear his voice. She was not a soft woman who took her opinions from others. She demanded proof. She had heard much of this Messiah, but she was not yet persuaded that he was different from other men who had taught and prophecied.

They looked up and met each others' eyes as they heard running feet in the courtyard. Young John Mark burst into the room, breathing in long, tearing gasps. Except for loincloth and sandals he was naked. His dark hair fell over his eyes; his face was streaked and soiled with sweat.

"They have—taken—the Master," he sobbed. "I tried—to warn him. But I was too late!"

Yod seized his arm. "Who made the arrest?"

"The Temple Guards. But the Romans know. They were many. They came with torches and swords."

Mark was almost hysterical, but Yod was reasoning clearly. He said scornfully: "The Temple Guard—to arrest a man who is never armed!"

Mary Mark and Talitha were weeping aloud. Young John Mark shook as if with a chill.

"Peter the Fisherman struck and drew blood. But the Master told him not to resist. The others escaped—but they took Jesus away. They seized me and would have taken me too, but I twisted out of my robe and ran."

Yod gripped his arm. "Calm yourself and tell us! You said you went to warn him. Who told you he was in danger?"

"The Roman sentry at the gate that leads out to Mount Olivet. I was trying to find the Master. The city is wild tonight. I asked the Roman and he said that Jesus had gone through hours before toward the garden called Gethsemane. He added, 'There were only a few men with him, and they did not look dangerous. But the guards of your high priests have just gone that way, armed to the teeth, and with witnesses.'

"Then I looked down where the valley slopes. I could

see the torches through the trees. They wound like a
serpent of fire, and I knew by the number that the entire
guard had turned out and that the matter was terrible.
I ran. I tried to overtake and pass them. My clothes were
torn. I fell in the brook. I climbed the garden wall. But
I was too late, I tell you! They came up to Jesus just as
I did. Judas the Iscariot stepped forward and kissed him."

Young Mark burst into stormy tears.

"The Master has been betrayed!"

16

EXCEPT for the reassurances of Yod and Servius, Procla
could not have slept that night.

Yod did not underestimate the danger. He was a practical man, and a man of affairs now. He had known all
along that in Jerusalem there were people in high places
who were determined to get rid of Jesus. But he also
knew his law and knew that, however high their estate,
all Jews must abide by it. Jesus in preaching and teaching
had broken no commands. He had done much toward
keeping peace. Even the Romans who ruled them
acknowledged that.

So he told the Roman governor's wife: "Whatever they
are trying to do, they can do nothing until the Passover
is ended. It begins with the next sunset and lasts for ten
days."

It was then some time after midnight and they were
back at the palace. The guard said that the governor had
come in several hours before. Servius went to his door
and came back to report that his apartment was dark.
Procla recalled that it angered him to be awakened from
sleep. She needed his good humor to win what she begged.

Servius reminded them, "Nor can the Jews at any time
impose extreme penalty without the consent of Rome,
Lady Claudia."

So she made up her mind to wait and speak with Pilate
next day. Sometimes he lost his temper, but she knew he
was not a cruel man. He had experienced the machinations of Caiaphas in the aqueduct business. When she
explained to him that this was more of Caiaphas' work,

he would be glad to thwart the high priest as well as
to order Jesus released.

Thinking of these things so earnestly that she forgot
even Draco, Pilate's wife fell asleep . . . and as she slept
she dreamed. . . .

Talitha and Mary Mark had come and taken her by
the hand and were leading her up a long hill whose stones
bruised her feet. Other women were weeping there, but
she did not yet know why they wept. And suddenly
Lalibela moved from them and toward her.

Come, said Lalibela. *I will show you the corn in the
ear. It is best you should see it before you see its bitter
planting.*

Lalibela first showed her an empty tomb in a garden.
The rising sun was shining into its open door, and instead
of sadness there was gladness all around it.

Before she could ask about it, she found that she walked
in an underground gallery. She shrank aside as Roman
soldiers tramped by with captives in their midst. *Who are
they?* she asked Lalibela. *Where are they being taken?*

*They are followers of Jesus Christ being taken out to
die in the arena where you have watched the games. But
the seed is alive and springing. Here is a man who is your
friend and who busies himself with the sowing.*

It was John Mark, and he was in Rome too. He said:
*Lady Claudia, I am writing the story of Our Lord. I know
little myself, but the fisherman he loved is telling me of
him.*

The scenes were so brief. Each went by like a glimpse
of something revealed by a lightning flash.

There was a forest where a man with a gentle face
talked to birds and beasts. *How can we love the gentle
Jesus,* he asked, *if we are not merciful to dumb and helpless things?*

Lalibela said: *The blade has sprung tall and green.*

She showed Procla great temples, unlike those of Rome

or Judea. They were built to the glory of Jesus Christ, and their choirs sang of Him as God's Son.

Procla heard then a thunder which she did not understand. She saw a sea lit by flashes of light, and ships like gray mountains on it.

In her sleep she heard Lalibela sigh. *It is the road of the cross,* she said. *He Himself is walking it now. But if you look, Procla, I will show you the corn in the ear.*

As Procla looked at the nearest ship, it was torn apart by a flash of light so terrible that she thought it must be lightning. There seemed to be hundreds of young men and the ship was sinking.

Then, on the slanting deck, she saw four men standing together shoulder to shoulder. One wore a yellow star and the others crosses of different shapes. But all four were alike in that they abnegated themselves and were thinking only of others. Procla saw they were giving to other men that which would have saved their own lives. . . .

Suddenly she and Lalibela were back on the stony hill, and now she saw three crosses. And although she had never seen Him before she knew the man in the center. She began to weep as bitterly as the other women were weeping—and suddenly Psiloriti was there and his arms were around her.

I did not know you were here, she said. *Who has done this? Can you not stop it?*

He swept one arm in a half circle to show her the great concourse. Thousands covered the hill called the Place of the Skull, and their multitude stretched beyond sight to eternity.

All the world is here, Procla, he said; *the dead and the living and the unborn.*

But who has done it? she cried again. *For this is the Roman way of death!*

Then the horror of it awakened her, and she sprang out of bed.

She remembered what had happened the night before, although the dream was more real. Her heart held onto what Yod had said about delay for the Passover. She said to Talitha: "Call Servius at once, and bid him tell the governor that I must see him without delay."

She was in such haste that she had dressed by the time Talitha returned. The girl's rose-brown cheeks were pale.

"The governor has already gone out."

"Where has he gone?" his wife asked. Her lips felt stiff as they shaped the words.

"He has been gone since before day. He was called to the garrison. Roman soldiers escorted him, and they carried the chair used for judgment."

"Bring my writing materials," said Procla. "And while I am writing go find a man to carry it to the governor."

She had so little time. If she could have seen Pilate and explained it all . . . there were so many things. She could not tell them all. But she must tell him enough to make him stop this catastrophe. Her fingers were shaking so she could hardly hold the stylus. He would even now be in the judgment seat, since it had been carried with him to the judgment hall. And he was the Roman governor and his word was final. The messenger would be coming, and every moment was precious.

So, trying not to tremble, she wrote her short message to Pontius Pilate:

Have thou nothing to do with that just man; for I have suffered many things this day in a dream because of him.

17

AFTER the messenger had gone, Procla tried again to reassure herself. Surely her dream had been only a dream. She thought of what Yod had told her, and she remembered that Servius had said final sentence lay with Rome. Rome served other gods—if Rome could be said to serve—but surely Rome stood for justice and bravery.

Talitha was in such a state of nerves that her mistress sent her away.

"Have Servius carry you safely to the house of your aunt. I shall not leave the palace, since I wait for the governor. You may stay with Mary Mark until tonight or tomorrow."

Yod had said the night before that he saw lightning in the east. This day the sun was overcast and the hot wind that came with spring was blowing. Procla, alone in the palace except for the household servants, moved as restlessly as the dust devils it was stirring. A young Cyrenian in training for house stewardship brought her midday meal.

She asked him: "Where is Servius?"

"He has not yet returned, my lady. Have I done wrong with the service?"

His dark face was so worried that, tense as she was, she tried to smile and give him reassurance.

"It suits me, but I am not hungry. Has Servius sent no message?"

"None, my lady, of which I have heard. There is such turmoil in the streets that he could be prevented either from coming or sending."

She asked quickly: "What has stirred the crowd to cause this turmoil?"

"It is rumored that the court has set free a man named Bar-Abbas. The people love him, and they welcome his release."

That seemed a merciful reason for turmoil and rejoicing. Besides, it sounded to her as if Pilate was in a merciful mood.

"Has the governor not yet returned?"

"I have not heard, my lady. But I have been in the kitchens since daybreak. From there I cannot see who comes and goes."

She sent another message, but the messenger brought back word that the governor was in private conference with the High Priest. Then in early afternoon she went down to the south garden. It was abandoned except for lone sentries at each of the towers. The running water was sorrowful in sound and the lilies were drooping. She was suddenly aware of close and intense heat. Out in the east, dark clouds boiled like a sandstorm up from the desert. As she looked lightning tore them, like the flashes of flame in her dream.

She hurried back by the climbing steps. Thunder was drumming steadily now, and darkness had spread to the zenith. As she reached the south door the wind swooped with black wings into the garden. Its roar was a furious background for the thunder's wild percussion. Looking over her shoulder she saw a pomegranate tree torn up by its roots and the lilies broken on their long stems and flattened against the ground.

She groped her way through the dark hall that was lit by the white pulse of lightning. A thunder crash so awful that it stunned her shook the whole palace. For moments she stood numb, then she made her way slowly on to the intersection of the west corridor. As she reached it the west door burst open with another explosion of sound.

Against the livid lightning outside figures of men were etched. Pilate was coming toward her while his guards fought to close the great door.

The lightning played so incessantly that she saw the awful fear on his face. He was crying out disjointed things.

"The Temple is struck by a thunderbolt! And I was passing as it fell. Jupiter meant to strike me!"

She stood still and watched him approach. He swayed, but he was not drunk.

Then the heavens were torn again by a noise too awful for ears to endure. The hall seemed full of white fire. She staggered and caught at the wall.

She saw Pontius Pilate fall at her feet. And then utter darkness closed on them. It was blacker than any night she had known. Through it she heard the thunder receding slowly with the sound of an army's chariot wheels on stone.

She could not see her own pale tunic. She felt arms catch her around the knees. They clung like a child's arms though they were Pilate's. Her husband's voice was no longer a man's voice. It was the cry of a soul in hell.

"Will you help me, my wife? I have only you. I am lost! For I have crucified a god!"

PART FOUR
Descent from Jerusalem

1

DESCENT by that long road was even steeper than Procla had imagined when she had looked out on the Judean hills from the north windows of Herod's house.

As she thought back upon it now, she and Pontius Pilate seemed to have been caught in an avalanche of disaster which was dragging them from heights to depths.

The fact that he, as Roman Governor of Judea, had permitted the awful deed which changed the course of his life only made his misfortune more bitter. To its regret and remorse were added the pangs of self-accusation and the formless terrors which now beset him.

The rest of their stay in Jerusalem had been like a time in delirium. He wished her with him at all times. He needed her beside him. She had been present when he was brought the news that the great stone had been rolled from the door of Christ's tomb. She had cried out: "In my dream the rising sun shone on an open tomb!"

Then she saw that his face was sick and his hands were shaking.

"Compose yourself," she advised him, "and answer these councilors. Remind them they had your permission to set a guard and they have only themselves to blame if that guard was lax. I was with you when you told them: '*Make the watch as sure as ye can.*' Throw it back now in their teeth, and show them that you are their master."

Her advice and presence had given him the manhood to do it. She rejoiced for him as he flung at them: "Why do you come to me? Did you set a guard so faithless that both men and officer slept? Or do you believe that this

man whom you made me let you kill has risen from the
dead, as he told you he would do?"

He had rallied himself for public appearance. In fact
he was sterner with the Jews than before. But alone with
her he kept repeating: "I did it for Rome, Claudia! Caiaphas said that the man must die!"

She did not add reproaches to the torture she saw him
enduring; but on the other hand she had no reassurance
for him.

"I had nothing against him—this man whom you think
the Messiah. When I saw him I was impressed by the
goodness on his face. I tried to save him. I swear it to
you!"

He caught at her hand and she did not withdraw it. But
he felt it cold and unresponsive in his clasp.

"I even sent him before Herod Antipas."

"Why did you do that?" she asked him. "You have yourself told me that Antipas has no power in Judea."

"I know! I know! But he has influence. Had he spoken
outright against the death penalty—which I hoped he
would do—the priests and the Pharisees might have
listened to him."

But Herod is weak, she thought, as you are. Like you,
he dared not take a stand. Aloud she said: "Antipas is
either a fool or a torturer, since he mocked true dignity
and kingship, which he himself lacks, with a purple robe
and a crown of thorns."

"You do not understand, Claudia! Antipas hoped, as I
did, that the sight of such punishment would satisfy the
mob. It is why I had him scourged. I told them he had
suffered enough."

He dropped her hand and put both his palms over his
eyes to shut out the sight.

"I tried to save him in more than one way. But he was
utterly fearless and refused to retract or deny. I had hoped
he would not claim he was king, since I knew that had

angered the councilors. But when I asked him the question he stood firm and answered: 'Thou sayest.'

"As he spoke, I almost believed it. He told me to my face: *'Everyone that is of the truth heareth my voice.'* It was then I asked him: *'What is truth?'* "

She shook her head slowly, remembering that Draco had said Pilate played with things like truth, things which were too great for him. If he had only been of the truth and opened his ears to that voice. . . .

"I gave him full benefit of a Roman trial. They had expected me to abide by the inquiry of the Jewish councilors and sentence him without further examination. But I demanded of them: "What accusation bring you against this man?"

"Did you then, in your formal Roman trial, find He had done such evil as to merit death?"

She was sorry as soon as she spoke, for she spoke in bitter sarcasm. She was trying to be kind to Pilate, for she saw that his suffering was real. The dreadful and wonderful events of three days had set a mark on her and brought out undeveloped traits of her character. In her ears still rang the remarkable words which Servius had told her were the dying words of that tortured man on the cross: *"Father, forgive them; for they know not what they do."*

She had always been fearless and honest but neither humble nor tender. Humility overwhelmed her at the thought of that great forgiveness. What right had she to blame her husband when Jesus Christ in His agony forgave him? Instead of blame, pity and tenderness filled her heart.

Pilate had cried out at her question.

"I found no fault in him! I told them so. I demanded to hear what evil he had done. You were not there, and you do not know how the people yelled around the judgment chair. They were determined to have his life."

"I know," she said sadly.

Since that terrible Sixth Day she had talked with Yod. She had sent for him. He had come and explained to her that the enemies of Jesus had laid their plans to seize Him and force trial and sentence before His friends could interfere. For they knew He had friends more powerful than the fisherman and artisans who left their tasks to follow Him. They knew He had friends in high places, but friends afraid to speak out. It all went back to hypocrisy, the one sin that He did not forgive. There was the great and intelligent Pharisee Nicodemus, who had visited Jesus and questioned Him. There was Joseph of Arimathea, who had voted in council against death.

But neither of these men had supported Jesus openly. To the surprise of the public and the indignation of the priests, Joseph of Arimathea had after the crucifixion come to Pilate and asked to be allowed to give the body of Jesus burial in one of his private tombs. Nicodemus had brought for its embalming one hundred pounds of priceless myrrh and aloes. But why had they and others not given Him open allegiance instead of waiting to give Him honorable burial after his martyrdom? Had His martyrdom been necessary to make them declare their belief? The answer was *yes*, and she was no better than they. She had been interested and strangely drawn to the Carpenter of Nazareth. Twice she had tried to go secretly to meet Him. But she had done nothing to help Him while he lived and worked. Not until He died on a cross had she been sure that He was God.

Pilate was crying out: "I tell you they howled! They howled around the tribunal as wild beasts howl for blood! Even so I might not have given in had they not shouted at me: *'If thou lettest this man go, thou art not Caesar's friend.'*"

That, she realized, was why he had sentenced Jesus to death. There had been no question of right or wrong in the mind of the Roman governor. He himself had said that he found no fault in the prisoner. But he had allowed political pressure to make him degrade his office. Caiaphas had been playing with him for years, like a cat with a mouse. The Jewish priests had a craft which no Roman could match. Caiaphas had beckoned in friendship and then shifted blame, as he had done in the matter of the money. But outside the garrison that day he had unsheathed his claws. That shout uttered by one of his supporters had practically told Pilate: If you release this man Caesar shall hear of it.

That threat had terrorized him into giving them their way. He did not wish Jesus to die. He was not a cruel man. The face and the voice of the Nazarene had made an impression upon him. He would have spared this prisoner if he could have done so without endangering his own career.

In the eyes of his wife that attitude was more contemptible than would have been an attitude of disapproval or hatred. Augustus' granddaughter could have sat in the judgment seat and sentenced any man she believed an impostor and criminal. But the yelling of all the mobs in Judea and the threats of all their leaders could not have made her sentence a man whom she thought innocent.

She had not said that to Pilate, and she would never say it. Her strange dream and the strange events which followed it had changed her. It was almost as if the Savior whom she had seen only in that dream had left her a legacy from His own inexhaustible mercy.

So she tried to give Pilate credit for the few points on which he had stood firm. She knew that he had refused to change the superscription on the cross. The centurion in charge had written *King of the Jews*. The priests, affronted, demanded that it be reworded *Who calls himself King of the Jews*. But by that time Pilate's anger and fear had hardened into the unmovable obstinacy of the weak.

They had made him inflict a felon's death upon a man whom he knew to be innocent. He had not the strength or courage to save Jesus; but he could at least insult all Jewry by leaving that legend above the head of the Crucified.

He was still trying to exonerate himself.

"It is the custom to set free some prisoner at the time of this feast. I remembered that and offered to release the Nazarene. But the crowd shook their fists and yelled: 'Give us Bar-Abbas!'"

She looked at him with pity, but a pity mixed with contempt—and he saw it in her eyes although she refrained from speaking.

He cried again, as he had cried in the darkness of the palace while storm and earthquake shook the walls and opened the graves of Jerusalem: "Claudia, stay beside me! I tell you, *I washed my hands!*"

2

THE unrest and rioting during that Passover kept the
Roman Legion busy. More than a million people were
in or around the city. Those who could not get housing
inside its walls camped on the hills just outside. To the
tension always present at a great public occasion were
added strange whispers about the Nazarene's death. Men
who had not known Him or before taken sides about Him
now stated their views aloud, and defended those views
with stones and sticks. Rumor had hold on the populace.
Many claimed to have seen dead men walking the streets
in their shrouds during the tempest and earthquake.
When others reminded them that darkness had been so
complete they could not have distinguished living men's
robes from shrouds, the argument progressed to a fight.

Procla stayed in the palace and got her news from
Talitha.

The disciples, who had scattered and hidden, were now
finding each other. They were only human. They had not
their Master's courage to face arrest and death by torture.
Many of them were unlearned and, like Roman ruler and
Jewish councilors, could not yet see the difference between a worldly kingdom and God's kingdom. It came to
them with a numbing shock that God's Son could suffer
and die. Until the last they had hoped for a miracle to
save Him, being blind to the greater miracle of His willing
sacrifice. Had He called on them, they could have stirred
a revolution to rescue Him. They knew that the country
was seething with threat of it. But they did not stop to

ponder that Jesus knew it too and submitted to a hurried death rather than incite men further.

Mark told Talitha this and many other things. There was even a theory that Judas Iscariot had not meant Jesus to die. A few said that he meant to confound the enemies of Jesus by forcing Him, when faced with arrest, to free Himself by a miracle.

Few believed that, and Procla did not. She did not even believe it when a pale-faced Talitha led her one morning to a blossoming tree in the garden. Its tiny, delicate buds clung to the still-bare twigs like snow.

"Judas who betrayed the Master was found at sunrise hanged on a tree of this kind outside the walls."

"Was he murdered?" Procla asked her. "Or did he commit suicide?"

"He took his own life. All men shunned him. Even the priests reviled him, Mark says. He tried to give back to them the blood money, and they drove him away."

"Poor creature," said Procla.

There had been a time when she would not have been so gentle in judgment.

"But, my lady—"

Talitha stopped, and Procla looked at her.

"One of the men who found him told my cousin John Mark that on the tree where he was found the flowers had turned purple-red."

"It is probable," said Procla, "that the tree blooms different colors, like the tree in this garden called 'Rose of Sharon.'"

Talitha shook her smooth, dark head.

"I have seen it all my life, and never yet seen one whose flowers were not white. People are saying those blossoms were stained by blood and shame. They are already speaking of it as the 'Judas Tree.'"

Later Pilate asked her if she had heard the story.

"Yes, I have heard it," she told him calmly; "but I do not believe all the idle gossip I hear."

"Neither do I," he agreed, a little too loudly.

There were times when he rallied and took that attitude. But his wife realized that it was as sad a symptom as were his fits of self-abasement and fear. One mood evinced as clearly as the other the anguish of his uncertainty. For he was still uncertain, in spite of that cry wrung from him in the dark of the palace hall. At times he shivered with the fear that he had crucified a god: a god like the pagan gods he knew, who would surely exact revenge. At other times, upheld by the crutch of wine, he strutted in a vain attempt to regain authority and tried to justify himself with loud and hollow speech.

But Augustus' granddaughter was no longer uncertain. In her childhood she had first heard of the Messianic prophecy. Lalibela had brought it from what was known as the "uttermost ends of the earth" to an island of exile in a periwinkle sea. Lalibela had returned to her in a dream upon the eve of the Messiah's martyrdom. She, Procla, had failed to save Him by her message to Pilate. But she had tried. She reminded herself of that and tried to take comfort in it. How could she have saved Him when His death was already forecast? About that she wondered. The Hebrew prophets had foretold it all, long centuries before an angel appeared to a Jewish maiden in Galilee. Among the sages who had arrived at Bethlehem on the night of the Christ Child's birth had been a prince of Egypt spoken of as Balthazar. His gift had shown that he had read the whole story in the stars. While others brought gold as tribute to the King, and incense symbolic of God's Son, the astrologer from Egypt brought a gift for the Martyr: that priceless resin known as myrrh, the reddish, aromatic gum which was used to embalm the dead.

Talitha knew all this, and Talitha had told Procla.

For thirty-six hours after the crucifixion, they and the others who loved Jesus Christ had remained suspended in a kind of sustained horror. Then had come the message of that Sunday morning. To Procla it brought no surprise, only a great wonder and a still, sweet certainty from long fear and doubt and hope.

The horror of Christ's followers was mixed with a real terror. They knew that the priests wished to exterminate Him and His teaching. In spite of the dissent of Nicodemus in council, Caiaphas had swung the vote for death by an immense majority. Now the priests could and would continue to destroy them. Rumors of Christ's resurrection made their foes more savage. The priests lacked heart; but they did not lack brain in regard to their own advantage. A man who had courage to submit to unjustified and tortured death, along with the power to rise from that death and appear to reliable witnesses, was a threat to their corrupt system.

Torn with horror and fear, the disciples remained in hiding. Talitha told Procla that some were still within the city walls. A few would gather that night at Mary Mark's house, and Talitha suggested that she and her mistress meet with them.

When they arrived two women sat with the mother of young John Mark. One was the wife of Cleopas, himself a follower of Christ. One was younger, with red-gold hair and a thin, white, staring face.

Talitha cried out at sight of her. "Mary of Magdala, I have been told that it was you who came first to His tomb!"

The thin-faced woman with fiery hair looked around with that fixed, fanatical gaze.

"Cleopas' wife was with me." Her voice was no more than a whisper. "So were Joanna and Salome. But I was so anxious I ran ahead. The stone was aside and the tomb vacant."

Talitha explained to Procla afterward that Mary of Magdala always ran ahead in life without taking thought. It was that unthinking recklessness which had caused her own village to look askance upon her. But Christ had looked deep into the heart of the red-haired girl, and had seen her longing for truth and goodness. He had healed her of the hysterical attacks in which her high-strung body and mind took refuge. Since then she had followed Him with the selfless and disregarding zeal of the visionary.

"Let us pray," said Mary the widow of Mark.

They kneeled on the rough limestone floor, and Procla heard them repeating words which had been spoken by the man who died on Golgotha.

The two older Marys were calm and sure. Talitha glowed like a lighted lamp. Mary of Magdala's hair escaped in burning locks from her dark head shawl, making her rapt white face look even paler.

It was she who remained on her knees when Mary Mark's prayer was finished. She looked around her with great smudged eyes which might have been green or blue or gray.

"The Lord is risen," she said in that faint, hysterical whisper. "What does it matter if we who love Him must suffer persecution and death?"

She threw out her arms, and her loosed head shawl released the mass of her blazing hair. It made Procla think of sacrificial flames. Were these men and women who loved Jesus, she wondered, to be victims of the same hate which had sacrificed Him?

"I am His to do with as he will," said Mary of Magdala. "What is there to fear from Roman or Jew? Jesus Christ has taught us that death has no victory."

Cleopas' wife and Talitha raised her up and soothed her. Mary Mark's words were practical.

"There is His work to carry on; but to do so we must

live. Both Roman and Jew are determined now to kill those who teach His precepts. Caution will better serve us than boast of fearlessness."

She looked gravely at Pilate's wife.

"Talitha should not have brought you here. You endanger yourself and your husband. It is even possible that spies may follow you; for it is known that you pleaded with the Roman to spare Our Lord."

"Perhaps you are right," said Procla. "I shall not come again. But I ask you whenever you meet together, to feel that I am with you; for I shall be with you in heart. I must go back the way I came, but I can carry remembrance. Wherever I go now and whatever befalls me, I will have faith in Jesus Christ and will serve Him in what way I can."

3

ALTHOUGH he had at last succeeded in transferring the governor's residence to Jerusalem, Pilate's restlessness now drew him back to Caesarea.

One place was to Procla the same as another. Talitha kept her informed of the movements of Christ's followers. They had organized and vowed to carry on His ministry. Already the men had scattered to teach in different places. The women worked too, and in spite of persecution their ranks were increasing. Talitha wished to stay in Jerusalem with them, but Mary Mark advised against it.

"You can better help us by being with the Roman governor's wife. He is half mad. In spite of remorse, he sets his soldiers on us."

"My lady tries to stop him. I heard him shrieking at her that if he could wipe from the earth all memory of Jesus Christ, it would prove He was not a god and would remove all guilt from those who had brought about His death."

Mary Mark nodded.

"The Lady Claudia is truly one of us. She will warn us by means of you if any new danger is afoot. That is one reason for you to stay with her. Another is that she is the loneliest woman I have known."

So Talitha stayed; and with her help Procla endured three years spent in vain journeyings between seaport and capital.

Infrequently Servius brought her letters from Draco. His leave from the Legion had been revoked after the Crucifixion. Palestine was even more in need of Roman

265

protection. His cavalry was deployed in desert fighting for the ruler he despised.

It suited Procla at first to wait. She did not wish to leave Pilate yet. His distress still tore at her heart and she tried at once to comfort him and to make him stop having the Christians hunted down. A strange and new feeling had hold on her since she had dreamed a dream and had kneeled in the house of Mark. Although she was certain that her husband had allowed the priests to make him crucify the Son of the True God, pity and gentleness grew in her heart instead of hatred for him.

She hoped that at Caesarea they could settle down again, and she could comfort and strengthen him before she left him for Draco. There had been no faltering in her love for Draco. But Jesus' teaching had given her a perspective different from her former pagan point of view. It had taught her to make love subservient to duty.

However, at that first year's end the Procurator of Judea seemed to have regained health and mental stability. I must be honest, she told herself. I must tell him what I am planning. So she sent Talitha to ask him to come to her apartment.

She went directly to the point. "Will you give me a divorce? I wish—and intend—to marry Andrus Draco."

His pale eyes seemed to protrude as they fixed their stare upon her. His fleshy face became the reddish-purple hue of the Judas bud. For the moment she feared that he was going to fall in a fit. Then he began to shout.

"So you have both been deceiving me! I was right to send him to battle. I had hoped that he would by now have died in the desert!"

"Lower your voice—unless you wish the servants to know your private affairs. Neither Draco nor I have deceived you. It is you who deceived us, long ago in Rome. You know that I never loved you but I had to stay with you. Since it had to be, I have tried to uphold the dignity of your office—and to help you when you were suffering."

He paused, scowling at her. But he was still proud rather than ashamed of the means which had gained his end.

"I will not divorce you! Draco cannot take you. Tiberius will uphold me. If you go to your lover I shall see that he is destroyed!"

She knew that he could do it with the Emperor on his side. She said coldly: "You had better go now. But I ask you to think it over. If you persist in holding me I shall not disgrace you. But I ask you now to leave my apartment and never again to set foot in it."

He went. But he took his revenge by never again even alluding to the matter of Draco.

Months passed, and Servius brought another letter. Draco told her his company was due a rest and there was a chance it might be replaced. If so, their summer quarters would be at Jerusalem. He would confront Pilate and demand her divorce. Although the Emperor was Pilate's friend, the great Legate of Syria was Draco's friend. He could and would protect them if she left Pilate and returned to Damascus with him. There she could remain under the Legate's care until Pilate saw reason and released her.

But before she had time to reply there came from Rome a letter which drove Pilate into frenzy. Tiberius was ill and suffering. Rome's doctors could not help him. But he had heard tales of a master physician in Judea: of a man named Jesus who healed when other physicians failed. He charged his governor in that province to send Jesus the Healer at once to Rome.

The demand threw Pilate back into terror as well as remorse. He sought his usual solace of wine. More excited by it he made Procla listen again to all that was tormenting him. She kept her bargain and argued with him. But each time the past overtook him, he lost ground. His horrors increased and were enhanced by imagination and drink.

She reminded him that the Emperor must be answered at once, and she urged him to send to Tiberius a detailed account of the trial and execution of Jesus. He did so. After it was done she saw that the writing had eased him a little. He took up his normal way of life, and he seemed to be trying to administer his office fairly.

She was glad for herself as well as for him. I can leave him now, she thought.

But trouble in the Judean desert had spread to Syria. Vitellius, the Legate of Syria, because he was a friend of Draco and because he knew the tribune's military ability, made an especial request for him and his division. It suited Pilate to accede. He told her of it mockingly. Both he and she realized that there would now be no chance for Andrus Draco to return on leave to Judea.

Procla was distracted from her grief by Talitha. The girl returned one night from her brother's house with news of an uprising in Samaria, hereditary enemy of Judea.

"The men of that nation are flocking to the village of Tirathaba. They have been told that the holy vessels used by Moses are hidden among rocks or buried in the earth on Mount Gerizim. In their error they still hold out that Moses stood on Gerizim."

"Can it be true?" the Roman woman asked her.

Could the great lawgiver, of whom she had first heard from Lalibela, have left physical evidence on a mountain which she had often passed and seen in traveling?

"I do not know. But the Samaritans claim to have proof in records set down by the hand of Aaron's great-grandson. One of their leaders has now offered to show them that evidence."

Gerizim was on the highway to Jerusalem. Jewish

leaders complained to the governor that mobs were forming on that road and obstructing traffic. Pilate, in his uncertainty, took it to be a chance to show authority and
reinstate himself. He ordered horsemen and footmen to
hold the roads and prevent the pilgrims from ascending
the mountain. But some of the pilgrims were armed, and
all were fanatically determined to reach their goal. No
one was ever able to say who struck the first blow, but
fighting broke out at once. Once started, the Roman
soldiers finished by slaughtering not only those who opposed them but many of the crowd waiting in the village
below.

Pilate's rage at defiance of his authority was so great
that he ordered survivors pursued and slain, and prisoners
put to death.

When Procla heard, she bolted her door and sat with
her face in her hands.

But when the Samaritan messenger reached Vitellius,
Legate of Syria and ruler of all the East, he acted without delay. He put Marcellus in charge of Judea, and ordered Pontius Pilate to Rome to stand trial for what he
had done.

4

PROCLA was so horrified by Pilate's brutality that she
could not regret their recall. She knew that if he stayed
in Judea he would only repeat his mistakes. It was better
for them to go and for him to suffer his punishment, rather
than leave him to inflict suffering on innocent people. It
would take her farther from Draco, she realized. But although she loved him even more, it was now a love that
could wait. The Messiah's skirts had brushed her as He
passed on His way, and that touch had given her strength
for abnegation of self before a greater need.

Talitha wept at the parting but would not leave Judea.
"As you know, my lady, Jesus has appeared to His followers more than once. He has told them to carry on His
work by preaching and teaching."

Procla knew that and knew it was best for Talitha to
stay. The number of Jesus' followers was now increasing
fast. Many too careless or fearful to attend Him during
His life now declared themselves openly. Many who had
not been able to believe while He lived had learned by
His death that He was God. In their eyes Procla had seen
the light she first saw in Talitha's eyes. She felt in their
presence a return of that great certainty and perfect peace
which had wrapped itself like a garment around her when
she had been brought word of His resurrection.

Her own lines were cast in different ways and she must
leave Judea. She knew that she faced a hard road, but she
carried His help in her heart.

As she was going aboard ship Draco's courier rode up.

Servius brought her the letter. It said: *I will follow and find you.*

Now she and Pilate were again in the house near the Temple of Vesta. Pride had sustained him during the slow journey. Over and over again he had told her that Tiberius was his friend. But even before they left the ship the centurion informed them that Tiberius had died under strange circumstances and young Gaius Caesar was Emperor of Rome.

Centurion and imperial guard escorted them to the house. They knew, as all Romans knew, what that escort could mean. The Praetorians were often used as a guard of honor. They also arrested persons charged with political crimes. Two of them were still stationed just outside the entrance. So Procla knew that Gaius had received the legate's report and that she and Pilate were under surveillance.

She knew that surveillance was often the prelude to prison. So she tried to remember all she could of the young cousin now on the throne. She had seen him a few times when he was a boy, but Rome had seen little of him. He was the youngest son of Germanicus and had spent most of his life in camps with his soldier father. There he was said to have worn a miniature uniform and to have been petted and spoiled by the legionaries. In childhood he had been proud of the nickname they gave him: Caligula, or Little Boots. Now he had rejected it and announced his title as Gaius Caesar Augustus Germanicus.

She knew practically nothing of him, but she did know that a pattern was being repeated, whether for good or for ill. Her mind went back to the time when she had come to Rome to find Augustus gone and Tiberius in his place. Now she had arrived with a husband instead of a tutor and found a cousin, a little younger than herself, instead of the Emperor Pilate expected to find.

The effect upon him was dreadful. Until now she had not realized how sure he had been of Tiberius' favor. He began drinking at once, and railing against misfortune.

"Tiberius would have cleared my name and reinstated me. How can I put my case to a man who is self-willed and half mad?"

She was surprised, for she had heard no wrong of this younger cousin. The fact that many of her old friends had already come to see her told her that he had not yet condemned her or Pilate in his mind. Rome was overjoyed at his accession, and Rome was doing whatever its citizens thought he would wish.

"Mad?" she asked incredulously, in answer to Pilate's words. "The people love him, and they rejoice that he is not like Tiberius. I have heard that he was his father's favorite, as well as favorite of the legionaries."

"Oh, yes! I saw him in camp, dressed like a monkey performing in a theater and strutting like a cock. The game he enjoyed most was catching insects or small animals and watching them writhe as he tore them slowly apart."

She was horrified; for that foretold some awful and deep-seated cruelty. But she knew that Pilate's status, and perhaps her own status, were uncertain and dangerous.

She made up her mind that she would do this last thing for her husband. It was possible that she could win Gaius. Pilate, shaky with drink and prejudiced, would only injure his own cause. So she requested an audience with the Emperor, reminding him that she was Augustus' granddaughter and his own cousin. It was granted after a few weeks.

She found him both attractive and easy to approach. He called her cousin and told her that he remembered her well.

"I came to Rome for my father's triumph; but the old

dragon Livia, who was your grandmother and mine too, made my father and Tiberius forbid me to ride in it."

She owed Livia nothing. "Our grandmother was stern. Why did she treat you so unkindly?"

He smiled with pure joy at a memory. "Do you recall a small steel-gray kitten by which she set much store?"

Procla remembered it. She had been kind to it, although she had no especial fondness for cats.

"I squeezed it and it bit me. So I threw it out of the window to a gazelle hound an Arab prince had given me in the East."

Procla tried not to shiver. The kitten was long since devoured. She must keep calm and work for Pilate's reinstatement and her own escape.

"From childhood," said Gaius, "I lived in camp with soldiers, and saw death and blood. You know my father's record. You must know of mine too, Claudia?"

"I know, my cousin," she answered dutifully. "I have found that you are admired and loved in Rome. Hearing such good of you gave me hope you would understand my husband's case."

He swallowed flattery as his hound had swallowed kittens.

"I soldiered in the East and saw its barbarous people. Vitellius writes that your husband is a butcher. But I can understand that Jews and Samaritans might have tried a governor beyond human endurance."

He looked at her and she bowed her head. She did not know what to say. Priests and politicians had tried Pilate sorely; but the populace had been innocent, and they were the ones he had injured.

"However, Vitellius will not keep him in the East, and I have no reason to keep him in Rome."

His eyes roved from her face to her feet. She thought of the kitten and wondered if it had felt as she did.

"But, cousin," he said, "I would like to keep *you* in Rome."

This is worse than Pilate, she thought. Have I failed again? Have I lost my happiness with Draco for nothing? Is the wretched man whom I am trying to help going to be sent alone to banishment and slow death?

But her voice was cool and composed as she answered Gaius.

"You are kind, and already I feel as if you were my brother. But I asked this audience to beg mercy for my husband."

"There is no hurry to decide," he told her carelessly.

But the sly, eager gleam in his eyes told her he was enjoying her distress and uncertainty.

She was afraid to insist. She rose. "Cousin, I thank you. May I go now? And may I go in the hope and expectation that your decision will show mercy to Pilate, who is a sick man?"

"Pilate is fortunate," he said, "to have both a wife such as you and a friend such as the tribune Andrus Draco to plead his case."

That surprised her so that she stopped, gazing at him with a new apprehension.

He laughed aloud. "Or is it that Andrus Draco is your friend?"

She chose her words carefully. "The tribune was Pilate's friend before I knew either of them. But he has been a good friend to me too."

"He is my friend, and a soldier—as I am," boasted Gaius. "I trust his judgment, so I shall do as he asks. I have had a dispatch from him saying he is on his way to Rome and begging me to wait and allow him to talk with me before I pass judgment on Pontius Pilate, accused of misgovernment, and Pontius Pilate's wife the Lady Claudia."

He rose too and put a thick, hairy arm around her, as he walked with her toward the door.

"What I decide about Pilate still hangs in the balance. But for yourself, you need have no fear of banishment, beautiful cousin."

5

DRACO followed his letter quickly. He went to Pilate's house directly as he disembarked, and he demanded to see Pilate as well as Procla. The ex-governor of Judea approached him with an uncertain smile.

"You are generous to come to my help, my friend Andrus Draco."

"I am not your friend," said Draco. "Has the Emperor given you a trial yet?"

Pilate dropped the hand he had raised in salute. The other two saw that it trembled and clawed at his toga.

"Not yet. But he told his cousin, my wife—that is, I still have reason to hope." His voice broke. "Andrus Draco, I hoped you had come to help me!"

"I have come to try to help you by sparing you death or disgrace. But I tell you here and now that I have come to take the woman I love away from you."

Pilate's face flushed. He tried to speak. But the soldier continued harshly. "Do not waste your breath in telling me that I take you at a disadvantage. I know now that you lied about me to Tiberius, in order both to get her for wife and to get your appointment in Judea. I shall ask Gaius to spare you; but I shall also ask him to grant her a divorce and allow her to marry me."

Pilate's face was a crumpled mask of terror and uncertainty. He looked at Procla. "Will you leave me? Do you love him?"

"I have always loved him," she said. "You know it. I never deceived you."

"I do not wish to die," he said. His voice was thin with fear. "But I cannot live without you, Claudia!"

"If you live at all," Draco told him, "you will live without her."

"Wait," she begged. "It is more than you think—more than any man's love for any woman. It is that remorse has tortured him since the crucifixion of Jesus the Christ. I have tried to help him, because I know that Jesus Christ preached forgiveness."

Draco stared hard at her and his eyes were uneasy.

"Are you mad enough to have become a follower of this Jew? Do you not know that both Rome and Judea are trying to stamp out his following?"

"I know," she said. "But I know He is God and I am not afraid to own Him. Did you not witness the events that followed His crucifixion? Has any one of the Roman gods lived as a man and suffered for men, and after men killed him risen from death and appeared to those who knew him?"

"I was not at Golgotha. They killed the man unjustly. He was good, but I have no proof that he rose from death." He paused and frowned, then continued honestly. "But this I know: there was a guard at the tomb—a guard of veteran soldiers who would not have neglected a watch."

Both had forgotten Pilate. He moaned aloud as he listened.

She was gazing at Draco without words. I love him so deeply, she thought. Before I knew of this Jesus Christ I was ready to go to his arms, as either his wife or his woman. Now there is a chasm between us. I love him. I shall always love him. But we can never be truly one unless he believes in my Savior.

"I have never held by the gods of Rome," he reminded her. "I am a Stoic. I believe that a man should be a man: self-sufficient and unafraid of either life or death. When the time comes that he can no longer be so, he has the right to end his own life. His only immortality is the reputation he leaves."

She shook her head. "Until Jesus came it was bravest and cleanest of our creeds. But do you not see what He offers us and what you are rejecting?"

She moved close to him, her pale face flushed and her eyes starlike with earnestness. "Have you never felt, Draco, that about you there is something more than muscle and bone? If I was no more to you than a body to clasp and a mouth to kiss, would you have waited so long for me? There are other women fairer."

He said stubbornly: "I made up my mind long years ago to have you. I tell you I am not yet sure about this Jesus of Nazareth. And I tell you to be silent about your belief in him. It will not help Pilate's case with Gaius if Gaius knows you are of a faith that his legionaries are hunting down."

Then he had gone, and all they could do was to wait for days in hope and fear. She tried to keep Pilate from drinking too much, but she had to pity his plight. In spite of Gaius' welcome to her, he had given her no assurance.

Morning, noon and night she said the prayers she had learned from Mary Mark. She thought of her dream. Already some of its scenes had become reality. She recalled that in it she had seen Roman soldiers arresting and leading Jesus' followers to death. Draco had ordered her not to speak of her belief in Jesus. But she felt that she could not deny Him—not even for fear of death.

When Draco returned she was waiting for him, tense with anxiety. He looked around the hall. "Where is Pilate?"

"He is so—so unnerved by suspense that I fear he could not discuss the matter with you. Will you tell me, and let me tell him the outcome?"

"He is drunk," said Draco bluntly.

She did not deny it. He looked at her, longing to take her in his arms and with his strength protect her from her own strength. He knew that she was trying to stand— slender, unselfish, unfrightened—between Pontius Pilate and the shock of the Emperor's verdict. It angered him, and yet it made him love her even more. He did not want a woman who was soft and weak and selfish. He was strong enough to deal with one whom he could look up to as well as love.

"He is drunk," he repeated, "and you are trying to shield him. But his absence simplifies matters. They need simplification; for a complication which I did not expect has arisen."

She put a hand to her throat and stared at him with unhappy eyes.

His own eyes blazed. "Why did you not tell me? What did that mad beast say—or do—to you?"

"Nothing," she whispered. "I swear that he did no more than say that he admired me—and put an arm around me."

"He admires you so much that before I could mention the matter of your divorce and marriage to me, he said that no cousin of his should remain the wife of a man disgraced and demoted. He added that although a cousin, you were not close enough to him for a tie between him and you to offend Rome's consanguinity laws."

"Gaius is mad," she said, "as mad as Tiberius was. I cannot think he really wants me."

"He wants you," said Draco frankly, "but not for his Empress."

"I loathe him! What can we do? What will he do to Pilate?"

"At my suggestion he will send Pilate away. I suggested it before I discovered his feelings toward you. When he spoke as he did about you, I reminded him that you were a Julio-Claudian and accustomed to respect. He fancies himself the Sun-god, and he likes to visit the South. I told him that if he gave your husband some small post in southern Gaul, he could keep an eye on you and even visit you there."

He caught her in his arms and hard against him. "I argued and flattered, when all I wished was to use my dagger on him! Oh, for Augustus to save Rome! She is going the road of empires. But you and I will escape, Procla. I can take you where Rome cannot reach us. Go quickly and quietly to the South with Pilate now. As soon as I have done Vitellius' errands here, I will come to you wherever you are. But go now, before Gaius changes his mind!"

She put her arms around his neck and clasped him as closely.

"I will go, and I shall be waiting for you while I try to help Pilate find his way. And my love—my only love— I will do whatever you ask throughout life if you will but give me the chance to make you believe in the Savior I love!"

6

IN the sunlands of the South Pilate fought for his sanity.
Like a child who glances behind him at some imagined
terror, he said to Procla, "I feel safe here." She saw he
was trying not to drink and to do all he could to please
her. But she felt each word and action binding her to
him with the cords of her pity and of his need.

Her heart ached with longing for Draco. That meeting
with him in Rome had not only shown her she needed
him but had stirred her love so long held in leash. She
kept telling herself he would come soon, and that by the
time he did she would have helped Pilate back to self-
reliance.

She saw at once that this appointment in southern Gaul
was a sinecure. They were in Nemausus, a settlement of
Roman veterans, and she felt that with Draco she could
have been happy there. It was a town of importance, with
aqueduct, public baths and temple.

But Pilate did not share her interest in the place. It
gave him only a brief asylum from his torment. The restlessness of a lost soul seemed to drive him on. He tried
to persuade both himself and her that his errand in
Nemausus was done.

"I am no longer needed here. I have delivered in person
the Emperor's messages and have sent their answers with
my report back to him. It is time for us to go on."

So they moved to the city on a lake which was capital
of Rome's earliest Gallic colony.

There was the residence of the proconsul, and there
the Roman fleet was frequently in port. For months Pilate

managed to busy himself. Then Procla saw the signs that she recognized too well. He could not sleep. He began once more to drink for a false forgetfulness.

This time she suggested the change before he did.

"Perhaps you could be of more service to Rome in Massalia. The proconsul is here; there he has no authority."

He brightened at the hope of some work to absorb him. . . .

Pilate's villa in Massalia stood on a rock overlooking the purple harbor. Wind from the three islands which had known Phoenicia's sails blew its soft salt through the shrubs and plants of their garden. The wharves below were busy with shipping from Egypt and Greece and Rome. There was nothing to remind her of a cross on a rocky hill—nothing except her heart which heard young John Mark quoting: ". . . *is faithful in that which is least. . . .*"

The moon rode full on that silver night when Servius brought her the letter. She went directly to Pilate and told him.

"Draco is coming for me, and I am going with him."

He looked at her in silence. When he spoke his voice was hopeless.

"I shall not try to keep you. You deserve a better fate."

"If you really mean that, will you try to regain your self-control and rebuild your life?"

"I will try. But I know that for me this is the end, Claudia."

He pulled himself together and begged her to go into the garden with him. Together they walked down steps cut in the stone from the terrace on which they had stood. On a shelf which gave level space was a half-moon seat of pink marble. As they sat, branches drooped blooms above their heads from trees that had root in the crannies.

He called the steward to bring wine, and he sent for the sand diviner.

The man came: an Arab, hostile as a hawk. He spilled the bright sand from his box and it glittered like gems in the moonbeams.

"What does the Roman wish to know?"

All of a sudden she feared this. It was no longer a game. She remembered Lalibela's hints of unknown abominations. What if something could break its way through that veil between life and death? She slipped her hand into Pilate's hand.

"Let us go. I do not wish to hear him."

"But I must hear," said Pilate.

He gulped his wine and drained the last drop from the pitcher into his cup. His mouth was twisted into a smile, but his eyes were not smiling.

"You will be gone and I alone," he said. "Why should I not know my fate?"

The wind eddied and built the sand up to a small peak. Servius had gone for more wine. The Arab spoke suddenly.

"You will not be alone in life. The woman will be with you until death."

She shivered and drew her cloak closer. The wind was cold, although it was spring and she felt the buds of the low limbs behind her caress her face. Pilate was already drunk. He laughed, and the sound was dreadful.

"You have made your first mistake," he said. "It would serve you right if I had you flogged."

The man squatted in the moonglare, and his hunched shadow fell behind him.

"You will have nobody flogged," he said. His voice was impersonal. "I have made no mistake, Roman; but you have made your last."

Something held Procla too frozen to resent his insolence. The wind blew stronger. She was watching the small hill of sand. Under her eyes it toppled and slid in a miniature avalanche.

"Although you climb mountains," the Arab said, "your road will go always down."

Servius came and set the pitcher refilled with wine on the marble. But neither of them saw it. They looked at the sand diviner.

"Where will this road that goes up and yet down lead me?" asked Pilate mockingly.

"To the donkey's head," said the Arab.

The bright sand moved in the moonlight.

Pilate threw out his arms angrily. He struck and upset the pitcher. The red wine ran on his hands and robes, but he did not notice it.

"You speak in riddles! Your own head is a donkey's head. Get you gone, fool!"

He waved his hand—and in that bright light he saw that it was crimson.

He screamed, and struggled to get to his feet.

"Claudia, there is blood on my hands!"

"Be still," she told him. "It is only wine. You overturned the pitcher."

He held them out before him.

"Blood on my hands," he moaned. "And the River Rhone and the Lion Gulf are not enough to wash them clean!"

The sand diviner had not gone. He spoke from where he still squatted.

"But there is a lake which will wash them," he said. "You are on your way to it."

Procla turned on him like a tigress. He rose and backed away.

"Leave this place at once," she said. "I will order you flogged, if the Lord Pilate does not."

She saw his eyes glitter, but he did not speak. His dark

shadow moved away with him, and it moved no more silently.

She turned to Pilate, and saw that he had lost all self-control. He was crouched on the bench and tearing twigs from the tree above it to wipe his hands. He rubbed them so hard that he tore the skin and his own blood mixed with the wine stains. He threw broken stems and flowers away from him as he used them.

Then he saw them in the full moonlight—and he screamed more terribly.

"What is it?" she asked him.

He tried to speak and choked. He could only point where the twigs lay.

"They are merely boughs from this tree," she said. "Come with me, back to the villa."

"It is the Judas tree," he screamed. "The tree on which the Iscariot died! I am damned; and nothing can save me and no waters can wash my hands! Look at it, Claudia! Look at it! People say that its flowers were white. Look at them lying before you! Now they are red as blood!"

7

WHEN he was himself again she reasoned with him. "I have questioned the old gardener. He knows the flora of this country."

"What help is his knowledge? You saw, as I did, that the buds of the tree were red."

"I saw they were red. They are still red. They have always been red."

"What are you trying to tell me, Claudia?"

"I am trying to tell you that the gardener has lived all his life in this land. Year after year he has seen that tree bloom, and always its blossoms were red."

"What of the one in Judea then? They said that Judas Iscariot . . ."

His voice trailed off, but his eyes held a gleam of hope.

"They said many things, Pilate; and they will say even more. You, yourself, are not unfamiliar with gossip."

He nodded. His eyes were eager now.

"Is it unnatural that about this Messiah such legends should grow? He did not ask for them. His life was clean and pure and full of common sense. But legends will grow, even about mortals like you and me."

"You think then it is a lie about the same tree blossoming white?"

"No. I saw it blossoming white in the palace garden. But there I also saw the Rose of Sharon bloom different colors. I think this tree blooms red or white according to the soil in which it feeds. The gardener tells me that plants often draw color from minerals deep in the earth.

But he insists that here it is known as the 'Red-bud' because it has always blossomed red."

He seemed to understand and he tried to be reassured. But she saw the veins in his temples twitch, and his cheeks were flushed with fever.

"I am not worth your kindness," he told her humbly. "I could not in this trouble have done without your help. But I know now that I am not worthy of you. I will not try to keep you. I will let you divorce me. You believe me; do you not, Claudia?"

She believed him; for she saw before her now the ghost of a man's self-confidence and aggressiveness. He had been large and full-bodied. Now he was thin and pale as wax, and he started at sudden sounds.

When she was not with him he would walk down the broad thoroughfare that led to the wharves. He would follow the curve of the water front, keeping always close to the sea. Water seemed at once to fascinate and terrify him. More than once she had sent Servius to follow and watch over him. The steward came back and reported that the one-time Procurator of Judea stopped as he walked on rocks or beach to wash his hands in the waves.

She knew that she must get him away from Massalia. A letter from the proconsul gave the opportunity. Rome was interested in the salt trade and wished a report on the salt pans of the Rhone delta.

It roused Pilate to a gleam of hope for usefulness and importance.

"I shall go into the dead seas and inspect the pans and the scrapers."

He looked at her and spoke wistfully.

"Will you go with me this last time? Or do you prefer to await him here?"

Draco had written that he would not arrive for a month or more. Pilate had promised to release her. She could repay him by this kindness before she went from him.

She knew that he not only dreaded to be alone, but that he might do something ill-advised without her.

"I will go with you. I do not need a maid, but let us take Servius."

Servius had become the mainstay of her strange and difficult life. He was strong and quiet and dignified, and he dealt with Pilate tactfully and kindly. But at the same time she knew that Draco had his love and loyalty. There was also between her and the veteran the bond of a faith different from that of all others around them.

The village they were seeking lay at the mouth of the Little Rhone, at that point where the dead seas met living sea. It was too small to have a name. It was merely a settlement of a score of huts built of reeds to shelter the families of fishermen and salt scrapers. She and Pilate were offered the largest and best. It was roofed by an overturned boat, and from it emerged a black-haired woman and a cluster of gypsylike children. But in spite of the woman's imperious gesture of invitation, Procla refused to accept it.

"Tell her," she instructed a guard, "that I thank her, but that my couch is prepared in the baggage wagon."

Pilate inspected the salt pans next day, and returned in better humor.

"I find that these scrapers are telling the truth. I shall report that to the proconsul. If anyone has lied, it is his tax gatherer. Servius checked them as I did."

So much better did Pilate seem that Procla dared suggest they return to Massalia. Flushed with the success of his inspection, Pilate agreed. But as they neared the city, his nervousness increased and before nightfall Procla knew they would have to wander on once more. Behind his locked door Procla heard him toss and moan throughout the long night, and he emerged in the morning pale and shaken, his eyes red from wine and sleeplessness. He was determined to depart with daybreak. He rode in silence: putty-faced, with slack jaw and staring eyes. When they reached the Grand Rhone he told her: "I will not go back to Massalia."

"Where then will you go?"

"I do not know. I think that all earth rejects me."

She put a hand on his shoulder, and she felt him trembling.

"Do not encourage mad fancies. If you fear Jesus' power, you should realize it is great enough to grant you forgiveness. Throw yourself on His mercy. He is kind and merciful."

"But I was not merciful to Him! It is for that I am accurst. I had hoped that He was an impostor, so I might be free of blame. I know now that He is a great god; for retribution pursues me."

It was a terrible choice for her. Draco must even then be on his way to Massalia. He was coming with her assurance that she would be divorced and would marry him. She knew his temper and pride—and loved him more for what he was. If he arrived and found that she had gone on with Pilate, he might misunderstand and give her up. How could he or anyone else understand her bond with this man who had deceived her, whom she had never loved, who was now half insane? Draco was a Stoic. He believed in the survival of the best, and thought it better for the world that the worst destroy themselves. If permitted to live her life with him, she could teach him Jesus' religion. It had courage and strength to appeal to his own strength and courage. But he was not yet a Christian; he would not understand; if she did not meet him she might lose him forever.

Had she not done enough for this weak, wasted creature, who stared at her with the eyes of an animal dragged by force to the sacrifice? Would it not be better for him and for her and for Draco if she left him to die

of memories alone, or if he returned to Rome, and Gaius
Caesar put him to death?

Procla paced back and forth in the garden, unmindful
of the rising wind that blew strong and cold from the east.
Oh, Jesus Christ, she prayed silently, if you send me your
answer, I promise you I will abide by it!

Faint in the moaning of the wind she thought she heard
John Mark's boyish voice: "*... that is faithful in that
which is least. ...*"

"We can go north by the river," she said, "inland to
the town of Vienne. If you agree, call Servius and give
him instructions. He will be able to terminate your affairs
here and then follow us."

And he can tell Draco, she thought. But what is there
to tell him?

A frantic hope leapt in Pilate's pale eyes.

"Do you mean you are going with me?"

"I mean that," she said steadily. "I cannot leave you
now."

"Procla, I am a damned soul! I no longer ask you to
stay."

She thought with a dull pain in her heart: I would not
stay for your asking. I have been told by my Lord and
Master what I must do.

8

So she and Pilate traveled up the river Rhone to Vienne. The city had long been romanized. It was walled and served by aqueducts, and it had an amphitheater and other public buildings.

She had recalled that when she suggested the place to him. She had reasoned that they would be surrounded by things Roman and familiar, and yet that the change would be great enough to distract his thoughts. He must have nothing to remind him of Judea or the waters that lapped its coast. Here were soldiers and merchants and travelers in the streets. Here were comforts and recreations to make a Roman think of Rome. But there was nothing to bring memory of a garden in Massalia.

She had hoped that Servius might bring her a letter from Draco. But when he finally arrived, the only letter he bore was for Pilate, and was an imperial dispatch from Rome.

Haggard of face, he took it unopened to his room. She turned to the travel-weary veteran.

"Did the tribune come?"

He inclined his head without speaking. She saw that he hated to speak.

"Was he—is he angry with me, Servius?"

"Yes, my lady—angrier than I have ever known him to be."

"Did he not send me a message?" she implored.

The veteran shook his gray head. She dropped her face in her hands.

"My lady," said Servius pityingly, "he will come back to you."

She looked up at him. "I fear not. I think that this time I have lost him."

"No; because he and I have arranged—" Servius stopped, frowning angrily. "I tell you I know the tribune. He will find you sooner or later. If I have aught to do with it, it will not be very late."

"Did he tell you his plans? Is he going back to the East?"

"No; he is now out of the Legion. But the Emperor has appointed him emissary to some mountain tribes."

To some remote barbarians, she thought. He is lost to me now. If I had waited for him in Massalia he would have taken me with him. But the sand diviner was right. I shall be with Pilate until death!

As she heard his voice crying her name she almost hated him.

"Claudia," he was wailing, "we are both destroyed!"

"What is it?" she asked him impatiently. For it seemed to her at the moment that no greater disaster could ever befall.

"Gaius has revoked my appointment. He writes that he has had bad reports of me from informers in Massalia. They told him that, instead of upholding Rome's prestige, I was seen in the streets with disordered robes and staggering from wine. Also he charges me with having taken too much on myself when I went into the dead seas to inspect the salt pans."

"The proconsul asked for a report on them," she reminded him.

But she knew in her heart that Gaius intended to accept no excuse, but was determined this time to ruin her husband.

"He charges me with having attacked Rome's authority by upholding the salt scrapers against his tax collectors. He orders us both to Rome: me to be tried on these charges, you to be put under his cousinly protection."

"There are lengths to which Gaius cannot go. There is still a Senate in Rome."

"He is the Emperor. Where can we hide from him? He will find us in any Roman province."

Servius was still looking on. He said, "The tribune told me—"

Procla turned on him. "Does the tribune know what is in this letter?"

"He suspects. It is why he hurried to Massalia. He—I advise that we leave Vienne at once, for some place beyond Rome's rule."

Pilate's drawn face showed a gleam of hope. "You are right. In Massalia you drew funds for me?"

"There were no funds," said Servius. "The bankers told me that you no longer drew any payment from Rome. They also asked me for the Lady Claudia's address. But the tribune had warned me of danger to you both, so I thought it well to tell them that you were returning to Rome."

The shock of his first statement was so great that neither Procla nor Pilate paid attention to what else he said. But Procla remembered it later as she sat alone, and told herself that Gaius was truly hunting them down. She had sent Servius out to sell her few jewels, and Pilate had bolted himself in his apartment.

I have lost Draco, she was musing, and I have brought Pilate harm rather than help. I was mistaken in thinking I had been chosen to serve. What the moneylenders give Servius for my ornaments will not be enough even to take us beyond Gaius' reach. He is indeed determined to have his way if he made the bankers inquire my address.

Oh, for a sign to tell me right from wrong, she prayed. Had I left Pilate, the Emperor might not have sought to destroy him. Had I gone to Draco, I am sure I could have won him to the following of Jesus by the very living of our life together. Have I done wrong, kind Savior? Send me a sign to guide me!

Without, night cloaked the city. She heard an occasional shout, or the sound of belated feet hurrying by.

She did not know how long she sat until she heard noises of entrance. The main door grated open and slammed shut again. She told herself that more foot-steps than those of one man approached. Have they caught up with us already? she wondered. Is this my sign?

Then Servius parted the hangings of the room. He said: "My lady, the man who asked your address in Massalia is here. He demands to see you. May he enter?"

She rose to her feet and braced herself for whatever might be coming.

"Bring him in," she commanded haughtily. "Bring him in—whoever he is."

Yod came through the long curtains. He looked at her with the same scowl with which he had regarded her long years ago on the island.

"I have had a hard time to track you," he told her gruffly. "You did all you could to evade me, but I have found you now."

9

S HE was so glad to see him and so grateful to have a
friend, that she listened submissively while he told
her what to do.

"You must leave Vienne tomorrow. If you journey east-
ward, you will soon reach countries beyond Gaius' reach."

She wondered how he knew that Gaius was threatening
them, but she was so weary that she still listened in
silence.

"There are places in the Helvetian mountains remote
enough for you and your husband to lose yourselves
from sight, yet near enough native settlements for you to
obtain provisions. There will not be comfort, but you
have never feared hardship, Procla."

She shook her head. "I am glad you remember that."

"I remember other things. I have not forgotten a debt.
There is no sum large enough to pay for escape from
slavery; for repatriation, wife, children, happiness. The
gold in this purse is only a token of what I owe you."

She looked at the velvet pouch he set on the table
beside her, and she felt the burning of tears she tried
not to shed.

"Yod, I did it for friendship! I cannot take return."

"Then you are more churlish than I ever was," he told
her. "I believed in your friendship enough to accept all
you offered. Does my friendship now mean less to you?"

She tried to regain her self-control.

"It means everything to me. I will take the gold, as
friendship's gift. It may save both my life and Pilate's."

He frowned in embarrassment at thanks, so she continued quickly. "But how did you know where I was, or even what had happened to me? What brought you from Jerusalem to Vienne?"

"All Judea knows of Pontius Pilate's recall. I feared that Gaius Caesar might intend to punish his wife with him. As you know, I am employed by international bankers. They have a house of business in Rome, and they had occasion at this time to send a man there. I asked for the mission and got it."

"You reached Rome after I had left?"

"Yes. I was told that you had gone South. There were conflicting rumors. Some said Pontius Pilate had been restored to the Emperor's favor. Some—" he looked hard at her— "said other things. I did not know just where you were and was undecided what to do, when I learned that there was in Rome a man who was your friend."

"The tribune?" she asked.

"It was he. He told me that you were in danger, but that the Emperor was detaining him in Rome. I followed you to Massalia, where the servants at your villa told me that Pontius Pilate would soon return. Every day I made inquiry at the bankinghouse. Then one day the bankers told me your steward had come and gone, and had said only that you were returning to Rome. Fortunately for me, the tribune came in to the bankinghouse asking for me before I left. He had seen Servius, and he told me what the steward had said. You must leave Vienne tomorrow."

So Yod arranged their departure and they went the next day. Pilate made no objection, for a terrible urgency drove him. He seemed not to care where they went. He did not even ask where they were when they came to a strange community which had first been built by lake dwellers. Some of its buildings still sprawled on stilts above water. But when they saw Roman ships at its river wharves, he cried out: "I must go on! I can stay in no place that is Roman."

From then on different and more difficult arrangements had to be made, for they began ascending the mountains. They left the town on the watery plain and went up through the Alpine passes. Ahead the ranges and peaks swept in immense crumpled arcs. Procla, gazing at them, was alarmed and yet exalted.

Even the loneliness seemed more immense than other loneliness. On their guides led them, on and up until her strong body ached. Pilate was carried in a chair, eyes closed, his head bent to his breast. But she walked whenever she could, keeping close to Servius. In that monstrous silence she thought of the ascent to Jerusalem. It was so short compared to this. Yet she and Pilate had spoken of it and she had warned him idly that descent was steeper than ascent. Since they had left Jerusalem their descent from fortune and favor had been as steep as the precipice they were skirting. What had the dark, hunched man told Pilate in the moonlit garden of the villa in Massalia? *"Although you climb mountains ... your road will go always down."*

When they came to a blue, deep lake dammed by moraines and walled by sheer heights of limestone, she begged Pilate to stop by its shores in the valley. But he pointed to the great shoulder of rock that rose southwest.

"The bearers tell me that there is on that mountainside a villa built by Romans who were encamped nearby a few years ago. We could occupy it, and I wish to go there."

She was accustomed to his changes of fancy. She knew he was a sick man and she must humor him. Moreover Servius approved. Servius had seemed all along to know where they were going, and had before this persuaded Pilate from some other change of way. She supposed it was because he had soldiered, and knew about marching.

But as they ascended that wind-swept, tilted plane of rock, she was alarmed by its wildness and loneliness. Their path wound up through dark conifers and emerged on mountain meadows. In the great silence she thought she heard a faint silvery sound of bells. It grew louder to meet them. Their bearers drew to one side, and rested the litters on a rug of moss and cushion plants.

Flocks of goats which pastured all summer on these high meadows were going down to winter in the valley. They passed in groups and singly, some scampering and some lagging. Herding them were tall mountain boys with long staves, and shaggy dogs.

She watched them, remembering Pandataria and Yod. Then the steep path was empty ahead and the bells were faint behind them. The bearers lifted the litter poles and bent for the climb to the villa.

To her disappointment and discomfort it was no more than a rude lodge of logs, set above tree level, and rough and inconvenient. Untrained mountaineers served them, and she had to learn words of their language. To her surprise she discovered that they used the Greek alphabet. The man who told her that told her the lodge had been built by Roman officers who hunted wolves and bear.

"Are such animals around us?"

"The wolf and the bear and the elk and wild boar," he told her proudly. "There are also the fox and the fierce stoat, and the terrible mountain lynx. I can buy dogs for you, lady, if you and your husband wish to hunt."

She shivered as she answered, "We do not wish to hunt."

She was thinking: We are the hunted. I would not pursue these wild creatures, for I now know the terror of being pursued.

In those autumn nights she heard the wolves howl, and the wind came through the log walls. But at first Pilate liked it.

"It is a safe hiding place for me," he said.

Then the snow began to fall steadily. For days and weeks at a time they could not leave the house. When it cleared enough to permit them to see, they looked out on a world of whiteness: a rugged, up-ended world of slanted planes and abutments. Here and there where the wind's broom swept, the black rocks outcropped and glistened. When the great drifts grew too heavy they overbalanced and toppled, and the roar of their avalanches became an accustomed sound.

High as was the lodge, several peaks were above them. That one nearest to them was steep. When it stood between them and the sun its dark shadow lay across their roof.

Pilate gazed wistfully at it in the brief daylight hours which revealed it between storms. "I shall climb it in the spring," he said. "I shall be strong and well again."

But Servius warned them that the servingmen had told him the pinnacle was treacherous and a deep lake lay at its foot.

That warning did no more than irritate the sick man. "I have climbed Apennines and Pyrenees. I feel more at rest here than I have felt for several years. It is the place I was meant to come. Something guided me to it."

Servius guided us to it, she thought. He must know it is safe and remote. If Pilate wishes to stay I will stay. I have now nothing else to do in life. But I am not mountain-born and I am not at rest. I dislike it and fear it—most of all this dark peak!

10

IT was a strange life for a woman who was granddaughter to Augustus and wife of the ex-Governor of
Judea. More than once the thought came to her that her
life had begun in exile and, it might be, was going to
end in exile stranger and sadder.

As far as eye could reach there was no sign of humanity.
No voice of a neighbor came to her. She found no human
footprint. Gaze as she might she never saw a feather of
smoke blown skyward, to witness that any man was even
within their reach.

Her eyes became weary of empty and incredible
distances. When the snow was not too deep she would
walk to the edge of the nearest abyss, and note on the
opposite mountain the belt of ice-sheathed conifers that
grew to timberline. Rank on rank they stood in their
glassy battle dress, as stiff and taciturn as a waiting
cohort. The sun rising higher behind her struck light
from their millions of prisms. The changes of the spectrum
played on them like colored flames.

Servius was invaluable. For not only did he share with
her a responsibility too great for any one human being,
he managed the crude house and the rough, uncouth
servants. He dispatched one of them at regular intervals
to get provisions from the nearest settlement. He wrote
careful directions for the messenger. She knew he was
proud of his learning, but she could not help smiling the
first time she found him busy with stylus.

"Can you write the Helvetian script?" she asked him

amusedly. "Or are the natives from whom you buy so learned that they read Latin?"

"My lady," he grumbled, "leave it to me. You have enough on your shoulders. I know what I am doing."

She had no reason to think otherwise. She was thankful for his support, and she prayed daily for guidance on her difficult way. But the little help that change of scene had given Pilate was over. Although he had planned to climb mountains, he stayed in the house now. More and more often he would go in his room and bolt the door. When she knocked and asked what was troubling him, there was no answer.

To add to her troubles just then, Servius told her that he must go down the mountain himself on matters of business.

"Can you not send one of the mountaineers?" she asked him.

"They are stupid and failed to deliver my last letter," he answered. "I tell you I must go in person, at once."

"I beg you then to return promptly. I am not a coward, Servius. Yet I fear the responsibility. I do not trust the Helvetians. I wish you were not leaving me. Suppose that you lose your way?"

"They have given me directions. I can better do this myself."

"Then do not stay away longer than you must, Servius. You see that the governor is worse rather than better."

"It is because I see that I must go. I shall stay no longer than I must."

So she charged him to buy for the sick man whatever could give him comfort. In his absence she tried to serve Pilate herself. She urged him to walk with her when the weather was good, but he still sat behind closed doors as if hiding from danger.

"Go when you choose," he said in piteous gentleness. "The servingmen can do for me what I need."

She did not consider them servingmen. They were proud and silent, although uncouth. She felt sure that they hated her and all other Romans and were only working for the gold Servius paid them. When he was there she had seldom come in contact with them; but now in her loneliness she talked more to them.

"Five days have passed since the steward's departure. Do you not think he will come tomorrow?"

The man shook his head.

"How far is the town to which he has gone for supplies?"

"The town is ten leagues away. But the Roman camp is almost again as far."

She cried sharply: "Is Servius going to a Roman camp?"

"The steward did not tell me where he was going. He asked me the way to the Roman camp."

Reconsidering, she decided that it was only natural a Roman veteran should seize the chance to visit any Roman camp within his reach. Servius, she told herself, must be as lonely as she was. Her insistence upon his immediate return had probably made him keep his intention from her. He had a right to his little holiday. The Helvetians were doing their work, and Pilate was quiet although morose. She would never let the faithful old soldier know that she had discovered his secret.

She stayed more closely by Pilate and made her walks shorter. One afternoon she hurried back because it was darkening for storm. As she entered the lodge she saw that the door of his room was open.

She searched that room and the other rooms. Far in the darkening distance she heard an avalanche thunder. She went outside and called his name and the names of the servants. One of them came around the side of the house.

"Where is your master? Is your brother with him?"

"No. My brother has gone down the mountain to meet the steward."

That news distracted her from fear. Pilate missed Servius as much as she did. It was not improbable he would have gone too to meet him.

"Is the steward already in sight? How do you know he is coming?"

"He is not yet in sight. His carriers are Helvetians. They call to announce their coming with a cry heard for miles through the mountains."

She remembered hearing an echo while farther up on the path. It had a strange, bell-like sound. She had thought it an elk calling. She was glad to think Pilate had taken enough interest to walk down the path. She said, as much to herself as to the man facing her, "Then the Roman lord followed your brother to meet the steward and the bearers of supplies?"

"No. He went the opposite way. He went to climb the peak."

A cold that bit sharper than rising wind clutched suddenly at her heart. He had planned to climb, but he was now too weak and ill.

"Which peak did he wish to climb? Why did he go so suddenly?"

The man turned and pointed at a jagged white silhouette which towered above them and against the lead-dark sky.

"He roused when he heard my brother go, and he came outside the house. The sun was then beginning to go behind that point. He said: 'Its shadow has lain on me since I came to this place.' He asked me its name, and I told him, and he started at once."

"What is its name, Helvetian?"

"It is known as the *Donkey's Head*."

11

SHE stood, colder than the snow beginning to fall from that swollen sky.

Up from the zone of the ice-cloaked trees came the cries of a wolf pack.

Her mind registered the thought that the beasts had probably scented the party ascending the mountain. But she had no fear for Servius and his carriers. She knew they always armed themselves against wolves when they traveled. She was giving herself these few seconds to decide whether to go down to meet and hurry them, or herself to follow Pilate.

She realized that the mountaineers could make better time than she could. But she had no idea how far away they were. This surly Helvetian who faced her seemed not to realize danger and certainly did not care what befell a Roman master.

She made her decision in that brief time.

"Follow your brother," she said to the man. "Reach the steward as soon as you can. Tell him the Roman lord is trying to climb the peak, and ask him to send at full speed the best climber in his party."

Then she was running with all her strength up the path—running and stumbling and rising again—and gasping for breath and struggling on.

She reached the foot of the upthrusting rock, but she could see no track. Neither Pilate's footprints nor a climbing path were visible. Snow that was newly fallen or that had been smoothed by the wind made a great pillar of untouched whiteness. She felt a sudden hope that

Pilate had turned aside. Perhaps he was now on his way down to the lodge by another path.

Then she remembered the name of the peak, and she knew that all such hopes were vain.

She tried in several places to climb, slipping back and falling, frantic with terror at the delay caused by each false start.

Now she distinguished several crude steps cut or worn in the stone. She could see nothing because of the snow, but she found footholds enough to make her way upward.

The storm was gathering, and the wind tore at her more savagely as she gained altitude. She went to her knees and caught with her hands at each jagged tread above her. They were so far apart and so irregularly spaced that she feared more than once that she had lost them. The wind was a blast, and dried snow and ice cut her face with their blown particles. She could not see above or below, but she knew the abyss was beneath her. She knew that one slip of hand or foot could precipitate her into it.

Her hands and knees were bleeding now, but she was too cold to feel bodily pain. All her strength and all her will made her cling to the stone and crawl upward. She knew that the stairway of the path must be circling the peak, so she could not guess how high she had come or what point of the compass she faced. She had no room for thoughts of herself and her own safety. She was thinking of a half-mad man somewhere ahead of her in this icy inferno.

All the sacrifice of the years she had given him concentrated in this hour. It had come to a focus here in a mountain storm, far from the sea he feared, on a peak known as the Donkey's Head. Neither she nor Pilate had known there was such a place, but they had been drawn to it as iron is drawn to a lodestone. The sand diviner had known. Each move of their restless journeying had drawn them nearer and nearer. . . .

At the last, Pontius Pilate had been possessed by a need to climb this mountain and seek sanctuary in the cruel shadow of that pinnacle.

Her hands, as they clutched for the next step, grasped only the deep-piled snow. She dragged herself up on the flat rock which capped the ascent.

The wind made her sway as she got to her feet. She dared not step backward or forward. She stood in a cloud of blowing snow, blinded to what might be within arm's reach, deafened by hissing particles and a great hollow roaring.

She shrieked Pilate's name again and again. But she knew that he could not hear her even if he were only a few feet away.

As she paused to collect herself, the storm paused. The wind fell suddenly. The opaqueness of the atmosphere thinned to a pale translucence. As it cleared, instead of a curtain of white she saw the snowflakes falling . . . falling more and more slowly . . . until she could see all about her.

She was facing a stormy sunset, invisible from below. One long ray burned its way from black clouds and reached briefly for the height.

In that interval which was lit as if by flame, she saw Pilate not far away. He stood with his back to her, on the sheer edge of the summit. Between and around them the snow seemed as red as blood.

She started toward him, afraid to cry out for fear she might startle him.

As she did, he raised his arms high and pointed his hands like a diver.

She shrieked his name then. But he gave no sign of hearing.

It looked to her as if he leaned slowly against space.

As she ran she reached out with her arms in a last terrible tenderness. Beyond him she was looking into immeasurable emptiness.

But while she clutched to save him, he went over . . . a dark shape sprawled and turning slowly . . . growing always smaller as it fell toward the ice-black mirror of the frozen lake below.

12

A RUSH of snow borne on the wind blotted that dreadful sight in mid-air.

But she put her hands over her eyes to hide it more completely. Tears ran between her fingers and stung her cheeks as they froze. I tried to be faithful, she told herself. I tried—but I was too late!

Instinctively she stepped back from the sheer drop that lay before her. Then she stopped—afraid to move further.

The snow in the air was thicker than it had yet been, and the wind howled like the wolves in the timber below. She realized that she must get down at once. She knew that she could not survive a night of that awful exposure and cold. The wind stabbed even through her thick garments and the blood in her veins was chilling. You will freeze, her numbing brain told her. You will freeze unless you act quickly.

Yet every movement had to be slow, for she knew she walked on the edge of death. She had no idea how large was the rock table on which she stood. In the short glimpse she had been allowed she had looked only for Pilate. Her next step might carry her into space after him.

The wind forced her to her knees, and she crawled by inches through the snow. In places where it was frozen to ice she slipped and sprawled and recovered. But she told herself that she had to go on and feel for the edge of the small plateau. If she found that, she could guide herself by following it around to the upper step of the path she had ascended.

She found the stone's edge, deep under drifts which

were growing deeper with every moment. She knew that
if she moved too far out and put her weight where they
overhung, they would give way with her. But she forced
herself on with the thought that it was better to risk
quick death than to freeze slowly, between earth and
sky, on this evil pinnacle which had drawn a man to
his doom.

She thought about Draco... that she had lost him
now.... Had she been wrong to send him away? Had
she failed to help Pilate and still lost the one man she
loved?

Through the wind's shouting she seemed to hear the
voice of young John Mark. He was speaking of Jesus of
Nazareth—of the man whose rule of life considered others
before Himself. Remembrance made her heart leap, and
she was warm again in the red-hung rooms at Caesarea.

"If thou canst believe, all things are possible...."

She had believed with all her heart in Jesus the Christ.
She had believed so deeply that she had tried to put that
faith into deeds, and to do her duty by Pilate. Perhaps
after all she had not failed. Perhaps she could call on the
Savior now.

Her lips were too stiff to shape words, but her heart
spoke: I have faith, Lord. Mark told me you promised
"According to your faith be it unto you." Because you forgave your enemies, I tried to follow your footsteps and
help the man who gave you up to death. Is it too great a
miracle to ask of you—since I have faith—to give me back
life and love?

She struggled once again to her feet and found that she
could stand upright. The tempest was lessening for another lull, and the instinct of self-preservation urged her
to take advantage of it. Her faculties were dulling, but
she thought of Servius. He might now be following
through the slanted, hissing snow. If only she could call
his name, he might hear and come to her.

With a last effort she gathered her strength and made her half-frozen lips obey. She heard herself calling his name. . . .

She was still calling him in a faint, hoarse whisper, when he seemed to materialize out of the thinning snow-flakes. He caught her as she swayed toward him and wrapped her swiftly in a cloak, but his hands were shaking her in order to arouse her, and his voice rang out: "Where is Pilate?"

"He is dead," she whispered. "He cast himself from the peak. I tried to stop him!"

Then the horror of what she had seen returned and overwhelmed her. As Servius lifted her from her feet, he felt her crumple unconscious in his arms.

13

PROCLA'S next sensation was warmth which tormented her half-frozen body. Something hard was hurting her mouth, and the heated wine burned it.

She had been so near death that her life's circle had almost closed, and her infancy was near and immediate. She set her teeth and whimpered: "I will not swallow it! It is too hot. You are choking me, Bruna!"

"It is I, not Bruna," a voice said.

Whose voice was that, she wondered, struggling to muster strength to open her eyes. It was a voice she knew, yet there was something strange about it. It was so gentle.

"Drink it," the voice begged. "You are safe in my arms. Do as I ask, my dear brave love."

Her eyes flew open, startled, to find Draco bent over her.

"Draco!" she cried. "How—"

"Hush, beloved. Later we will talk."

She drank from the cup he held, then let her head fall back against his shoulder. Her eyes began to focus, and she saw she was in the lodge. Servius stood close by, and at sight of him she remembered all.

"Oh, Servius, if you had not gone you might have saved your master!"

Servius looked at Draco. "This is my master," he said. "I went to the Roman camp to tell him you were in danger from a man who had lost his mind."

"You did right," said Draco.

She was trying to get to her feet. But her struggles were weak, and he only held her closer.

"Hear me, Procla," he said, with the new gentleness still in his tone. "Servius knew that my errand brought me near. I was inspecting both the Roman and the Helvetian camps. Yesterday when he came to warn me of your danger I sent him straight back and followed within the hour. I reached you just as Servius was carrying you into the lodge."

"Then it was to you Servius was writing all these weeks?" she asked in faint surprise. A mist of unreality, like snowfall, was still around her.

"It was. In Massalia I told him to report regularly to me."

"But how could you know we were going to Helvetia?"

"It was your only escape from Rome. Nathan Bar-Jonas and Servius saw that as clearly as I did."

She closed her eyes, recalling that everything had seemed to point to that steep road for Pilate.

"Do not blame yourself, Procla. No one is to blame. All we can do is to make the best of what means we have." His voice had grown soft again, and to her amazement, humble. "I have learned, and learned the hard way, that there is a power stronger than that of an empire's legions —a power which fights on the side of right rather than might."

He stopped suddenly, as if ashamed of the admission. But her heart was leaping. She knew from its tone that it came from his heart. Humility was a strange new garb for him. He was still more at home in battle dress. But she told herself that the One to whom she had called had granted her even more than her prayer for life.

"Once I told you I could not make up my mind about Jesus of Nazareth," he went on. "I knew He was a good man, a man who had been killed unjustly. But I could not accept Him as God without some proof."

"And you found the proof?"

"I did. I found it again and again in the men and women whose faith grew stronger as our legions relentlessly hunted them down. Pain and death were as nothing to them, and as they fell others took their places in ever greater numbers. Their weapons were faith and forgiveness, against which no sword can prevail. Faith and forgiveness—and love. All this I came to believe in, and it has brought me back to you."

She looked up, and their eyes met.

"You were watching over me all the while I thought I had lost you."

His arms tightened. "It was all I could do until the time came when I could make you my wife and take you away. It has come now, Procla. I have served Rome faithfully. My report will go to the Senate by a Roman officer. But you and Servius and I will make our way to some land where the beast who rules Rome cannot reach us."

"You and Servius and Yod planned it all?"

"Yes. I hoped that in the remoteness of the Alps Pilate might remain undiscovered. For I included him in the plan, since you would not leave him."

He felt her shudder. He said, "It is better so, Procla. He is at last at rest."

She answered very slowly, "I think he has washed his hands."

Now she felt herself warm with happiness and strong with love. Again she tried to rise, and again his arms tightened.

"Once on Pandataria," he said softly, as if to himself.

She looked up at him in question. His head was bent toward hers.

His voice went even lower. "Once in my villa, once in Herod's palace by the Galilean lake. . . . "

"What do you mean?" she whispered.

"I mean that three times, my only love, I held you in my arms. I mean that three times they took you away from me. But I hold you now, my own love, and nothing shall take you from me!"

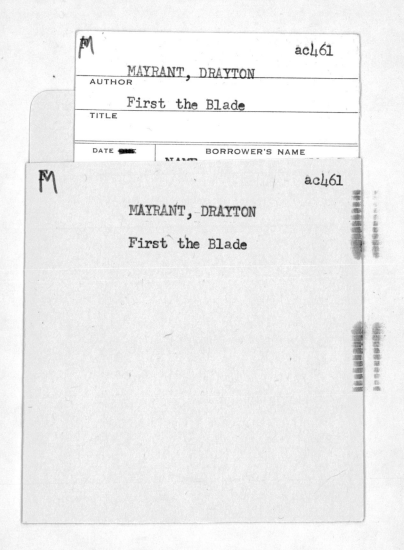

FM   ac461

MAYRANT, DRAYTON
AUTHOR

First the Blade
TITLE

DATE ~~DUE~~ | BORROWER'S NAME

FM   ac461

MAYRANT, DRAYTON

First the Blade